Praise for *Summ[...]*

"I'm in love with Corrello's voice. [...] hers is a voice that's been missing from the rom-com pantheon. wonderfully real characters, unexpected heart-twists, and knee-buckling humor makes *Summertime Punchline* a surprising standout. What a delight. Please welcome to the stage . . . Betty Corrello!"

—Julia Whelan, author of *Thank You for Listening*

"A vibrant sunbeam of a book—I simply inhaled it. Betty Corrello's writing is both achingly vulnerable and wildly funny. The ideal summertime (or anytime) read, guaranteed to make you crave both a funnel cake and a cute single dad."

—Rachel Lynn Solomon, author of *Business or Pleasure*

"Funny and keenly crafted, *Summertime Punchline* is packed with messy people, perfect chemistry, and a satisfying amount of heartfelt forgiveness. I tore through it, you will too."

—Annabel Monaghan, author of *Nora Goes Off Script*

"*Summertime Punchline* is killing it! Betty Corrello brings a fantastic and fresh new voice to modern rom-coms with sharp writing, nimble humor, and an enchanting romance. I can't wait to read what's next."

—Amy E. Reichert, author *The Kindred Spirits Supper Club*

"Humor, heart, and steam collide in this charming story about how people and places change and grow whether we're there to witness it or not. Betty Corrello's debut is the rom-com equivalent of a tight five—everything hits exactly how you want it to. My spouse kept asking what I was laughing at, and the answer was always just 'This book!'"

—Sarah Adler, author of *Happy Medium* and *Mrs. Nash's Ashes*

"A charmingly heartfelt and genuinely funny second-chance romance. *Summertime Punchline* is a wonderfully witty love letter to stand-up comedy, true love, and there being no place like home. Betty Corrello is a hugely exciting new voice in rom-com. I absolutely loved this book!"

—Georgia Clark, author of *It Had to Be You*

"*Summertime Punchline* is the funniest rom-com I've read in years—while also delivering all the chemistry, angst, and emotional depth I could ever want. I was torn between wanting to savor it and devour it as fast as possible. I'm officially a Betty Corrello superfan."

—Ava Wilder, author of *How to Fake It in Hollywood*

"Betty Corrello writes big-hearted, hot romance and perfectly crafted jokes that kick your ass; reading this book was like taking a beach vacation with an extremely hot single dad and the funniest person you know."

—Lex Croucher, author of *Infamous*

"Betty Corrello's hilarious and sincere debut completely swept me away. The beautifully messy heroine narrates with a dry wit that gives way to a surprisingly earnest and tender core. I laughed, I swooned, I dabbed my eyes. Corrello is a voice to watch."

—Rachel Runya Katz, author of *Thank You for Sharing*

Summertime Punchline

A Novel

BETTY CORRELLO

AVON

An Imprint of HarperCollins*Publishers*

SUMMERTIME PUNCHLINE. Copyright © 2024 by Betty Corrello. All rights reserved. Printed in the United States of America. No part of this book may be used or reproduced in any manner whatsoever without written permission except in the case of brief quotations embodied in critical articles and reviews. For information, address HarperCollins Publishers, 195 Broadway, New York, NY 10007.

HarperCollins books may be purchased for educational, business, or sales promotional use. For information, please email the Special Markets Department at SPsales@harpercollins.com.

FIRST EDITION

Designed by Diahann Sturge-Campbell
Title page illustration © John T Takai/Shutterstock

Library of Congress Cataloging-in-Publication Data

Names: Corrello, Betty, author.
Title: Summertime punchline : a novel / Betty Corrello.
Description: First edition. | New York : William Morrow an imprint of Harper-Collins Publishers, 2023.
Identifiers: LCCN 2023031958 | ISBN 9780063329584 (paperback) | ISBN 9780063329591 (ebook)
Classification: LCC PS3603.O77235 S86 2023 | DDC 813/.6—dc23/eng/20231010
LC record available at https://lccn.loc.gov/2023031958

ISBN 978-0-06-332958-4

24 25 26 27 28 LBC 5 4 3 2 1

*For anyone who finds this book in the midst of wandering.
I hope it makes for good company on your journey home.*

You were the hot one, I was the weird one.
You only got hotter, I only got weirder.

—Matt DeCaro, "Hot One Weird One"

1

The worst day of my life began like most: with my roommate, Misty, swinging open my bedroom door to drape her seven-thousand-foot-long limbs all over the cramped rectangle that constituted my part of the apartment.

"God, it smells weird in here."

I blinked through the dried remnants of sleep in my eyes and pushed my short, choppy bangs out of my line of vision. "Can I help you?"

"Cool shirt." Misty delivered this observation with the taut restraint of a serial killer. I'd fallen asleep in my work uniform—a *Gimbley's Irish Pub & Comedy Club* fitted T-shirt and a pair of black leggings—after collapsing on top of a pile of clean laundry that had covered my bed since the 2020 election cycle. After waitressing a double, I'd stayed to host a four-hour-long open mic, and I could feel the echoes of twelve hours on my feet all the way up to my hips.

"What do you want?" I groaned, rolling over onto my back and slapping around for my phone. Ingram was probably looking for me. We'd been dating for three months, and I was still adjusting to the concept of someone wanting to talk to me.

"Few things: The *Post* is coming by in two hours to photograph the living room, so make sure you're not here; you left a mug in the sink last night which is *fine* but I thought we discussed boundaries? And here's your mail." She dropped a pile on my overcrowded nightstand before pirouetting toward the door. Misty might have been an interior décor micro-influencer, but her heart was with the American Ballet Theatre.

"Thanks," I said, before pulling myself into an upright position and checking the time on my phone. Ten A.M. I'd slept for five hours. Not bad.

Across from my bed, I spied myself in the full-length mirror and raked my fingers through my chin-length bob, readjusting the shell-shocked layers back into something more effortlessly tousled. I swiped at the dried mascara under my eyes until it came away and smoothed at my cheek until the pillow lines disappeared. The way Misty treated me, you'd think I was a bell-tower gargoyle sprung to life, squatting over a pile of dead pigeons in the middle of Times Square. But I was just a normal person with a relatively attractive face and normal—what did the kids call it? Midsize, like a five-door hatchback?—body. Misty was sinewy and permanently tanned terra-cotta orange, her shiny blond hair snatched into a low bun. She lived under the tutelage of ever-changing trends, running herself ragged trying to keep up with a consumer landscape that wanted her devastatingly insecure or, I don't know, dead.

I couldn't blame her for hating me when she spent so much time trying so damn hard.

I yawned at my reflection then stumbled up and around my room, hunting for a clean tank top and my favorite pair of breezy summer pants, my mental to-do list already forming.

Before I grabbed the train from Queens to Hell's Kitchen, I needed to stop at the post office and mail Sam, one of my best friends, her birthday gift. Then, I had to stop at Cyrus's to use his laptop to print my Brainwave Comedy Festival welcome packet.

Brainwave Comedy Festival. The words jumped into my mind as I laced up my sneakers. I paused to breathe it in. *You got into Brainwave Comedy Festival.* I still couldn't believe it. Out of thousands of comedians who had submitted audition tapes, I'd actually done it.

I, Del Silva-Miller, had landed a spot in *the* comedy festival. Held annually in Vancouver, Brainwave was known to start—or end—professional comedy careers. That was part of the reason I'd stayed to host the entire open mic last night. It had been my good-bye to Gimbley's—my bon voyage. After four years, I'd officially quit. It was a huge risk, but with the festival only forty-five days away, I needed to book as many practice shows as possible.

Deciding to leave Gimbley's had been hard, a bittersweet series finale to a sitcom starring a bunch of PowerPoint comedians and a kitchen full of OGs who found us insufferable. I'd worked there with my best friends, Cyrus and Tucker, and even though our boss sucked and the kitchen smelled like mold and we had to clean up *so* much puke, it had been special.

But I needed my set to be perfect. This was it. My last shot to repot my lifelong dream like a grocery store houseplant and make it bloom. To step into the life I'd been working toward since I was twenty.

I looked around my messy little room hunting for my purse and keys. To say I'd decorated the space would have been a lie, but I had collected knickknacks over the years: the sunburst tapestry pinned behind my bed; the string lights wrapped around my bookshelf; and Buster the Weeping Clown, a dementedly jovial ceramic clown permanently trapped mid–high kick as he clutched a bundle of colorful balloons. His balloons lit up, casting an iridescent honeycomb of primary colors across my bedroom ceiling, but he was *never* happy about it. If anything, the balloons, his oversize red shoes, the jaunty little hat on his head were all a burden—a curse.

Buster and I had a lot in common.

I grabbed my keys from under Buster's shadow and swung my bag over my shoulder, ready to brave the strangling, moist heat of New York City in August.

There I went, swan-diving into a bright new day and the crystal-clear pools of my future. What I didn't know was that, when I hadn't been looking, someone had drained the lake.

I'D MET Ingram at Gimbley's open mic night. Most servers couldn't handle working to the continuous soundtrack of comedians bombing, but it had been my favorite shift of the week. All the nervous first-timers would show up with sweaty palms and a ferocious need to get as drunk as possible, as soon as possible.

Ingram had been sitting in the front row at one of the small bistro tables with a red votive candle in the center, legs crossed and head in hand. The whole time I performed he kept his eyes trained on me with this *look*. Like he wanted to laugh but wasn't sure. I wouldn't have noticed if it hadn't been for his eyes—they were so green, almost feline. They glistened under the hot overhead lights, watching me with a conspiratorial sweetness. Like we already shared a secret.

I was breaking open a new box of beers and dumping them into the well when I looked up and there he was, leaning against the bar. Head still in his hand. Eyes still flickering.

"You're funny." He said it in a flat, monotone voice. His mouth was small and twisted into a cheeky little grimace.

I raised a brow. "Oh wow, thanks so much."

"I mean it." He was wearing the most ridiculous orange hat. But still, he was magnetic.

I slid the top of the well shut and leaned forward, resting my elbows on the bar. "Can I get you anything? A daiquiri? Maybe a hot dog? They're buy one, get one. Wanna find out why?"

Finally, he gave in to a smirk, tapping the underside of his silver thumb ring against the bar. "What about dinner?"

Behind me, Cyrus had made a sound like he'd swallowed a fly. And I agreed to dinner.

Ingram and I didn't make sense. His father ran Canada's premier cable TV business, and his mother was a French model. He'd grown up between Alberta and Switzerland, often revealing alienating details about his life. Annual Christmas ski trips; a familial horse farm in Aruba; a distant cousin named Thierry. He found my Jersey accent endearing and my big tits novel. I never thought we would get married or anything. I didn't even really do relationships.

I *thought* I wasn't fooling myself.

I *thought* I knew exactly what we were doing.

But as I stepped out from the Forty-Ninth Street station, my favorite song in my ears, I guess I wasn't thinking at all.

I could have texted or called before showing up at his place, but on my way to Cyrus's I remembered I had left a very important pair of slippers at Ingram's. It was on the way—why would I have not stopped? He was my boyfriend.

I pushed my key—the key he'd given me—into the door and turned until the door clicked open.

And there he was. In his little orange hat. Nestled between Misty's knees.

FOR MANY years, I'd had a single goal in life: never *ever* move back to Evergreen, New Jersey.

But as I went ballistic on Ingram and Misty, who scrambled to disengage from the throes of a type of oral sex too complicated for my simple mind, time went concave. Around me, they moved at hyper-speed: Misty lunged for her knit-sweater crop top; Ingram spun around so fast, he nearly lost his hat; his cat, Cheddar, screamed frantically from the loft space. The slick white walls of his apartment rounded around me and my mind went as still as the surface of a frozen lake, my thoughts falling like snowflakes, floating on humid air, drifting until they landed on the ice with an echoless *plink*.

Misty. Plink.

Ingram and Misty. Plink.

I just quit my job. Plink.

I have to move out. Plink.

Where the hell am I going to stay? Plink.

Oh my God. Plink.

I'm going to have to go home.

Plink.

SOMEWHERE BETWEEN Hell's Kitchen, Queens, and back again, the humidity broke, and the dark skies roiled like quicksilver, opening up and producing a violent summer storm. Stepping out of the subway station into the night, I was immediately drenched in sticky rain and the smell of hot concrete.

I wanted to pull out my notebook and write a half-hearted joke about how I was doing Alanis Morissette better than Alanis ever had. I wanted to immediately take the material facts of my life and spin them into a sardonic, painless fictionalization. But my head was pounding, and my throat was sore from screaming at Ingram. I was crying in an unending, choking-on-air sort of way, like a toddler after too many hours at a theme park.

I tucked into the overhang of Cyrus's apartment building and jammed my finger into his buzzer until the slick, wet tip of my finger turned white. No response. Not even a crackle over the intercom.

"Cyrus!" I called out, up toward his window. When he didn't surface, I pressed his buzzer again and again. "*Cyrus, answer me!*"

Thunder cracked in response.

I dropped my suitcase and guitar by the door and backed away from the building. He lived on the second floor of a redbrick house on a side street. Everything around me was eerily quiet for a Friday night. The only noise was the *swooosh* of cars skating through rain puddles and, of course, my voice. His living room light was on, and I knew his shift had ended about forty minutes ago. *Why the hell is he ignoring me?*

I snagged a rock from a potted plant beside his front door and aimed for his window. I nailed my target with a satisfying *ting*.

"*Cyrus!*"

Immediately, the window flew open, and a familiar head of glossy black hair popped out, flooding me with relief. "What in the fucking—*Del*?"

"Cyrus, I called you like, five times," I panted, waving my arms over my head to make sure I didn't lose his attention. "Did you get my calls?"

"Um, yeah." He threw a shifty look over his shoulder, leaning farther out the window. "I did. You rang my doorbell like, thirteen times."

"I'm sorry, I know," I rushed to explain. "I walked in on Ingram with Misty and I didn't even think he liked blondes—can I sleep on your couch tonight?"

Cyrus blinked at me. "My couch?"

"Please." I clasped my hands in front of my chest. "I caught them together, doing oral. It was so gross. I think I hate sex now,

and I have nowhere to go and I'm *so* tired and there aren't any
buses back to Evergreen until—"

He suddenly looked heartbroken. Actually physically hurt.
Please, please, please, I begged silently. He ran a hand over his
hair. "I'm sorry, but you can't stay here tonight."

"Did you not hear me?" The choking tears were starting again.
"Oral sex! Nowhere to go!"

"Del—" He shot an anxious look over his shoulder before
sticking his entire torso out the window and making very intense, long-distance eye contact. "I love you. You're one of my
best friends, but I have a girl over and please never bring this up
again, but you're *way* too hot to bring upstairs."

My face collapsed into an outraged sob. "*Gross.*"

"Yeah, well!" He slammed a hand down on the windowsill, di-
recting his next sentence at the sky. "If I bring you up here, she's
going to think I'm trying to orchestrate some sort of threesome."

"You're going to let me die on the streets of Manhattan because
I'm *too hot*?"

"Jesus, Del. Here—" The rain had stopped, and now I could
see clearly that he was digging around in his pockets. Then, he
yanked out a key fob. "Take my car. Keep it for however long you
need. Sleep in it, drive it, whatever."

"*What?*"

He dangled the keys over my head. "I'm parked in the lot by the
bridge. You know my car."

"A rotted green Hyundai," I said quietly.

"Exactly. Your rotted green Hyundai now." And he dropped
the keys. I held out my hand and caught them easily before they
could crash onto the sidewalk. "I'm so sorry, but I need to get laid.
Like, clinically."

I stared down at the metallic mass in my hand. He had one of those license-plate-nameplate key chains. "Don't apologize, I guess." I tightened my grip on the keys, using the backs of my hands to push the last tears out of my eyes. "Thank you."

Cyrus nodded solemnly and threw me a quick wave before disappearing back into his apartment. I heard him laughing nervously then shouting, "So, how was the bathroom?"

The guy had zero game.

I gathered up my things, shifting my guitar onto my back while maintaining an ironclad grip on the keys. They were my lifeline.

I was exhausted, soaked, and sad. I was stuck in a minefield of disaster.

2

Y̶ou *slept* in a *car?*" Nan's voice echoed over the phone line.

It was a new personal low—even for me, a burgeoning woman of twenty-eight once described as "vibing" like a "depressed Deadhead who flunked out of art school."

But, indeed, I had. I had slept in a car. A rotted green Hyundai with a sticky steering wheel and a dusty dashboard. This was a fact that could easily be twisted in my defense or further evidence that I was, in a spiritual sense, not doing great.

I shifted the phone from one ear to the other as I flicked on my blinker and turned into the gas station, pulling up to an empty pump. I was officially ten minutes from Evergreen and I had run down the clock on telling my grandmother, Nan, about the hell that had been the last twenty-four hours. "It's not like I *planned* to fall asleep. It just sort of happened."

"Why didn't you call me?" She sounded absolutely horrified.

"Nan," I said, my voice hard with anger. "Let it go, okay? Remember the part where my boyfriend was in the middle of getting freaky with my literal roommate?" I gritted my teeth and aggressively raked at a knot that had formed on the back of my head. "I survived, and I'm almost home."

She went silent on the line. I could hear the TV in the background—the earsplitting caw of a local injury lawyer demanding we all act now—so I knew she hadn't hung up. Not yet at least. *Wait till she finds out I'm also unemployed.*

Nan was the only parent I'd ever really known, and I, like any devoted child, found the thought of disappointing her worse than material failure. She'd given me her life. The least I could do was eat her weird Christmas cookies with aplomb and not be a total flop.

Finally, she spoke up, soft and quiet. "Did she kick you out, sweetie?"

"No," I replied. "I saw myself out." The image of Ingram sitting on his couch in his too-small, too-white boxers clutching a throw pillow to his chest like a scandalized maiden came swimming back to me, and I felt every part of myself involuntarily tense. "I'd rather drink straight from the bay than spend another second around either of them."

What had I been to him? It was the question that had chewed at the back of my brain for eighty-nine and a half miles. An adventure? A joke? A quirky anecdote? A checkbox on some long-haul journey to fuck every type of woman that's ever existed? When his eyes met mine, he'd had this *look* on his face. He wasn't stricken with terror that he'd ruined a perfectly great relationship or squandered the best thing that had ever happened to him.

No, Ingram had looked *annoyed*—peeved I'd interrupted his Friday night plans to get his dick wet.

I slammed the car door behind me, maybe a little too hard, as I jumped out and made for the gas pump. I didn't care that I was breaking New Jersey's most sacred law—today, I would pump my own gas.

Misty could have Ingram. She could keep the apartment that

had never even felt like a home to me in the first place. I had way too much self-respect—way too much venom coursing through my veins—to subject myself to either one of them. I'd felt more alone being around them than I had when I was actually alone.

"Good for you," Nan declared, pride cresting in her voice. "You're a Silva. You've got that hot Sicilian blood in you."

I pushed the gas nozzle into the tank. "Is that why I'm always so sweaty?"

The Shore was distinctly less humid than New York, but the sun was still blindingly strong, baking the blacktop of the highway and sending up a heat that bristled my skin through my leggings. Under the gas station overhang there was a gentle, warm breeze that danced across the back of my neck. I leaned against the car, watching a steady stream of people go in and out of the Wawa, a strange mash-up of locals in their flip-flops and lifeguard hoodies and day-trippers with their pale legs and bucket hats.

"No, that's probably high blood pressure from your father's side." She punctuated this with a phlegmy cough. "What time do you think you'll be home? I can make whatever you want for dinner—or we can order a pizza—or we can go to the diner. They have this new thing called a shrimp burger."

I roused at the sound of the nozzle clicking. "Your pick. And your treat."

"Oh, come on . . ." Nan kept talking, parsing through the mechanics of how one actually made a burger out of shrimp, as the convenience store door swung open and a man in a pair of reflective aviator sunglasses stepped out into the sun.

The first thing I noticed about him wasn't the curvature of his arms or his full, brick-colored lips. It wasn't even his cheekbones—high and flat—or his jawline, which would have brought Caravaggio to tears.

No. The reason I noticed him was because he was tall. Ridiculously so. Not like a Harlem Globetrotter, but tall enough that he drew my eyes to him. Tall enough that if he had walked right over to me, yanked the gas nozzle right out of my tank, and told me to beat it, I would have replied: *Absolutely, of course, sir.*

He was commanding.

I almost dropped my phone as I pushed myself away from the car. He had his credit card in his mouth while he juggled two water bottles, attempting to shove his wallet into his back pocket. His eyebrows were pulled forward into a deep furrow that looked perpetual, a fact that only added to his air of competence.

"I gotta go, Nan." I cut her off someplace in the middle of a soliloquy about the structural difference between the diner's cheesesteaks and cheesesteak hoagies. I didn't even wait to hear her goodbye before I hung up.

His head tilted vaguely in my direction, and I reflexively took a big step behind the pump, out of his view. No way I was letting someone that hot see me this gross. He probably could have smelled me from half a parking lot away, if he concentrated hard enough.

From my hiding spot, I watched as he turned to dab someone hello. They were laughing and chatting loudly, giving me a perfect and uninterrupted view of the back of his head. He had one of those haircuts designed in a lab to ruin straight women's lives. Faded all around the sides, but left long enough on top that you could really dig your fingers in. If you needed to.

His hair was curly, radiating upward in a soft mass of black corkscrews, the sun moving through the far-reaching twirls and giving him a halo. If I hadn't been busy trying to roll my tongue back into my mouth, I would have laughed out loud. Had anyone this gorgeous ever been within a fifteen-mile radius of Evergreen?

He must have been a wayward perfume model, lost on the Garden State Parkway after wandering blindly out of a Nordstrom's beauty department.

Hot Man was still struggling to get his wallet in his pocket, his T-shirt sleeve pulling back and forth to reveal the colorful lines of a half-sleeve of ink and the swell of his biceps. He was muscular in a pragmatic way, like moving heavy objects was part of his everyday life. There was something about his hands—his knuckles. They were so *square*. Sharp like the edge of his jaw.

Was it normal to find someone's knuckles attractive? I wished I knew what four out of five doctors thought.

I flattened my hands over my hair and pushed my sunglasses down onto my face in an attempt to hide my mascara-smeared eyelids.

No, nothing about this was normal. Nothing about *me* was normal—I had twelve hours of hard evidence. At this point, I needed to just get comfortable with the freak show I'd become. Really lean in. Learn to juggle. Grow a tail. Buy a big, striped tent—

My plans were interrupted when the single-most-attractive man in New Jersey suddenly turned around, sunglasses now hanging from the front of his shirt.

Face completely revealed.

"Oh my God," I gasped. Loudly.

The words shot out of me like a bark from a beached sea lion groaning in agony. His eyes flashed toward me. I clasped my hand over my mouth and spun around, bracing myself against the car.

"No," I hissed. "No, no, no."

It couldn't be.

It was impossible.

It could not be *him*.

3

It was the coldest first day of school I'd ever experienced, and I was having a hard time not seeing the weather as some sort of omen about what my high school experience would be like. Fog was rolling in off the shores, encasing Nan's Jeep and the entire Malaga County High School parking lot. A Volkswagen Beetle had blasted through a stop sign, cutting Nan off and skidding to a self-conscious stop two spots over. *Yep, definitely an omen.*

After Nan got all the necessary cursing and lecturing out of the way, I turned to her and revealed my truth: "I hate high school already. Everyone's going to call me mean names like Big Foot and Mrs. Yeti."

"Delfina Marie," Nan chastised me, pulling her Clinique lipstick away from her mouth. She was reapplying, using the rearview mirror to make sure she stayed in the lines. "Why would anyone ever call you that?"

"Look at those boys, Mom." I pressed a finger flat against my window, pointing at a gathering of nervous-looking fourteen-year-olds at the base of the wide, tall steps that led to the main doors. "They're like twigs."

She leaned across me, squinting at the crowd. "They look a little underfed."

"Underfed. Skinny. Short." I sunk down low in my seat, attempting to rightsize my five-foot-eight frame. I was wearing a pair of JCPenney Little Miss skinny jeans and an Iron Maiden T-shirt I'd found at the Goodwill. Nan wouldn't let me cut my hair, so it was in an impossibly long, thick braid, wiry black hairs frizzing around my forehead.

"You're gorgeous. You look like Gene Tierney." She was always doing this. Who the hell was Gene Tierney?

"No one cares about her," I whined, hugging my lunch box to my chest. "They care about Paris Hilton and Lindsay Lohan."

"Lindsay? Paris? *They* sound underfed."

I couldn't fight back my smile. Nan was hilarious, a minor annoyance when all I wanted to do was experience righteous anger and pout tragically. "You're obsessed with food. You would turn into a doughnut if it wasn't for me."

"What kind of kid loves carrots?" She smiled affectionately at me, swiping a thumb under my eye, clearing away some smudged eyeliner.

"Don't forget, you promised we could go to FYE after school today."

"Honey, if Dr. Moscow has late appointments, I have to stay late and then I have to cook dinner—"

"Nan, please," I said, voice tight with emotion. "Jim Gaffigan's new special is out on CD. I just want to listen once all the way through—"

"Oh, don't beg. It inflames my GERD." She reached over and pressed a cold hand to my cheek. "You're going to make friends. You may even make a boyfriend."

"Boo." I leaned over and pressed my lips to her cheek. She tasted like CoverGirl compact powder and rose water. "Ciao."

"Ciao," she replied as I jumped out of the car. "Be good!"

SIGNS AROUND the campus directed all freshmen toward the northeast entrance, and by the time I reached the steps I'd spied from the car, the crowd had quadrupled.

All around me everyone buzzed with conversation—catch-ups from the summer, introductions, even laughter. All the while a man with a dusty blond mustache and a clipboard stood on a step, arms spread out wide as he shouted at us to form a line.

I joined the group, keeping to the edge where I felt like I could make a run for it, if necessary. There was a boy (short, of course) a few feet from me, leaning against an enormous and oddly shaped instrument case plastered with band stickers. He was wearing a Sixers hat pulled down to his brow line, a poofy ponytail sticking out under the back.

"Dream Theater," I blurted out, in place of a greeting. "On your case."

The boy slowly peeled his eyes away from mine and looked down to the case. "Oh. Yeah. They're like, my favorite band."

I nodded sagely. "My dad likes them."

He started nodding, too. We bobbed our heads like two mallards pecking at crumbs. "Do you like them?" he asked eventually.

"Um, I don't know. I'm more into Dashboard Confessional and stuff."

"Ew," the boy said definitively with an air of ease and expertise. "Emo is for girls."

"No. It definitely isn't. Emo is like, international."

"Totally," he pivoted. "Have you ever heard of Tool?"

An upperclassman with painfully red pimples on the apples of his cheeks ran past us grinning and shouting, "Fresh*meat*! Fresh-*meat*!" His eyes connected with mine and he tossed me a disturbing open-mouthed wink.

I tightened my arms over my stomach. "Um, kinda."

"Okay, yeah." He pointed a finger gun at me. "*They* are a real band."

"Oh." I scrunched my nose. "That doesn't really make sense."

"Yeah, it does."

"No, it doesn't. All bands are real bands. Just because they're not meant for boys doesn't mean they aren't real."

He had no counterargument, but from the way he was staring at the pebbled stone path, I could tell I'd really given him something to consider. "I'm Eddie, by the way."

"I'm Delfina, but I go by Del."

"Is this the freshman line?" Eddie and I both spun around toward the pinched voice. It belonged to a girl, way shorter than me, with a head of barrel curls. Despite the anxiety pulling at her voice, she was smiling like her life depended on it. Her skin was deep brown, a coat of pink blush dusted expertly over her cheeks. We began our nodding again—in unison.

"Have they started the hazing yet?" she asked.

"The *what*?"

She adjusted the straps of a heavy-looking backpack on her shoulders. "My brother told me they force all the freshmen to strip down and swim across the lake to their first class."

The well-trained alarm bell that lived in the pit of my stomach immediately went off. The creepy crawl of anxiety started up the back of my neck and over my ears, no doubt turning my skin pink in its wake.

"No way. That's so illegal," Eddie said.

"Yeah, totes illegal," I parroted with a fraction of his confidence. She finally stopped smiling. "That *fucker* lied to me."

I tried to keep my mouth from falling open. I'd never actually said *fucker* out loud—even though it was Nan's favorite curse, second only to *sonuvabitch*—but I had thoughtfully considered it once or twice. "My *stupid* older brother said I was going to have to swim to class." She pulled aside the neck of her hoodie to reveal the edge of a bathing suit. Before I could react, the teacher with the clipboard clapped twice.

"Hello, freshmen! Welcome to Malaga County High." He grinned. "Are all y'all ready for the best years of your life?"

THE HIGH school cafeteria was huge. All of the tables were picnic-style, lined up one after another after another. There were groups of friends everywhere. It seemed like everyone had someone. It was the only way to make this type of seating work. You either had friends or you starved.

Eventually, after my fifth or eighteenth lap, I found the boy with the ponytail. Teddy or whatever.

"Hey," I called out to him, nodding at the open spot at the end of his table. "Can I sit with you?"

He shot a sidelong glance to his lunchmates. They dropped their eyes to their trays, snickering under their breath. "Um . . ."

"Never mind." I flicked my braid over my shoulder. "Forget it."

"It's just . . . there's probably not enough space," one of his friends piped up. Then, they all dissolved into laughter. I tightened my grip on my lunch box and looked right at the boy with the ponytail.

He wasn't really laughing, just letting out a few dry, hard *haha*'s to avoid accusations of being so *totally* homosexual—or worse, friends with me. He'd had no problem talking to me earlier, subjecting me to his mostly bad opinions about some band my loser dad listened to. Somehow this hurt way more than any insult I could have imagined, including Mrs. Yeti.

I narrowed my eyes at him. "Seriously? You're a fucker." I turned to leave and took a half step before I decided I was *not* done. "Also . . . Dream Theater sucks. My dad likes them, and he's at least forty." The table erupted into a chorus of *ooooooh*s, but I was already walking away. *Bunch of nerds.*

And as if the heavens were on my side, I immediately spotted the curly-haired, toothy-grinned girl at a table by the windows that overlooked the football field. She was eating alone, wrestling a straw into her Snapple.

"Hey," I sang out, racing over to her. "Mind if I sit with you?"

Her eyes lit up. "Mind? Oh my God, I would love it. Please. I feel like such a dork."

I slid onto the bench opposite her. "You? That guy with the ponytail is the dork." I pulled a deformed tuna sandwich out of my lunch box and tossed it onto the table. "I think his friend called me fat."

"Ew," the girl hissed before biting into a baby carrot. "That is so *pathetically* middle school. Your boobs are huge, and that's awesome."

I smiled at her. "I love carrots."

"Cool." She flashed her smile at me again. "I'm Sam."

4

Mayor Pollard Memorial Dog Beach

Some relationships are beyond subconscious—they're elemental. Molecular. Like the protons inside you are charged differently, and no matter how hard you try, there is no besting the invisible hand that moves your pieces. There are organic puzzles that exist throughout the entire molecular world. So why can't humans—full of molecules—also reject each other? Because of logic or human will? Because of our stupid brains?

My brain, famously, was full of shit. Shit thoughts. Shit habits. Shit ideas.

Like the shit idea that Edgardo Rodriguez was the sexiest man I had ever laid eyes on when I knew, *I knew,* in an elemental, molecular way we were incompatible.

I continued to brace myself against the car, pretending the back door handle was the most interesting mechanism I'd ever laid eyes on, while a lifetime's worth of shame and embarrassment pulsed through me, congregating in my neck and turning me the color of strawberry jam. I yanked at it, hoping—*praying*—Eddie hadn't seen me.

I kept up my charade until I could just make out that he was walking away in my peripheral vision. Then, I looked again.

Yep, it was Eddie. Undeniably. Much taller than the last time I had seen him ten years ago, now a full-fledged man.

He even drove a fucking SUV.

I dropped my gaze and shuffled around Cyrus's car as fast as I could, throwing myself into the front seat. Then, I ducked my head down between the window and the steering wheel, running a fake script through my mind, attempting to give my absolute bizarro behavior some backstory.

Oh no! My shoe came untied. Ugh, gotta take care of that before we drive again, Del! Safety first, you absolute safety nut.

I had not seen this guy—man?—in a decade, but a Silva-Miller never cedes to her enemies. I would know. I've interviewed every single Silva-Miller in existence (one—me), and we all agree.

I'm not just some ledger-keeping psychopath. I had four years' worth of high school memories that proved exactly why someone like Eddie Rodriguez was not the type of guy you ogled at a gas station. The number-one reason being, if he knew I was ogling him at a gas station, he would never let me forget the ogling or the gas station. The Eddie I knew would have purchased a billboard or adopted a highway to commemorate the moment (and my ensuing humiliation) for his pleasure and the pleasure of generations to come.

As I was swimming in shame while hiding in a borrowed car, there were only two things keeping me from melting into a blubbering panic attack:

One—erasing the mental proof of *everything* I'd felt about Eddie's face, arms, tattoos, shoulders, and knuckles from my memory.

Two—texting Sam.

I hit send on a long text to her that read something like Ajdh-fjdshfjksbdohmyGOOOOD and flicked my eyes back up to where there'd been a white Honda SUV containing the man who had once been the bane of my existence. And maybe the most devastating crush I'd ever had.

"Thank God," I sighed out loud.

Thank God, Eddie was gone.

I watched the back of his car speed by, over the final bridge that stood between me and my hometown, past a sign that read: WELCOME TO EVERGREEN! SOMETIMES SUNNY, FOREVER GREEN.

I STARED at the sign for a long time. Until I saw two and a half signs.

The last twenty-four hours had finally caught up with me, and I was punch-happy. Slap-drunk. The exhaustion had skipped over my body and settled directly in my brain. I was slack-jawed and sleep-deprived, unable to move. Unable to pull out back onto the two-lane highway and finish the longest journey I'd maybe ever taken.

My mind was ping-ponging between New York and Evergreen, dinging off Brainwave and circling around to hit me in the gut, reminding me that *I'd been cheated on*. Sure, that hurt— a solid blow to my ego—but all I could think was: *my jokes*.

I slammed on the gas and peeled out of the lot, cutting across the highway and turning down a roughly paved side road. I just needed a second—a moment to catch my breath from what felt like wave after wave of pure, uncut life crashing into me, pounding me back and making my bones feel like sand. My hands were sweating, and my heart felt like it was growing bigger with each pulse, expanding rapidly to fill my entire rib cage.

Just as the gravel and sand road came to an end and I'd unofficially given up hope of things ever working out in my favor again,

I spotted the narrow, uphill footpath among some overgrown reeds. A crooked metal sign, mostly hidden by brush, stuck out at a forty-five-degree angle.

MAYOR POLLARD MEMORIAL DOG BEACH.
IF YOU BRING IT IN, YOU CAN BRING IT OUT.

Finally. A place I could stop and catch my breath. A place I'd always been able to stop and catch my breath.

I'd been frequenting Mayor Pollard's dog beach since I was a kid. It held thousands of memories that flashed through my mind in a hazy blur, like photographs through a viewfinder: Nan dragging a cooler across the sand as her sun hat caught in the wind. A three-legged race that ended with burns on my elbows and hands, all to save a border collie named Cricket. Slightly wet ham-on-focaccia sandwiches, sand in my teeth, and a bichon-Maltese staring expectantly, inching forward with every bite I took.

I kicked my sneakers off before getting out of the car and scrambling up the hill.

The air smelled the same as it always had: the salty staleness of the ocean inlet mixed with sunshine and echoes of dog pee. The sun danced tirelessly on the surface of the ocean, stretched like a cobalt-blue canvas in every direction. This inlet was calm and shallow, warmer than any other part of the Atlantic this time of year. The water pulled me in with its rhythmic whisper and glistening calm.

I pulled my tank top over my head and pushed off my pants. The tides were little more than a frothy *swish-swish* across the gray-brown sand and I waded into the water with little resistance. As the water lapped at my chin, and my feet lifted from the velvet-smooth floor, I pushed into a butterfly stroke that took me to where the water turned ice cold beneath my feet. Then, I closed my eyes, floating onto my back and letting the sun warm every inch of me.

I could hear Nan's voice in the back of my mind.

Are you insane? Are you out of your mind? Swimming alone? Do you have a death wish?

I flipped over and took an enormous breath before diving under the surface, pushing out my breath, and letting the frigid water surround me.

I MADE it back to shore, teeth chattering wildly, where the sun had turned the sand molten, and I knew I'd be dry within minutes. I was squeezing water out of my hair when my phone chirped from underneath my pile of clothing. I snagged it, along with a handful of sand, and hit accept.

"You ghosted me," Sam shrieked across the line. "Did you say hi to him? Did he say hi *to you*?"

I squeezed my eyes shut and turned away from the ocean. "Sorry, I had to pull over to have a complete mental breakdown. Do you remember how I told you about my Ingram jokes? And how good they are?"

"I think so," she replied slowly, cautiously.

"I . . . I don't think I can joke about him—or us—now. And that was my whole set for Brainwave. All of my set—the entire thing is just . . . it's just trashed. Sam, it's trash."

Sam inhaled sharply like she'd just given herself a paper cut.

"Every joke is about us as a couple, what we're like together. How I'm all, I don't know, poor and weird. And he's a fancy prince-bitch from Alberta." I kicked at the sand, watching it catch in the wind and blow back at me, sticking to my salt-slick legs. "Each show I did, it just got bigger and bigger laughs. *Fuck*." I pressed the heel of my hand into my eyes, pushing back the full-ness. "I didn't think it would end like *this*. When did the universe decide to end me?"

"Hey, listen." Sam rushed to keep up with me, her voice tight and frantic. "You are going to be okay. You are a professional co-median. You have jokes for days. You make fun of things all the time. What about—what about when you called the—the store—you called it something *so* funny, do you remember? The joke about the store?"

"What store? What *something*?"

"Never mind—forget it. What about the material you did that got you into Brainwave? Your submission tape? Use that!"

"No matter what I do, it's like I'm starting over." I turned back toward the bridge over the inlet that led directly into downtown Evergreen. The sign was behind me now, technically. "I'm back in Evergreen, starting over."

That was all Sam needed to hear. "Eddie has you spooked."

I gritted my teeth, snagging my clothes off the beach and shak-ing out the sand. "Forget about Eddie, Sam. I'm an unemployed adulteree. I slept in a car."

"Yeah, you did," she started slowly, her voice building with the confident precision of someone who told people what to do for a living. "And you broke up with your toxic boyfriend, who you should have ditched a month ago. And you left your craptastic job. You *also* finally got out of a hostile living situation. Good job. All your life problems have been solved in the last twenty-eight hours. Enjoy your mulligan."

My mouth fell open and closed a few times, soundlessly wob-bling with shock, until I got it together enough to stutter out, "Mulligan?"

Sometimes I thought Sam became a psychologist just so she

could more competently school me. She always knew how to lovingly snap me out of it, à la Loretta vis-à-vis *Moonstruck*. Though I did still have my hand and could, one day, have my bride.

I wanted to tell her that she wouldn't get it, that she would never really get it. Sam had both her parents and what felt like never-ending access to good luck. I loved her with my whole heart; she was the closest I'd ever gotten to a spouse, a sibling, a soulmate. But there were so many parts of myself plastered with Do Not Disturb signs. Parts of myself that were hard and dark and no pep talk could pull them forward.

I had to backtrack the conversation to a more comfortable place. "I guess I could find some tables to wait here," I offered meekly.

"We'll get there. Consider getting home step one."

Sam didn't have time for a *we*. She had a baby, a husband, and a career. I'd made it this far on my own, couldn't I manage the rest? Or I could have stayed on the dog beach, in Cyrus's car, forever. Grow that tail I'd been talking about.

"I'll see you soon," I assured her.

She gave the phone a noisy kiss. "Bye, sister girl."

We'd started calling each other that after an assignment our senior year of high school wherein we had to describe our best friend using just a single word. Sam had chosen *sister*, and I had chosen *girl*.

"Bye, sister girl," I replied before hanging up.

5

507 *Crestfallen Lane*

Evergreen, New Jersey, was surrounded by water. To the west was Malaga Bay and to the east was the Atlantic Ocean. The northernmost tip of the island was home to Evergreen Lighthouse State Park.

If you drove south long enough from the lighthouse, you would hit 100 percent of the most important landmarks from my childhood—the Evergreen State Research Reserve, where Tully Martino told me I was too tall to be a girl; the boardwalk where Sam and I spent every weekend of our adolescent lives swapping precious secrets over funnel cake; Santorini Café, where I began working as soon as I was old enough to pronounce *marinara;* and the Pier Point Diner, where Nan and I ate eggs every Sunday after mass. Then, you'd hit Surf City, Long Branch, and finally the last town on the whole island: Beach Paradise. Therein you would experience a gorgeous irony: no paradise, very little beach.

The only things that truly tethered us to the southern half of New Jersey were a few bridges and the velvet fist of democracy. Evergreen was a free-floating slither of marsh, sand, and water-logged jetties bobbing recklessly along with the tides.

I pulled up to the first traffic light, and everything was alive with an August beachside heartbeat: a freckled teen with a thick blond ponytail and tomato-red shoulders pedaled her bike barefoot through the busy intersection, using the hood of my car to help propel herself with a lazy shove; vacationers unloaded their cars at the Bay Breeze Motor Lodge, the first motel on the island, waiting like an overeager host; an army of American flags flapped in the wind for as far as I could see, from the bay to the ocean. I couldn't remember if Evergreen was always this patriotic or if we were just stuck in that hazy, jingoistic hangover that made up the days between the Fourth of July and Labor Day. Every inch of downtown hummed, and when I put down my window, it all sounded like a song.

Ten years ago, Evergreen had mostly been filled with check-cashing businesses and pawnshops. The boardwalk was dark except for a few pizza places with nearly identical names—Jim's, Jan's, Genie's. Formerly unoccupied row homes were now Froyo shops, escape rooms, Korean fried chicken joints, and trinket shops completely dedicated to the majesty of wind chimes. I could hear the merry-go-round on the boardwalk from a mile and a half away, the merry-go-round that had been out of commission for more than half of my life, a handwritten *See you next summer!* sign slapped on the ass of a vacant-eyed horse. Someone must have finally coughed up the money to have it repaired.

As a kid, I'd felt trapped at sea, longing to be on solid land—*connected* land—close to a Hot Topic and wherever Green Day was performing. Not some soggy paradise for the pathetically criminal and criminally pathetic.

But now Evergreen wasn't just a place. It looked *and felt* like a destination. Like people came here on purpose. Not because they took a wrong turn on their way to rob an Arby's.

Maybe I can pretend like I'm here on purpose.

At the exact moment this thought entered my mind, an elderly woman in a salmon-colored pantsuit standing on the corner turned around to reveal that she was carrying a sign.

ACCEPT CHRIST!!! GO BIRDS!!!

Never mind.

Technicolor motels and houses whizzed by. The old red and white brick house on the corner of Brambleberry and Washington, home to The Billiards (Evergreen's oldest dive bar, est. 1962), had undergone a bit of a face-lift. As the road turned to a sandy dead end, I pulled up alongside an L-shaped building built around a parking lot and swimming pool, ruby-red doors facing the street. A cherubic sun grinned down at me and beneath her baby face the sign read: BEL SOL CONDOMINIUMS.

Home.

I WAS lugging my suitcase up the wooden steps that led from the parking lot to the second-floor apartments, sweat beading under my nose, completely dried from my swim. Every granule of salt and sand shifting against my hot, sensitive skin was pure hell.

"Fuck. *Shit*." I pushed a tuft of tangled, ocean-blown hair behind my ear. A single droplet of sweat ran down the side of my face, spiraling toward the ground before crashing into the tip of a shoe I didn't recognize.

"Need help?" a voice, thick with a Jersey-Italian accent, growled from above me.

I looked up, shielding my eyes from the sun, directly into the face of a man who appeared to be Danny DeVito's stunt double, so tan he was roughly the same shade as a grilled hot dog. He stood shielding his eyes with a calloused hand, toothpick hanging out of the corner of his maw. I wasn't sure how *he* was going to carry my suitcase if *I* couldn't. I was twice his height, no comment on width.

I pushed my sunglasses back into my hair. "I'd love some."

With my approval, he lifted the suitcase like it was loaded with cotton balls. "You Annetta's girl?"

"Yes, sir." I followed behind him on the steps.

"She don't need your help."

"No, I'm not here to take care of her. I actually need her help."

He paused, staring down his bulbous nose at me. "Your husband leave?"

"No," I said, more defensive than what the poor guy probably deserved. "I just . . . I dumped my boyfriend."

"And he made you leave?"

"No! Why does everyone keep asking that?"

He clunked my suitcase down in front of apartment 205 before dusting his hands off. "I'm Alfonzo. I live down there." He pointed across the bend in the building to the last apartment facing the swimming pool. "You need something, you get Annie to call."

I smiled at his use of her nickname. "Thanks, Alfonzo."

He flapped a hand at me as though I'd insisted Mars was a state. He muttered goodbye and took off in a bowlegged hustle.

I inhaled deeply for a moment, steadying myself for a tornado of energy that was my beloved grandmother. Questions, comments, clanking bracelets, neighborhood updates, too much perfume. Before I could even knock, the door swung open.

"Oh my God, you stink!" Nan announced—a grinning vision in powder blue. She was glowing with her summer tan, her fingernails painted, alternately, coral and pink. She'd grown her pixie cut out into a bob that looked *very* familiar, gray waves tucked behind her ears.

"Nice haircut," I quipped, pointing at my own bob and using my knees to push my suitcase over the threshold. "I just met Alfonzo."

"That old crone," she remarked, pulling me into a quick Chanel-scented hug. "*Muah, muah!*" Sometimes Nan just made the kissing sound, assuming that was enough to substitute for the actual act.

"He's handsome," I teased, ending the embrace quickly so she didn't feel my wet bra through my shirt.

"He's a joyless little complainer who eats too much ice cream." She gave my suitcase a fruitless yank before huffing away, back toward the kitchen.

The apartment was exactly as it always had been—the living room still painted a shade of screaming cantaloupe, followed by our little kitchen and balcony that hung dangerously low over the end of the boardwalk. The couch was still covered in intricately embroidered pillows featuring sequined fireflies, cross-stitched owls and fairies, and bedazzled gnomes. Over the lacquered oak entertainment center hung a set of the metal butterflies that, as Nan loved to emphatically remind me, worked *perfectly* and *really tied the room together.*

Family photos hung in ornate frames around the room, mostly of my mom and me at various points of our schooling. Here, we existed as Nan's two daughters, decades apart, neither one of us ever older than seventeen.

My mom's, Michelle's, school pictures had a yellow tint to them—her gaze fixed softly on something in the distance. Her eyes were a murky shade of gray brown and her mouth tended to settle into a grumpy, conspiratorial pull. Next to her I was softer and rounder, more palpably pleasant. I was pale like my dad, with a splash of brown freckles over my stubby nose. I had her murky eyes, but mine were larger, wetter. While my mom stayed frozen in a pubescent tomboyishness, I seemed to always be firmly situated in womanhood. In my fifth-grade school photo, I even wore a blazer. I looked like a very tiny, very scared HR representative.

As far as I knew, Nan only kept one photo of my parents and me as a family. It wasn't framed. It wasn't hung over the TV. It was buried deep in our kitchen junk drawer. I had found it a few years ago when I was hunting for chopsticks.

Nan returned from the kitchen, fists pressed into her hips. "Unfortunately, you do look like Roger's side," she observed.

Roger is my dad, but mostly, he was just Roger.

I dropped my purse onto the couch. "Unfortunately?"

"You know what I mean. He's a handsome man!" She turned to walk away, adding under her breath: "But my God, what a prick."

I rolled my eyes and began dragging my suitcase farther into the apartment, toward a small dining room table laid out with cream-colored doilies and a spread of cured meats, cheeses, and crackers.

"Lunch," she announced, bustling back over with a pitcher of pink lemonade.

"Nan, thank you so much, really." I gestured at her meats. "But I'm a vegetarian."

"Oh no. You're still doing that?"

"Of *all* the decisions I've made in my life, being a vegetarian is the one that bothers you?"

"It's really inconvenient, bub," she said, observing the spread with concern.

"I have *Semi-Charmed Life* tattooed under my butt cheek," I reminded her, snagging a triangle of provolone before turning down the hall toward my bedroom.

"Well," Nan called after me. "You and your butt cheek can order something 'cause this is all I got."

"I'm not hungry, but we appreciate the offer." I was already halfway down the narrow hall. "My butt cheek and I need a nap."

I woke up to the sound of a live studio audience laughing faintly and the sun setting through the curtains, casting my room in a dreamy pale purple light. I rolled out of bed—a knotted pine day-bed I'd picked from a catalog during Dubya's first term—and stumbled down the hall to find Nan sitting in her usual corner of the couch poking at an iPad.

"Good morning," she teased. "There's rice pilaf on the stove."

I rubbed the sleep from my eyes, swallowing against the dry-ness in my throat. "What time is it?"

"Just after eight." She peered up at me from over the tops of her reading glasses. "You were exhausted."

I nodded through a yawn, flopping on the couch beside her be-fore lying down and weaseling my head under her iPad and into her lap. "I don't want to be here, Nan."

"I know," she hummed, nails clicking against the tablet screen. "You'll be okay."

"Will I? Or will I end up on one of those reality shows about adult women who hoard Cabbage Patch dolls?"

"One second, love." She had the tip of her tongue pressed into her Cupid's bow, like typing on an iPad was a physical act of ex-treme strength. "Just doing some admin for St. Agnes's Facebook page. Frankie D'Alessandro posted some crazy crap again."

I dislodged from her lap, sitting up straight again. "I think I'm going to go for a walk on the beach."

"Okay, honey," she said without looking away from the glow-ing screen. "Be careful of jellyfish. Mating season went unregu-lated because Mayor Cisco spent the whole freaking budget on his mistress's *boob* job. Those little things went hog wild. We're drowning in pups."

6

I took a quick shower and pulled on a well-loved black-and-white-checkered sundress before heading out into the dense, chilly night air. Down by Bel Sol everything was quiet, save for the laughter and chatter of the few who'd meandered all the way to the end of the boardwalk, where planks became sand and road again. I was outside Nan's apartment, leaning over the railing and letting the breeze fall over me while I felt sorry for myself. It felt different to experience self-pity while at the helm of the ocean. Much more satisfying.

I was interrupted by the sound of a plastic chair being dragged across concrete. I spun around to find Alfonzo slowly hobbling toward me, chair in tow.

"Need help?" I called out to him, only to be met with silence.

When he finally reached me, he shouted, way too loudly for how close we were, "What're you doin' here?"

"I don't know?" I replied, embarrassment traveling from my belly to my cheeks. "I needed fresh air, I guess."

He flapped a hand at me, easing into his seat and pulling a piece of wood and a pocketknife from the front of his board shorts. "Why? Forget the boyfriend."

"You remembered."

Alfonzo ignored my attempt to forge a bond. "All the kids go down to Billiards for music and drinks," he said, offering me an opportunity to take his heavy-handed hint.

"What if I want to hang out with you instead?" I countered. I didn't care if being small and grumpy was his thing, I suddenly very much wanted Alfonzo to comfort me. To give me a black-licorice-scented hug.

He looked up at me through his big, wiry eyebrows. "No."

"Why not? I can whittle."

He nudged his head toward the street. "Go play with your friends."

"Alfonzo, I don't have any friends."

"You're blocking my view."

"Fine," I whined. "I'll go drink and listen to music." I pushed off the wooden railing and shifted my bag up high on my shoulder. "But I won't like it."

"Don't be home late," he called to me over his shoulder as I made my way down the steps toward the parking lot. "Annetta gets up very early."

FOR EVERGREEN'S "one true dive," The Billiards was looking awfully respectable these days. The once famously gross bar was on the first floor of an old-school shore house—tall and narrow with a wood-shingled awning over the front door—situated on a grassy lot far away from the street. A few bucket-hat wearers sat around the picnic tables that dotted the lawn, smoking cigarettes and playing checkers.

I attempted to spy the crowd through the door before making my way in, but it was almost entirely covered in posters. Freshly taped over the center of the door was the largest—and most obnoxious—featuring the faces of two disembodied men vomiting rainbows.

WE'RE BACK, BITCH. EVERGREEN'S ONE AND ONLY COMEDY OPEN MIC NIGHT—EVERY TUESDAY. HOSTED BY JAMES & DUSTY.

BRAVE SOULS ONLY.

I sucked down a shaky breath.

Would this be the place I rewrote my Brainwave set? It was better than nothing—which was what I had right now. No jokes, no other place to practice.

I snapped a picture of the poster.

Between the signs, I scoped out the bar. I could make out some high-top tables and metal stools, a headless mannequin wearing a T-shirt and leaning against one of those old-school cigarette machines. Behind the horseshoe-shaped bar was a small stage just big enough to fit a band. A group of women had gathered around it, sitting on the edge and sipping from cans with willowy arms covered in tattoos. Why did stepping into this bar feel like the first day of high school? Arming myself with faux confidence, I pulled open the door.

The Billiards was definitely not a dive.

First of all, it didn't smell like a dive. It smelled like pulled pork, fresh mint, and brick-oven pizza. People weren't just drinking at the bar; they were eating. For pleasure. Visibly *savoring* it. Nary a BOGO hot dog in sight.

Instead of the usual Philadelphia sports regalia that plastered the walls of every other bar in this area, various Caribbean and South American flags were lovingly pinned to the walls. Brazil,

Puerto Rico, Paraguay, Guyana. Sure, the owners had kept the old cigarette machine and Budweiser neon sign. But they were dusted and shined, charming vintage centerpieces instead of scrap garbage no one had ever taken out.

I slid onto an empty stool at the curve in the bar and pulled out my notebook. This place was vaguely inspiring, wasn't it? All I had to do was push through the wiggly feeling in the depths of my tummy and focus. *Time to write the joke that will change my entire life, catapulting me to fame.* I clicked my pen. Flipped to a blank page.

Across the bar a man in an Eagles hat was telling an enthusiastic story, yelling so loudly that his face was tuna tartare pink. I chewed my lip, then put pen to paper:

You ever look at a man's face and think, damn, that'd be a good sandwich?

"Can I get you anything?"

I closed my notebook, praying the bartender had horrible vision or a very generous sense of humor. "Um, just a Maker's on the rocks. Actually, no, I'll have a Coke." Then, I lifted my eyes.

"Delfina?"

My breath caught in my throat. Edgardo Rodriguez. Wearing a different shirt from earlier today. No sunglasses on his nose. No credit card in his mouth. Just . . . Eddie.

"Eddie."

Only five feet of waxed mahogany bar between us.

The long part of his hair was pulled back into a little bun. All except for one single jet-black curl, hanging in front of his forehead. He looked winded, cheeks flushed and his chest rising and falling quickly.

Eddie's eyebrows flickered deeper into a contemplative pull. "It's you."

God, he's handsome. I could barely look at him. It was like staring directly into the sun. "Me, indeedy," I said. *Indeedy?* Humiliating. "You, uh, remember me."

"How could I forget you?" He shifted from foot to foot then quickly added, "They had to bring in that hat specialist to custom-make you a softball helmet."

My jaw seized into a metallic clench. "We all got new helmets that year."

Eddie mirrored my expression, folding his arms over his chest. Just like that, the molecules kicked in. "C'mon, I'm sure you remember something unflattering about me."

Was that a challenge? A flagrant, bold challenge? Was Eddie, ten years older and wiser, ready to pick up exactly where we'd left off?

I steeled myself, ready for battle. "Just that you were roughly five-foot-three for most of high school."

"Wow." His lip curled as he flicked a stained dish towel over his shoulder, backing away slowly. "You remember my stats."

Motherfucker.

As soon as he turned his back to me, I grabbed my phone. Help, I texted Sam. Realizing that probably wasn't prudent, I followed up immediately with another text: Not real help. Sorry. I just bumped into Eddie Rodriguez??? He tends bar???

Three dots popped up. Lol.

What was she laughing at?

Get with it, Del, Sam wrote back as if she could read my mind, he owns The Billiards.

I let loose a gasp. The man beside me glared at me from over the top of his Yuengling. Why did I keep gasping? I'd never been a gasper.

"So, was it a whiskey or a Coke?" I jolted again, shoving my phone out of sight. Eddie was looking over at me, leaning forward,

the width of his palms pressing into the bar, every muscle in his
forearms jumping to life. I wasn't sure if I wanted to paint him or
tell him to kiss my ass.

"Whiskey," I fumbled. "Or a Coke. Coke-whiskey. Whiskey-
Coke?" Suddenly, the entire bar made sense: the stage, the Caribbean flags, the persnickety attention to detail and well-curated
coziness. This was the adult version of painstakingly wallpapering
your locker with band pictures. The Billiards had *Edgardo Rodriguez* written all over it.

Owns!!!!!!! I wrote back.

A waitress with an abundant, curly ponytail saddled up to Eddie and tapped him on the shoulder with a landline phone. "More
mama drama," she announced.

"Not now, Chels," he growled, stalking back toward me with
my drink in his hand. He set it down on my napkin but didn't let
go. "I thought you lived in New York."

I reared back at his tone. "Um, I do."

"But now you're back in Evergreen?"

"Very observant." I flexed my hand in the direction of the glass,
hoping to coax it out of his death grip. "You've got a keen eye for
detail."

Eddie let out a dry laugh and ran his tongue over his teeth like
a hungry python eyeing up its prey. "You really are a comedian
now, huh?"

My stomach lurched, a shuddering reaction to his words. "Who
told you that?"

The confidence drained from his eyes. He batted his long lashes
left and right, opening and closing his mouth, hoping the words
would arrive if he just moved like they already had. I reached for
my glass again, but he snapped it away.

I rolled my head on my shoulder, exhaling a wave of frustration. "Is there a problem here?"

"No problem at all." He shrugged. I could see the pads of his fingers turning white around the glass. "I just thought you were never *ever* coming back to—what did you call Evergreen again? A shithole?"

Anger bucked in my chest at his recollection. "Am I allowed to visit my family? Or have you and the Council of Elders put an embargo on outsiders?"

"Huh." I watched the weight in his jaw shift from one side to the other. "You're a regular Lenny Bruce."

Lenny Bruce? How *dare* he. The heat was back, creeping up my neck now and overtaking my features. My pulse quickened. "Are we done here? I have things I need to do."

"Done," he repeated, cold humor clipping his voice. "Yeah. I'm done." With that, he pushed my drink toward me.

Now it was my turn to death-grip the poor, cold glass. "Know what I remember about you?" I fired back. Eddie paused mid-step, eyes flicking back to mine. There was something in them— familiar enough that it made my heart feel like it'd snagged on its last beat. "You told everyone you thought you were 'creatively' 'probably' a guitar prodigy."

Eddie flinched like I'd lifted my sundress and revealed a loaded gun. "Alright, I *never* said that."

"Oh yes, you did. In front of like, fifty people—in study hall."

"I was probably joking."

"Okay!" I leaned forward onto the bar, baring my teeth in a victorious grin. "And I was probably joking when I said I wasn't coming back."

"No." He leaned forward, flashing his own grin. His smile was bright and white and ice cold, but there was no way to not notice the glint in his brown eyes. The little wink of acknowledgment. The *you can't lie to me, I know you.* "You meant it." Then, he swiveled on his heel, flicked the bar towel over his shoulder, and walked away, leaving me to breathe loudly through my teeth.

"Drink's on the house," he called over, eventually. Just when I'd calmed down enough to take a sip.

EDDIE STAYED on the other side of the bar for as long as it took me to finish my drink. The smell of pizza was replaced by spilled cranberry juice and shaken tequila. I watched him count ones, shine glasses, and pop open beer bottle after beer bottle. When a young server ran up to him with two receipts in hand, panic all over her face, he leaned close and placed a calming hand on her shoulder, talking her through whatever it was she was freaking out about. I swallowed against the sudden, throbbing lump in my throat.

I was just embarrassed, that's all. I hadn't seen him in ten years; it was normal to feel this way.

His shirt was a little too short for his torso and shoulders. Every time he yanked the top off a bottle, the bottom pulled up and I could see the muscular planes of his lower back.

Maybe it was the whiskey. Maybe it was the August beach feeling.

Either way, I needed to get the hell away from Eddie.

7

Sam's House

To the untrained eye, Sam and I didn't make sense as friends. She was a pastel-wearing, designer-purse-carrying sweetie from a big Guyanese family. Her smile was bright, radiating joy and happiness. It was the smile of someone who had been loved fiercely by a mom and a dad in a big house by the bay. I couldn't remember a single year of Sam's life when she wasn't enrolled in some sort of extracurricular activity. She swam; she played lacrosse; she was a tristate mathlete champion. She was student government president in high school and the head of the South Jersey Collegiate Ecology Conference throughout her bachelor's and graduate program.

Sam's eyes were like an oil-slick puddle sitting in the sun. Rainbow refractions that with a tilt of her head revealed a glimpse of something else. Something darker. Slick, murky heaviness. I'd always seen beyond the initial brightness into her darker side. The part of her that liked to drink and swear and obsess over every guy with soft brown hair and dimples.

It was a tale as old as time: she started off drinking on the weekends in high school; then she progressed to smoking pot and rolling; then there was the treacherous Burning Man bender of 2014, followed by a secret relationship with a Manhattan real estate broker twice her age that nearly caused her to flunk out of her doctorate program.

Then, two years ago, she met Devon at a club in Miami. And ten months later, Devon Junior was born.

Leave it to Sam to find the one way to deeply disappoint her parents and "fuck up her life plan" while still meeting the man of her dreams and giving birth to an objectively perfect baby.

I sat at her kitchen island, baby DJ swaddled against my chest, in her and Devon's gorgeous cottage right on the edge of Malaga Bay. Soft-focus portraits of DJ sleeping in various positions were hung lovingly across the walls. Just like Sam, her home was bright and light and joyful. Maybe you'd expect me to be jealous—but I wasn't. There'd never been a situation where I saw myself owning a house at twenty-eight. Or ever. It was just me and Buster the Weeping Clown, enduring endless discomfort.

Every time we hung out Sam made our customary reunion meal—the Sad Salad. It was a meal that was mostly nutritionless, but in possession of every comforting flavor and texture we could think of. I ran a hand up and down DJ's back absentmindedly, alternating between pushing a pacifier into his mouth and chips into mine.

"It's simple," I said, summarizing my grand plans to toss my mulligan back in the face of fate. "Step one, secure a sublet within the next week. Step two, move in and immediately refocus on writing. Step three, write the best jokes of my life. Done. Easy."

Sam raised her eyebrows as she dumped freshly washed iceberg lettuce into a big wooden bowl.

"Okay, what does that face mean?" I dragged a tortilla chip through an enormous bowl of guacamole. "That's one of your little clinician faces."

"If you can believe it, Delfina Marie, I'm just having a normal reaction to this"—she twirled a finger in my direction—"insanity right now."

"*Inshanity?*" I shouted through a mouthful of chips and guac.

"Yes, girl," she replied pointedly. "You don't have a job. You're living off your savings—which is great that you even have. But you need it for a plane ticket, your phone bill, your health insurance, your student loan debt."

"What do you mean *even have?* Where I come from two thousand dollars in a snow boot is generational wealth." I straightened my back, cocking my chin in the air. "I'll have you know I even have a credit card now."

"Watch out, world. She's ready to spend six hundred dollars on a chair shaped like a hand."

I froze, mid-chip-in-dip. "You told me that chair was cool. Look, I can't keep sleeping in that damn daybed. It's like an adult-size crib. *Also* my high school bully owns the only freaking bar where I can practice new material."

Sam gingerly set the salad tongs onto the counter, as if holding them any longer might have resulted in her using them against me as a weapon. "You think he bullied you?"

"Yes. He was my mean, mean bully, and now he's very, very hot."

"Nope." She held up the bag of shredded cheddar cheese and I actually flinched. "You have absolutely mythologized your relationship with this man."

My mouth dropped open. "*Mythologized?* Who am I, Aesop? Quick, get me a stone freaking tablet. I have some fiction to transcribe."

She tossed a crouton at my head, and I narrowly dodged one of its incredibly sharp corners. "Your memory is failing you."

"He totally bullied me! Even last night." I leaned forward and whispered, "He brought up my special helmet."

Sam shot me a look of exhaustion she'd perfected over the years while slowly mixing the contents of the bowl. "You called him 'Soft Serve' for three years after you saw him eating soft serve *once*."

"It . . . was funny," I replied weakly.

"You signed him up for the talent show—"

"He's a talented musician!"

"To play the spoons."

I pulled my mouth into the universal expression for *yikes*. But Sam was on a roll. She kept rattling off memories as she tossed the salad with one hand and sprinkled the mixture with shredded carrots with the other. "He signed you up for a children's choir. You forked his lawn. He called you Pat and then Pat-ass for two years all because you played Mrs. Viola's original character, Patricia, in *Cinderella Junior*. You forked his lawn . . . again."

Did we really do all of that to each other? That was not what I remembered about Eddie at all. I *did* remember that he always possessed the unique ability to hurt my feelings unlike anyone else.

"Sam," I said, desperation peaking in my voice. "Am I evil?"

"No," she managed through laughs. "You two just tortured each other."

I relaxed back into my chair, relishing the realization that I was probably not totally evil. "Well, I've matured. Not sure about him." I picked up DJ's pacifier and turned it over in my hand. "He was obsessing over the fact that I'm back in town. He kept bringing up how I thought Evergreen was a shithole."

Sam slapped the bottom of a bottle of ranch until a glob flopped onto the lettuce. "Evergreen is kind of a shithole. It's like, part of the whole deal."

"Thank you!"

"Eddie's always been like that—so sensitive and protective of stuff he likes, you know?" There was a part of me that woke up when she said that. His face had been so severe—thick eyebrows pulled into a solemn, downward slope; the dramatic angle of his jaw even more pronounced with what was clearly an omnipres-ent clench. The only time his face seemed to relax was when that server needed his help. And maybe when he was talking to me. His eyes had softened around the edges, hadn't they? Or maybe I'd imagined it.

I couldn't read Eddie like I could read Sam; I had no idea what was behind the shimmer in his eyes—so dark they were like pools of ink. It was embarrassing to still crave his affection—crave the feeling of his fingers on my shoulder. But Eddie and I had a thing—a schtick. We disagreed, we argued, we sometimes found ourselves alone and then things happened that were *never* meant to happen. That was it.

"Toxic hetero-masculinity."

Sam gave me another clinically approved look—this one full of appreciation. "Sure, but he was also a kid. Not socialized or given the vocabulary to properly express himself."

"Ugh, you're so smart." I rolled my eyes, holding a protective hand against DJ's back as I slid off the stool and rounded the island toward Sam. "Why are you even friends with me?"

She handed me a set of plates. "Because you've got a great ass and incredible lips for a white girl."

I puckered my incredible lips before waddling off toward the sliding glass doors that led to the yard and eventually, the bay. She trailed behind me, hauling our disgusting feast. We settled around her table on the deck, facing the placid azure surface of Malaga Bay.

Sam popped the tab on a hard seltzer and leaned back in her chair, taking a sip. "What did Nan say when you told her you quit your job?"

I froze, tongs suspended over my plate. "Oops."

"*Del.* You're so convinced you'll be able to move back that you haven't told her you're *unemployed*?"

"First of all: ouch, my feelings. Second of all: I'm not hiding it from her, I swear. I genuinely forgot," I rushed to defend myself. "There was so much happening all at once. The Ingram thing, the sleeping in Cyrus's car thing, the Brainwave thing—which made her so happy, by the way."

"You are the most chaotic Libra I've ever met."

I pointed the tongs at her. "You need to meet more people."

We spent the rest of lunch talking about other things, but I couldn't stop thinking about Sam possibly being right. She must have noticed that my mind was elsewhere because her chatter slowed until we were eating in silence. How was I going to be able to get back to New York? My master plan was held together with bubblegum and toothpicks. I barely had enough savings to get me through Brainwave. If I spent the next forty-some days apartment hunting or job hunting, when was I going to have time to write my new, perfect material? The pressure was building in my chest again, the same way it had moments before I pulled over at the dog beach and walked into the ocean.

DJ began fussing and whining against my chest, and Sam came to retrieve him from where he lay against me.

"Let's go make a bottle," she whispered into the side of his head, placing a noisy kiss on one of his chubby cheeks.

I gave his chunky little foot one last squeeze before they headed back inside. "I'll miss you, peach."

It was a perfect August day. The air was buzzing with a dense humidity, but the sun had slipped behind a set of cotton candy clouds, giving us a brief reprieve. Here on the bay, there was no noise, no chaos. Just my favorite person and a seagull trying to lift an entire slice of pizza out of her trash. I closed my eyes and slid down in my chair, letting the sun warm my chest.

I hadn't slowed down like this in months.

I hadn't been home in months.

Since Christmas, to be exact. I'd nearly missed my bus after the ferry from Manhattan to Jersey got stuck behind a Frank Sinatra–themed booze cruise. Then, December 27, I was gone again—on a train to Baltimore, where I performed at a local festival.

It wasn't like I purposefully avoided coming back here. It was just that the thought of doing so left my heart feeling leaden. Nan never pushed the issue—she understood better than most that, for me, Evergreen wasn't just the sweet-sour smell of the ocean and quirky dive bars and guys like Alfonzo popping up out of nowhere.

It was the ghosts that clung to the shoreline; all the parts of myself I'd closed off at eighteen.

"Do you ever see Roger around?" I asked, once Sam was back.

She blinked hard, adjusting DJ in her arms. "Your dad?"

I nodded, shifting my eyes out to the bay. "I should probably let him know I'm in town before we bump into each other."

"Do you . . . miss him?" she asked tentatively.

I forced out a tinny laugh, embarrassment pulling at my stomach. "God, no. I was just curious. I haven't spoken to him or seen him in . . ." *Ten years.* I couldn't even say it out loud. We texted and emailed sometimes. He tried in that way, but that was about as much credit as I was willing to give him. No amount of *I'm so proud of the young woman you've become* texts would ever stop reminding me that the woman I was today had everything to do with how little he tried. I finished my sentence with, "Forever."

"It's okay if you do."

I shook my head. "Was just a thought." I didn't want to think about Roger, and I sure as hell did not want to think about Eddie. Not right now when I had jokes I needed to write. Happy, funny, good jokes. "A silly thought."

But they were like twin vines, wrapping around my brain and digging their thorns in.

8

salt & sage boutique

Sam's words had a way of working through me, slowly moving through my bloodstream until I absorbed them completely.

I got back to Bel Sol just after sunset, the parking lot now full. Two boys swatted a shuttlecock back and forth, chasing each other between the tightly packed cars. Their laughter and the tumbling of the tide against the sand were the only sounds in the air. I made my way up the wooden steps that led to the second story, passing in front of apartment 235. Alfonzo's door was ajar and the Phillies game playing at high volume; the smell of roasted peppers and grilled fennel-stuffed sausages drifted through. Evergreen felt like a tear in the time-space machinations, filled with smells and sounds that teleported me back to a time that wasn't simpler, but maybe I was. I breathed in the moment, willing myself to not puzzle out how much I'd missed Bel Sol's comfort.

Then, I felt the gentle thud of the shuttlecock against my shoulder.

"Sorry, lady!" one of the kids yelled from where he was now standing, fully clothed, in the shallow end of the pool.

I tossed it back. Since when was I a *lady*?

When I opened the apartment door Nan was lounging in her corner on the couch, knitting what looked like a set of oversize mittens. She looked peaceful in her buttercup-yellow housedress printed with lighthouses and sailboats, pedicured feet propped up on the coffee table. Her hair was freshly permed, hanging around her ears in rich gray, white, and brown shining swoops like a brown pigeon's plumage.

I'd spent the entire car ride home from Sam's working myself up to this conversation, and now that I was here my heart was hammering so hard, I was afraid it might actually get tired enough to stop.

Nan and I had only ever had one real fight. And it started with comedy. Or maybe, it really started with my mom. Either way, it all came to a head when I'd told her I was dropping out of college to focus on stand-up full-time.

When I told her, Nan was so angry she couldn't even speak. She just set down her cardboard cutout of a donkey and left me alone to finish putting together the St. Agnes Nativity pageant backdrop. She got in her Jeep and drove all the way to the drive-in movie theater in Delsy and stayed for five hours, through their entire Katharine Hepburn marathon. She told me this later like it was a war story; she'd been a prisoner of crackling, fast dialogue and soft-focus cinematography.

Two days later, she opened the door to my bedroom while I was getting ready for Christmas Eve dinner and said, "You better be the hardest-working comedian in New York City." Those two days without her were the longest, loneliest days I'd ever experienced. I'd never wanted to see her look at me like that again.

Nan looked up at me from over her needles. "Angela's got her telekinesis back."

"Um. Very cool." I slipped out of my shoes and joined her on the couch. She was watching the same soap opera she'd been following for the last twenty years—*Magnetic Touch*. Angela was the main character.

I took a deep breath. "Nan?"

"Hmmm?"

"I'm going to need to stay with you for a little while." I flicked my eyes over to see if she had stopped knitting or pulled her eyes away from the TV. *Nothing yet.* "I quit my job. To focus on the festival, so I could give it my all." I paused. She kept on knitting, but her needles were moving slowly, pulling tensely at each stitch. "I'm sorry. I don't want to disappoint you any more than I already have."

Okay. *That* got her to stop.

"*Disappoint* me?" She flicked her gaze to me, peering over her glasses. "I've never been disappointed in you, Delfina."

I narrowed my eyes at her. "You sure about that?"

"Angry, maybe. Concerned, definitely." She set down her needles and muted the TV. "But performing is your passion, always has been. My gosh, you sang before you could talk." She tutted at me in faux annoyance, a smile in her eyes. My heart hurt with love for the way she remembered tiny bits of me.

"I promise it's just temporary—until after the festival," I rushed to explain. "I need this time to focus, then I'm gone."

"Sweetie." Nan pulled her glasses off her face, smoothing her hair away with the back of her hand. "Why would you think I'd want you to leave?"

"I-I . . ." I shook my head. I didn't have a good answer—only the same feeling that those vines were squeezing me tighter and tighter. *You don't want me to leave. I need to leave. Again.*

Nan didn't wait for me to figure it out; she picked up her needles and unmuted her program. "This is your home. Heck, after I kick the bucket, it'll literally be yours."

My entire chest relaxed, melting from the inside out, until I was leaning my head completely against the back cushions of the couch. *Relief.*

I would never know how she truly felt—if she ever forgave me for dropping out of college—but she sounded like she meant it and that was enough for me right now. I leaned over and pressed my lips to her cheek. "Thank you."

She chuckled gently, leaning her head against mine. "James doesn't know that Trisha's baby is actually his twin brother reincarnated."

I closed my eyes, wrapping my arms around her shoulders. "Please tell me we're talking about the TV show."

THE NEXT morning, I was awoken by the sun, which greeted me by slipping through the cracks between my blinds and shining directly into my corneas. Vengefully—as if I owed it money.

Despite the abuse, I didn't mind the relationship I was forming with the sun; I'd never been a morning person, but now I had shit to do. A timetable to adhere to! Tasks and goals! Important, life-altering art to make!

I snuck out into the living room, where I did some morning stretches, unloaded the dishwasher, made a fresh pot of coffee, and enjoyed said coffee on the back balcony, lounging in a beach chair while watching the morning runners and surfers. The ocean smelled the sweetest this time of day, when the air was still cold and wet.

The sun and I made up.

I started running through some new material inspired by my environment, scanning like a sonar system searching for whales. Maybe I could do a whole bit about the sun. Was that too boring? Maybe a little too experimental.

I tried to identify some runners worth lampooning. There was a spritely, shirtless old man booking it down the planks. He was sort of hot for being definitively in the grandfather age range. Maybe I could do a bit about going to the Vietnam Veterans Memorial just to scope out potential boyfriends.

No. Too edgy.

I sipped my coffee, watching the sand slowly turn from white to gray as the tide went from low to high. Around seven-thirty, Nan popped her head out and said goodbye, heading to her job at Dr. Keizer's office. Then, my coffee was finished and I . . .

Paced.

Sat on the couch for thirteen minutes and forty-seven seconds.

Waved at Alfonzo until he waved back and then shouted at me to "stop, please."

Considered ordering a bagel.

Blow-dried my bangs into the perfect swoop.

I did *everything* but open my notebook and finally begin working on the jokes I *needed* to rewrite.

Like, *had to*. Because just knowing there was an Ingram-shaped hole burning its way through my pages of jokes made my throat feel tight and my pulse pick up.

Brainwave was coming. Whether I had jokes ready or not.

MY PROCRASTINATION led me to the boardwalk to admire the new crop of stores that had opened for the summer. Winters at the beach brought heavy windfall, frozen ocean foam, and the closure of many pipe-dream businesses that hadn't made enough during peak season to sustain them through the months when the shore turned back into a series of sleepy small towns. It was a huge bummer; when the Locked Up: Abroad—themed escape room was forced to close, I'd taken it particularly hard. But each summer, my first walk down the planks was like Christmas morning.

A new boutique on the north end caught my attention right away with a window display of rattan lanterns and rose quartz crystals. A cappuccino-colored sign above the door displayed the store's name: salt & sage btq. All lowercase. The font equivalent of blowing cigarette smoke in someone's face.

The store wasn't like most beach boutiques. No hokey signs or seashell key chains for sale. The clothes were arranged by color on wooden racks around the perimeter of the store. Behind the counter, a woman with tawny hair was tapping at an iPad.

"Hello," she sang out in a twinkling voice as I passed through the door.

I flashed her a nervous smile. "Are you open?"

"Of course." She smiled brightly, setting the iPad aside and standing up. She wore the same jumpsuit that was on the mannequin in the window, but in a warm terra-cotta shade. Her hair was so long it swung around her waist as she slid off her chair and to her feet. "Looking for anything in particular?"

I was thumbing through the hot-pink section of clothes, the display closest to the door. "Just browsing."

"I'll leave you alone." She wrapped her hands around a mug and lifted it to her lips. "I hate when boutique owners breathe down my neck."

That made me laugh. "I appreciate it."

She moved as softly and soundlessly as air, shifting out from behind the counter and halfway across the room. "You want a coffee? A juice or water?"

"A coffee would be great, actually."

She returned shortly after with another mug, steam twirling off the surface. "I'd offer you some champagne, but unfortunately I usually make customers wait until ten."

I took the mug with a look of gratitude. It smelled divine. "I hope I don't look like someone who enjoys booze before ten."

She threw back her head and let out a laugh. "No, I promise, you don't."

I wandered over to the section of the shop that was made up entirely of green items.

"You probably look amazing in that shade," She immediately clamped a hand over her mouth. "Sorry! I keep doing the thing!"

"You never have to apologize for complimenting me." I shrugged, pulling an emerald satin skirt from the rack. "I just moved back to town and I haven't really talked with anyone other than my best friend and grandmother." I held up the skirt. "You like?"

"Ugh! I love it," she gushed, reaching out to thumb the silky fabric. "That's from a new line by an Indigenous designer out of Santa Fe. I love her stuff."

Maybe a new skirt will help get my creative juices flowing. I imagined myself lounging in the lush material, reflecting more keenly on the nature of grandfathers being hot. "Mind if I try it on?"

She showed me to the dressing room, tucked in the back corner of the shop. I slipped out of my shorts and pulled the skirt up over my thighs. It did look amazing on me. Hugging the width of my hips perfectly, following their dramatic curve. I could hear Nan's voice in the back of my mind—I did look like Roger. I was tall like him, built solidly and broad in every way. Wide hip, sturdy shoulders, pronounced cheekbones. I had his button nose. What I *didn't* have were his forest-green eyes; that would have been too generous of him. Classic Roger.

I changed back into my shorts and took the skirt to the front register. "I'll take it."

"Yay!" The woman literally beamed, clapping her hands together softly. "I'm so happy you found something."

Being a comedian meant spending 90 percent of my time with people who feared earnestness like it was an airborne brain-festering pathogen. It was exhausting to exist around people who consistently skirted intimacy and then, I don't know, *gave you their car*. An unfortunate personality trait that I also suffered from. But her enthusiasm was so warm, just like the ocean air she seemingly had bottled and infused the entire shop with. So, I grinned and clapped my hands, too, like a dumb little baby. "*Amazing*. I can't wait to wear it out."

"Well," she said as she carefully folded the skirt, wrapping it in tissue paper and setting it into a brown paper bag. "I can't wait to see you wear it out. So, make sure you come by when that happens."

"I'm Del, by the way," I said.

"Meghan," she replied, extending a tanned hand for me to shake. "Welcome home."

After I paid, I stepped back out onto the boardwalk. Now, the air smelled like bananas Foster pancakes and sunbaked seaweed. The early-morning runners had been replaced by midmorning strollers. I leaned against the railing and tilted my head back, inviting the sun to warm my neck and face.

Welcome home. Despite my pale limbs and band tee, I was a local. And weirdly—perversely—that made me happy.

There was a weightlessness in my chest, like I'd been carrying a cowbell around my neck and someone had finally taken it off. I'd spent multiple hours partaking in small, loving rituals when I was supposed to be writing jokes. But how the hell was I ever going to do that?

Who has *ever* written jokes from a place of peace?

9

Before my alarm could go off the next morning, I was jostled
awake by the undeniably catchy downbeat of what sounded like . . .
reggueton? I was stumbling out of my bedroom and down the hall,
still trying to scrub the sleep from my eyes when I realized the
music wasn't coming from the thoughtless ingrates in apartment
210; it was coming from our stereo.

"Nan, what the—"

"Del, come dance!" she yelled, flicking her wrists to the beat as
she shuffled in a neat little two-step around the living room.

"What is happening?" I grunted, too tired to stop her from
hooking her hands around my wrists and pulling me out into the
middle of the living room.

"Tuesday's 'Rhythm of the Caribbean' day at aquarobics, and
I like to warm up my hips!" She pulled at my arms like she was
operating a backhoe. "You're stiffer than a glass of whiskey."

For a woman in her seventies, Nan moved deftly, hips and
shoulders gliding together in a little harmonized cha-cha as her
hair swayed with her to the beat.

"My hips usually are pretty warm," I defended myself, letting

Nan use me as a mostly willing partner for her geriatric pièce de résistance. "I haven't had a chance to stretch yet."

"Those pajamas are *awful*."

I looked down at myself—an old pair of Ingram's boxers, stretched to the point of rupture over my haunches, and an enormous Hulk T-shirt I'd stolen from a comedian after a brief but ruinous tryst.

"If you sleep sexy, you'll feel sexy." She was wagging her eyebrows at me now, shimmying her shoulders toward mine.

"Alright, no more reggaeton." I pulled my hands away, heading toward the coffee machine. "You're misbehaving."

She let out a laugh. "You thought I wasn't capable of being naughty! But I'm just getting started!" Before I had enough time to react, the doorbell rang, and she let out a little chirp. "Coffee's here."

I quirked a brow. "Have you been Grubhub-pilled?"

She pulled open the door and trilled, "Hola, cómo estás?"

"Buenos días, Annie."

I turned slowly in the direction of that voice.

There he was again. Standing in Nan's doorway, aviator sunglasses hanging from the collar of a devastatingly sexy knit polo shirt, the type of shirt you might see on a chisel-jawed Gucci model slinking along the cobblestone streets of Havana or Capri. That was, in fact, exactly what Eddie looked like. Except he was standing in my living room, two coffee cups in hand.

"Delfina, you remember your little friend Ed, right?"

"Friend?"

His mouth twitched into an inscrutable little smirk, a single dimple creasing in his cheek. "Sorry, I wasn't thinking, I only brought two coffees. You can have mine—"

I crossed my arms over my chest. "No, thank you."

He nodded curtly. Nan took her cup and held up a finger. "Gracias por el café con leche." And with a satisfied grin she bustled down the hallway.

I watched her walk away, silently cursing her name while hoping and praying my nipples weren't trying anything experimental.

"Nice shirt." Eddie's voice was different when he spoke English; lower, with an omnipresent sarcastic lilt. His Spanish had sounded so sweet—like my ears were being drilled by a honey-dipped jackhammer.

I swung my head back toward him. "What the fuck are you doing here?"

Eddie was leaning against the doorframe, staring down at a picture of me from a third-grade trip to Colonial Williamsburg. There I was—prepubescent, miserable, and dressed to churn butter. "I deejay the Caribbean class so I give Annie a ride." He lifted the frame off the end table. "Nice bonnet."

I raised my brows at him. "*Annie?*"

He set the frame down, careful not to disturb Nan's couch-side gnome collection. "Annetta. She's been trying to learn Spanish from watching novelas, so we practice together."

"Huh." I clicked my tongue. "Teaching old women Spanish. How wholesome."

Eddie pulled back at *wholesome* like the word had a stinger. "It's not wholesome. Annie's my friend."

I let out a bitter laugh, a burst of air from between my teeth. "I never really thought of you as the *friends with the elderly* type."

"Oh?" He smirked, smoothing a hand over the arm of the couch before sitting gingerly on it. He was wearing a pair of shorts I would describe as *European* in length. A pair of shorts that was *acquainted* with his mid-thigh. The curvature of his thigh muscle flexed as he sat. "Do you think about me a lot, Del?"

My mouth dropped open.

"Here I am!" Annetta sang out as she emerged from her bedroom, beach bag in hand. "Jesus, Del, close your mouth."

I snapped my jaw shut and skimmed Cyrus's car keys off the coffee table, stomping toward the door, past Eddie, giving fuck-all if he could see my nipples or my butt cheeks or my Third Eye Blind tattoo. He could stare all he wanted—but he would not shoehorn himself further into my life with his stupid, sexy, six-inch-inseam shorts and *asinine* comments. "Nan, I'm driving you."

She wrinkled her nose at me as she slid out of her house flip-flops and into her outdoor flip-flops. "Why? Eddie's already here, love."

"We're family, and family doesn't just let family walk out the door," I vamped. Eddie tilted his head back and brought his eyebrows together in a look of poorly hidden amusement. It took everything in me to not flick the sunglasses off his shirt. "Family takes care of family."

Nan shuffled toward the door, waving for him to follow her. "Sweetie, go back to sleep."

"Seriously, I don't mind," Eddie chimed in. He stood, sliding his sunglasses onto the bridge of his nose. I swore he gave me one last sweep, eyes glazing over my thighs before they disappeared behind a reflective stretch of blue green. "This is kind of our thing."

"Oh, *your thing*?" I replied in a nasally, little voice. "Well, here's a *thing* for you. Nan's my grandmother and I would like to see what sort of crowd she's hanging out with."

"Violent psychopaths addicted to easy movement," he said, stepping back outside.

"Ted Bundy loved a splash."

Nan pointed her country club swipe card at me. "Stop being weird, it's making us late."

"Fine." I shoved my feet into a pair of Crocs I usually reserved for emergency situations, like retrieving a package or proving a point. "I'll just tag along."

She and Eddie exchanged a look—a conspiratorial, *ain't she something?* look that I detested. And of course, Nan grumbled, "This is all Roger's side."

EDDIE'S SHORTS were short, his forearms were toned, his hair was perfect, but his car? His car was a fucking mess. He must have known I'd barely fit between the various piles of random crap in his back seat, which totally explained the evil, twitchy little grin he flashed me as I swished past him to the car.

So, there I was, crammed in the middle seat among some bed frame slats, a pile of *Nat Geos*, and a freaking car seat. It looked like he'd carjacked a soccer mom then looted his local Goodwill. My knees pressed into the backs of their seats; Eddie kept throwing dodgy looks at me every time he made a turn, and my knees were forced in a little deeper as I braced for impact. I wanted to tell him to keep his eyes on the road—one bad turn and I was getting a free lobotomy. But instead, I stayed calm, keeping a look of distant serenity on my face. *Oh, Eddie Rodriguez is friends with my grandmother? What a silly, fun joke.*

If I wasn't still stuck on how he'd treated me the other night, I would maybe have found this moment hilarious. Because they were yammering away. In *Spanish*. Was this what she'd been doing all those months I wasn't able to visit?

Eddie drove with one arm resting across the windowsill, fingertips just barely grazing the wheel. With his other, he gestured as he spoke—pointing here and there, rotating his wrist in rhythm with the cadence of his speech, languid with a distinct Puerto Rican accent. It was an objectively sexy way to drive, and I couldn't help but let my eyes linger on the way his lips pooled when he rounded them around vowels.

"Qué está haciendo el perro?"

"El perro está caminando," Nan replied in a measured, even tone. Her accent was quite good, and she could even roll her *r*'s.

"Brava."

"Isn't *brava* Italian?" I chimed in as Eddie dodged a pothole and I grabbed on to an iPhone charger cord for stability.

His eyes flicked to the rearview mirror and his gaze snagged mine, holding me there.

"El café es muy bien, Ed," Nan said, pulling his eyes away from mine and back to the road. He shifted in his seat, reaching over and fiddling with the AC.

"Ah sí? Yo también creo que el café está muy bueno. Lo compré en Dunkin'."

"Dunkin' es muy bueno! Mi favorito."

"El mío también."

I dislodged something from underneath my butt cheek. A wire hanger.

NAN INSISTED that I enter the country club by climbing through the hedges that separated the parking lot from the pool rather than through the front with her and Eddie.

"You look like you just hitchhiked here from Atlantic City after a cocaine bender," she said as she pushed me toward the shrubs.

"And climbing through the bushes is going to help my case?" Nan ignored me, threading her arm through Eddie's and shuffling off toward the front gate.

I removed my Crocs and forced my body through the dense, interlocking greenery until I emerged on the other side, next to the lifeguard stand, hair mussed. I humbly flopped down onto one of the blue-and-white-striped chaise loungers by the edge of the pool, but only after I was certain no one had witnessed my arrival.

Generally speaking, Evanstone was a locals-only establishment focused on servicing the upper echelon of Malaga County.

There was this unspoken divide between people who lived beachside and bayside in Evergreen. Beachside was made up of apartments, motels, and condo buildings that, until recently, had been considered rough. Bayside was outfitted with cottages and townhomes with waterfront backyards, nuclear families, and happy, flapping flags that said things like HOPPY EASTER or KISS ME, I'M IRISH. In the summer, Evergreen hosted plenty of upper-middle-class city folks staying at their second homes—both bayside *and* beachside. But when I told locals I'd grown up beachside, they usually winced.

Thankfully, there was no one around the pool and I was left alone to kick off my shoes and lie back. The sun gleamed off the opal surface, sending a dancing stream of light over the bay windows that faced me. Behind them, men in white polos and ladies in wide-brimmed hats nibbled at bagels with lox, hard-boiled eggs, and yogurt parfaits. A woman with an immobile blond Rod Stewart shag lifted a coffee cup to her lips, and I regretted denying Eddie's coffee with my whole soul. My stomach and I groaned in unison.

At least I'd grabbed my sunglasses and phone before scrambling out the door. Maybe I could actually get some writing done. Pretty unfortunate that it had to happen while I was wearing my pajamas in public. *Didn't I have a nightmare about this once?*

Right as I pushed my sunglasses up into my hair, Nan emerged from the club in her jewel-toned one-piece and matching bathing cap, flanked by two women I recognized from church—Terez and Lucinda. *But no Eddie.* I spotted his deejay booth, kitty-corner to my chair, overlooking the shallow end of the pool from under the shade of a poplar tree. I imagined what he looked like, hands working deftly over the mixing board, lip pulled between his teeth in concentration.

Ugh. That asshole.

The gals were making their way into the water. Terez and Lucinda dragged a toe over the surface and shivered away, flapping their hands. Below the warm surface of the pool, the depth was probably still freezing. Nan followed suit, but instead of shying away from the water, she lowered herself to the edge and then slid in, letting out a high-pitched *ooooooh!* as the water lapped at her belly. I couldn't help but smile, though I was still very angry with Miss Annetta.

"You wild girl!" Terez shouted after her. Then, she waved toward me. "Hi, Del!"

"Morning, Ter. Morning, Lu."

"Del!" Nan shouted. "Come down to this end so you can watch my samba!"

Before I could shout back, the chair next to me scraped against the ground, and I snapped my head toward the sound *just* as Eddie lowered himself to a lounging position beside me.

It was incredible how smooth his curls were. Back in high school, Eddie had worn his hair in a low frizzy ponytail and then, later, in two chin-length poofs that he'd tuck behind his ears. Now his curls were silky, neatly defined. Except for that one curl. It hung recklessly over his forehead in a backward-zigzagging loop.

"I felt like I owed you one," he offered, handing me a plastic cup. *Iced coffee.*

I grunted, taking it from him, pushing down any urge to forgive him for Saturday night.

"This class is fifty minutes long, you know that, right?" He wrinkled his eyes against the sun, his bright teeth glimmering. His skin took on all the sun's warmth, shining like bronze. I could see the edge of his tattoos curling out from under his shirt sleeve, and another around his left wrist. It looked like words—a cursive font, twisting around itself.

I yanked my eyes away and focused back on Nan, floating on her back at the end of the pool. "Perfect. Just enough time for me to burn."

Eddie laughed, low and deep. "You don't mind everyone seeing your Calvin Kleins?"

"They're my ex-boyfriend's, actually."

"Nice. Did you two trade?"

I whipped my gaze back to him. "What if we did? Would you underwear-shame him?"

"Absolutely not." He uncrossed his legs and turned to face me, sitting sideways. We were a lot closer than I thought. I wanted to hate it. "I'd be impressed. All the women's underwear I've seen looks very uncomfortable."

I scoffed. "Nice casual brag, Eddie." I could imagine what type of underwear he'd seen. I was sure he had a favorite type. Red lacy dental floss, size double zero. I'd made up this fact about Eddie, but it felt real enough for a wave of rage to crest in my stomach.

"That came out wrong."

"No, no." I took a noisy sip of coffee. "I get it. You fuck."

"Jesus, Del. It's not even nine yet."

"I would just like to note that I'm also wearing women's underwear," I snapped. "I'm not just free-balling at the country club in my ex's briefs."

"*Free-balling?*"

"You know." I flicked my hands out toward the water. "Lips to the wind."

"*Lips* to the *wind*?" His face twisted rapidly between horror and amusement. "Not sure how Pastor George is going to feel about that."

I flashed him a nervous look. "He takes your class?"

Eddie leaned toward me, resting his arms on his knees. "Everyone takes my class."

"They'll make you mayor next."

Another flicker of that dimple. "You're not making fun of me, are you?"

"I don't know, have you been secretly hanging out with my grandma for the last ten years?"

"Definitely not ten. Maybe a year, year and a half?" He sounded like he was kidding, but was quick enough to pull back when he caught what faltered in my eyes. We both knew why I hadn't known Eddie and Nan were hanging out—I'd barely seen Nan in the last year and a half. He cleared his throat and swiped a hand over his chin—quickly, anxiously. "I was, uh, kind of a dick Saturday night."

"Just Saturday night? *Kind of?*" I snorted. "That's like saying the *Challenger* sorta went *boom*."

Eddie winced. "Damn, that bad, huh?"

I watched him for a moment, smoothing my fingers through my bangs. "Wanna know what your problem is?"

"Oh, man." He squared his shoulders, leaning back to showcase their full width, dragging a hand back and forth over his chin. "I'm an asshole dickhead?"

"Besides that. You're a *freaking* elephant. You never forget anything." He held my gaze. I didn't look away; I wasn't backing down to all the memories tucked underneath his perfect head of hair. Eddie knew as well as I did that every interaction we had was a millefeuille of subtext. "We can be friends—or strangers. Everything that happened was years ago. A decade plus some."

He watched me intently, jaw jumping as he clenched and un-clenched. He was going to say something serious; I could feel it. "You want me to forget about the helmet?"

"Jesus." I laughed. "No, I want you to forget about . . ." I in-haled deeply. "Who I was ten years ago. That's all." And then I took a sip of my coffee—a long, nervous sip as he pressed his lips together until they disappeared into a thin, pink line. Condensa-tion rolled down the cup and splashed onto my thigh.

"Okay," he said finally. His voice sounded different—all the joking gone. "I can do that." His Apple Watch beeped. "Aight, Miller. That's my five-minute warning."

I released my iced coffee, swallowing roughly. "Buena suerte."

He stood and watched me, mouth still pulled into that inscru-table little line. "Gracias."

10

Eddie's Bar

That night, against my better judgment, I went back to The Billiards. According to the blurry picture on my phone, tonight was their open mic and if I was ever going to get back to working on my Brainwave set, I needed to jump back into the game.

This time, the bar was almost completely empty. Nothing cleared a room like the threat of a white man with a microphone. It was a very far cry from Gimbley's open mic, which frequently resulted in a line down the block, all unknowingly competing for Best Ed Kemper Look-Alike.

The Billiards servers were chatting by the kitchen, standing around a dish cart and throwing dodgy looks before leaning in and trading gossip, manicured fingers running through their ponytails. A longing for my life as a server passed through my chest as quickly as a heartbeat, and for a brief second, I missed all of it. Every excruciating night I spent on my feet, running french fries back and forth until my pinky toes hurt. Kvetching with the kitchen guys and my best friends over a shared cigarette. Passing out in my dirty clothes and knowing I deserved to sleep for fourteen hours, because I'd earned it.

Eddie probably let his staff take breaks and days off when they didn't feel well. He probably let them cry in his office and encouraged everyone to stay hydrated. Not like any boss I'd ever had. They'd all wanted us parched and emotionally constipated.

I skirted my way through tightly packed tables toward the stage; I spied a yellow legal pad on the edge of the stage and a skinny, awkward man in baggy jeans milling about. *That must be the sign-up sheet.*

The skinny man was scratching fiercely at his ears while staring at the legal pad so hard I wondered if he was trying to set it on fire with his mind. Eventually, he gave up on pyrokinesis and turned to me.

"You signing up?"

I nodded, pulling a pen out of my tote bag and adding my name to the list. Evidently DeeJay Bernstein had taken the first slot, and I was number two.

"Yep." I dropped my pen back into my bag. He was staring at me from behind his transitional lenses. My neck itched. This was the part of comedy I did not miss.

"Your first time, right? Mine, too. I'm so nervous."

How much time did I really want to waste being his mentor? I tucked a stray hair behind my ear and replied, "Not my first time, no. But I get it. Just remember you're supposed to be making people laugh."

He nodded vigorously. "That's what they're saying on the forums."

My eyes involuntarily widened. "Right. The forums. Exactly."

Eddie emerged from the kitchen carrying a bin of clean glasses, eyebrows contorted into a look of deep concentration. The servers immediately scattered back to various, random jobs. One girl started shuffling menus like they were playing cards.

I made a beeline for the bar. Eddie was back in bartender mode, curls pulled back into the little ponytail at the crown of his head, wearing his Billiards T-shirt. I preferred him like this; this Eddie was a little bit closer to the nerd I used to know. It was a strange realization that hit my chest with warmth and a burst of comfort, like taking a long sip of chamomile tea. I didn't let the feeling slow me as I swished over to the same stool I sat on the other night.

"Hey, stranger," he drawled, unloading the glasses at lightning speed—hands and voice wholly out of sync. Cyrus could never.

"Very funny." I pulled my notebook out of my bag.

He caught one of his server's eyes. "Chelsea—glasses," he commanded before picking up a towel and turning back to me. She rolled her eyes and dragged herself away from dusting the cigarette machine, throwing her compatriots a knowing look. What did that look mean? I needed to know. At Gimbley's we'd had a series of loaded glances we used to communicate a variety of things about our boss like, *he's doing the gross thing again* and *no, the other gross thing*.

"What can I get you?" Eddie asked, interrupting my thoughts, eyebrows tented in anticipation of my order.

I clicked my pen on and off, on and off. "Is this the trick to getting good service? Being a stranger?"

"Aw, *ouch*." He brought a hand to rest over his heart, mouth twitching into a lopsided frown. "*Not* my customer service skills."

I let out a snort of a laugh.

Eddie looked incredibly satisfied that he was able to make me laugh. In fact, he was smiling hard enough that I could see the two twin dimples at the centers of his long, angular cheeks. He flicked his towel over the bar top, pushing away some crumbs and taking special care to skirt the edges of my notebook. "You changed."

It took me a second to realize he meant my *clothes*.

I contemplated firing back something about his short-shorts, but I could not risk Eddie knowing I'd taken any note of his corporeal form. "Yes, but I promise I'm still wearing multiple pairs of underwear."

"Lucky us," he replied, sliding a napkin in front of me. "Maker's on the rocks?"

He remembered. It caught me off guard. He was a bartender. This was what he did. Cyrus remembered all his regulars' drinks. *But I'm not a regular.* "I'll take a Miller Lite."

A thumbs-up and he was turning away, punching my order into a screen next to the register, under a mirrored shelf covered with half-filled bottles.

I resisted the temptation to pull out my phone and immediately text Sam. She was already busy and exhausted without me, her elder child, constantly bombarding her with overdramatic updates about what were, objectively, a series of meaningless and normal conversations.

But I wanted her professional take so badly. I didn't know *this* Eddie well enough to know how he was really reacting to our conversation earlier at the pool.

The Eddie I'd known was mercurial, if not predictably so. He'd tease me, ignore me, chase me, and forget I existed all within one class period. He made me feel special and yet totally, utterly alone. When he felt particularly humiliated, he'd duck his head and rub his cheek against his shoulder, as if he could push the blush back into his body.

Kind of like what present-day Eddie was doing right now. I watched his shoulder rise and meet his cheek.

He spun around, freezing mid-step with a little bowl of popcorn and my beer in hand.

"Were you just staring at me?"

"E-excuse me?" I sputtered. "*Absolutely* not."

He made a little tutting noise. "That big city's made you a menace, Miller."

"You're obsessed with New York."

"Nah." He shrugged, setting the beer and popcorn down in front of me. "Maybe just a little jealous."

I huffed, dropping my eyes to the blank pages of my notebook. "Don't be."

He narrowed his eyes at me as he popped off the top of my beer with a pointed *fzzzz*. "Cryptic."

"I prefer *mysterious*."

"Alright, Nancy Drew." He pushed my beer against my closed hand until I dropped my pen and took the bottle.

"She wasn't mysterious. She just solved mysteries."

The front door banged open, and a gust of hot, humid beach air sent a stream of napkins fluttering across the bar like a swarm of butterflies. Suddenly, the bar's noise level jumped from zero to one hundred. We were surrounded by a never-ending deluge of pasty-legged, Natural American Spirit–smoking rabble-rousers. They grabbed seats up front by the stage; others came directly to the bar.

"Yo, Ed!"

"Ed-*day*!"

"Wassup, big guy?"

He got a few stray dabs and one heartfelt hug.

"Who are all these people?"

"Your people," Eddie replied, snagging an empty cigarette pack off the bar. He held it up. "Already making a mess."

"Like, white people?"

"Close." He smirked, leaning forward onto the bar and nodding his head at the stage. "Comedians."

Comedians. Duh. How had I not realized that? And there was a whole pack of them. I felt a lump rising rapidly in my throat. "Oh God."

"Yeah." Eddie rolled his eyes. "They don't tip well, either."

"I'm second on the list . . ."

"So what? You're a real stand-up. These are just a bunch of college kids from Philly and North Jersey." He jabbed his thumb toward a short guy with horn-rimmed glasses, a red hat away from looking like Waldo. "He's the host. Still intimidated?"

I shook my head, craning my neck to investigate better. *All dudes.* "No, you don't get it. Comedians don't laugh at other comedians. Especially if the comedian they don't know is a woman. They only laugh at their friends."

Eddie's expression shifted. "You sound like a bunch of assholes."

"Exactly." I smacked my open palm against the bar. "Comedians are *dicks.* I have to get my name off that list."

"These kids suck. I fell asleep during last week's show. You'll be fine."

I could feel his eyes on me, big and warm, full of that distinct Eddie thing that made my heart feel like it was being filleted with a hot knife.

Eddie didn't know why I was home. He didn't know about the avalanche of bad luck that had sent me running for cover. As much as my situation had started with what Ingram had done to me, and taken away from me, it had somehow become about Evergreen and this *damn* writer's block. The way I couldn't stop thinking about everyone I'd left behind ten years ago. The vines that had wrapped around my brain.

I guess I had to try and explain. At least a little bit. I took a swig of beer before I started.

"The issue is I can't do any of my act because my ex—"

Lights went up on the stage. Feedback erupted from a microphone as Waldo yanked it from the stand with a loose grip. The lights over the bar dimmed. Applause broke out as everyone turned toward the stage. Everyone except Eddie. He was watching me, worrying at his lip.

My pulse quickened, dread rippling through my entire body like a church bell's *gong*.

"Ayo, aye! How y'all feeling tonight?" the host called out. "Welcome to Brave Souls Night at The Billiards!" I clapped along with everyone else, but my hands felt numb. "This is the best weekly stand-up open mic at the damn Jersey Shore, so please give it up for yourselves!"

Eddie finally turned away from me, cupping his hands around his mouth and letting out a hoot.

"So, I was scanning the list"—the host held up the yellow legal pad—"and I saw a name I know. I actually saw this comedian live at the Portland Chuckles festival, and I know she's got a big gig coming up—" *Oh God*. Oh no, no, no. My heart was stalling out in my chest—alternating beating faster than it ever had before and slowing down close to a stop. "So, I'm going to just bring her up." This couldn't be happening. No. No way. "Please give it up for Delfina Silva-Miller!"

The host beamed into the audience as they shifted in their chairs, clapping and *wooh*-ing and waiting for *me*.

Eddie stared at me, excitement in his eyes. *Go*, he mouthed. I pointed at myself. "Yes!" He raised his voice to meet the applause. "Go!"

I jumped up and made my way across the bar to the little stage, up the steps, and met the host under the spotlight.

"Huge fan," he whispered, gripping my hand. I said something. I'm not sure what.

Then, I took the mic.

"Hello," I whispered.

The audience let out a crackle of laughter. *Well, then. Maybe this won't be so bad.*

"I'm very nervous," I continued. "Because my high school bully owns this bar. But joke's on him." I widened my eyes, gesturing at myself. "I'm doing really well. I'm a hot and sexy career . . . comedian."

Another wave of chuckles.

"Not to blow your minds, but I am kind of going through something right now. I just broke up with my boyfriend. Turns out his favorite part of dating me was fucking my roommate." More belly laughs. I paused, letting the laughter peak and valley as I took a moment to adjust to the stage. "That's not a joke. It's just a fact, but I said it with the cadence of a joke. Industry trick. Here's another: a dentist once told me I have the mouth of a sick child and then *he asked me out.*"

That kept them going for a bit. Vamping bought me some time as I mentally scrounged through my entire life for a joke I could grab ahold of. Unfortunately, I wasn't fast enough. Their laughter came to a stop, and I knew I had to start talking. One too many moments of silence and you're dead.

"I don't have my usual material prepared for tonight, because I wrote a lot of jokes about my ex. About me and him, but the jokes were mostly about me." I shook my head. "After what happened, I just can't do those jokes. Because he hurt me, you know? It was like he proved me right. They stopped being jokes."

Crickets.

"I have this one joke about how when we go places people

think I'm his wet nurse. Genius, right?" A few big laughs. "But now it's just . . . he cheated on me with someone richer, thinner, blonder, more *adult* than me. Someone more like him. I don't want to keep making fun of myself—of my body—after that. I want to do material that's more . . . *something*. Maybe more honest or, I don't know. Something about Evergreen or about . . ." I took a deep breath. "Jokes that feel like they *are* me. Not just *about* me."

Why was I saying this out loud? I'd never verbalized any of this before. Hell, I barely even knew that this was really how I felt. But the lights were hot and the three sips of beer I'd taken were sloshing around in my stomach like battery acid. Over the audience, I could make out Eddie's frame behind the bar, arms folded over his chest. He was watching me—I had his full, undivided attention in front of a crowd.

Wasn't this what I always wanted—a chance for my *Ten Things I Hate About You* moment? Instead of a poignant speech, I was spilling my soul like I'd tripped with an overflowing mug, a bunch of twenty-one-year-olds watching as I face-planted in front of my Patrick Verona.

And I couldn't stop.

"It's hard to remember how things *actually* happened, how they really felt when you're only ever reliving those memories through the jokes you wrote about them. And if I'm only ever writing jokes where I'm a fool, where does that leave me?"

"This isn't funny," someone shouted from the back of the room.

"No shit," I fired back. "Maybe not everything needs to be funny all the time. Maybe I just need more time." I licked my lips slowly before turning to the host. "Would you laugh at my jokes if they weren't about my ass?"

He nodded, terror waxing in his eyes.

"Cool." I shoved the mic back into his chest, sending a trill of feedback through the air. "I'll work on it."

Then, I stormed offstage.

"Del." Eddie was looking at me, hands pressed firmly into the bar. I couldn't place what it was I saw in his eyes. But it was enough to knock the air out of my chest.

I yanked my bag off the seat. "I bet you loved that."

I WAS halfway down the block, wearing my shame like a heavy cloak, when I heard his feet catching up to me.

"Del, *wait*."

I spun around at the sound of his voice, shoulders sagging. "What, Eddie? I'm not in the mood—"

"You forgot your notebook." He came to a breathless stop, holding out the tattered spiral-bound book that contained every thought, anecdote, and one-liner I'd written since 2018. "Figured it's pretty important to you."

It was. How could I have forgotten it? I took the book out of his hand and tucked it against my chest. He watched me, worrying at his bottom lip with his hands on his hips.

"Thanks," I said softly. "I promise I'll pay you back for the beer."

"Forget the beer." He shoved his hands into his pockets and brought a shoulder to his cheek. "Look, you were right."

I snapped my eyes up to his, holding my breath for the second half of the sentence. There were too many things to be right about when it came to me and Eddie. He kept his gaze fixed on the moon, hanging low and bright in the sky. "You're not the person you were ten years ago, and I'm sorry I tried to treat you like you were." He brought a hand to my arm and gently placed his fingertips on the edge of my shoulder. "I'm proud to know you, Del."

It was the gentlest touch—so soft I had to look at his hand to make sure I wasn't imagining it. It was the same gentle hand he placed on his server's shoulder the first night I passed through The Billiards, when all I had wanted was for him to see me, to reach out and comfort me. Seeing his hand against my arm, hearing him call out to me, I felt something—something I'd left behind in Evergreen.

11

Whatcha listening to, Patty?" Eddie said it like the word had two syllables—*pat-tay*. He was twisted around sideways in his chair, tapping a chewed-up pencil against my desk with a weird little grin on his lips, dead set on annoying me.

I tightened my grip on my iPod Mini. "Mind your business, Edward."

He pouted, scribbling on the edge of the algebra homework I'd swiftly abandoned. "How many times do I have to tell you that my name is Edgardo?"

I mimed counting on all my fingers. "Seventy-eleven." He took this as the moment to try and snatch my iPod off my desk but I yanked it away in time with a satisfied grunt.

"Why won't you tell me what you're listening to?" He was twisted all the way around now, long limbs folded over the back of his chair, head practically on my desk. Eddie had gotten his hair cut recently but his curls were still wild and long, sticking out of the bottom of a beanie in coils that hugged his ears. I spied a little gold stud in his ear, catching the light from the fluorescent overheads. He was still giving me that faint smile, a deep dimple in his cheek winking at me.

"Because I'm *not* listening," I pointed out with an exaggerated eye roll, broad enough that I could sneak another glance at his earring. "And I don't feel like hearing your corny opinions."

"Why?" His smile deepened, eyes disappearing into joyful commas. Eddie had the coolest eye shape—angular and intense like a fox's—and my interest in it was purely scientific. "Danity Kane?"

"No way." I laughed, picking at the nail polish on my thumb. It was a screaming shade of femme-fatale red, a shade that had made me feel like a woman in the moment I'd chosen it. A fact that had once excited me and now haunted me.

"Taylor Swift?"

"We're gonna get in trouble."

Eddie lifted his head, stealing a glance at Mrs. Traeger. Her nose was still buried in a Spanish reader titled *Vamonos! Level Four.* She was, famously, the most lax study hall proctor. If you needed to smoke a cigarette or get pregnant, now was the time to do it.

"Gwen Stefani?"

"You're just naming pop stars, loser." I lifted an uncapped pen and poked it into his hand. I expected Eddie to pull away with a dramatic shriek, but instead he kept his hand there, perfectly still, until I'd finished drawing a daisy. My hand looked corpse-like next to his deep olive skin. Another reason to be embarrassed, freshly unlocked.

Once the flower was complete and I'd pulled away, tongue sticking out of the side of my mouth, Eddie lunged for my iPod. "Got 'em!"

I gasped. "Fucker!"

Mrs. Traeger snapped her book shut, beady blue eyes sweeping the room like a radar until they fell on us. "Delfina. Edgardo. Don't make me separate you."

I glared at Eddie and whispered, "If you get my iPod taken away, I will never forgive you. Ever. Not even when we're thirty."

He flipped the metallic device between his thumb and middle finger. "Who are you taking to the winter dance?"

I narrowed my eyes at him. "Don't you have English homework?"

"I'm taking Rachel," he gloated.

"Good for you," I mimicked back in his singsong tone.

"So." He dragged out the *ooh* as he scrolled through my iTunes library. "No date?"

I leaned forward and yanked my iPod out of his hands. "No date. And I don't want one, either."

"Miss Silva-Miller." My heart lurched and I looked up to find Mrs. Traeger staring at me again from overtop her reading glasses. "Why are you touching Mr. Rodriguez?"

A giggle rippled through the rest of study hall and my cheeks rapidly began turning, no doubt, the color of a tomato. "He took my iPod."

"Mr. Rodriguez, give back her eye-posh." She snapped her eyes back and forth between us. "And do not touch each other."

Eddie had turned all the way around in his chair, shoulders shaking with silent laughter.

Somehow, he'd managed to scribble on my math homework in a wobbly, sloppy boy script: *No Date Del Waz Here.*

WE HAD orchestra practice for the Christmas concert after school. We were on our seventh repeat of a jazzy rendition of "Hark All Ye Faithful" when Mr. Desiderio finally let us take a break. In most high schools, orchestra was for losers, but at Malaga County, orchestra functioned as a microcosm of the larger high school ecosystem. Anyone worth remembering was in the orchestra.

And there was a clear pecking order. All the popular girls played wind instruments. If you were hot, you played the clarinet. If you were bookish, you played piccolo. If you were a horse girl, your only option was the flute. Hot, popular guys were in the percussion section. Self-serious debaters and young Republicans made up the brass section, plus or minus a few Lisa Simpson types, but they were numbered and prone to quitting due to "scheduling conflicts." Last and least, the string instruments were reserved for artsy kids, international students, and . . . me and Tully Martino.

I was the only freshman girl who played a string instrument, drowning in a sea of sweaty boys and senior girls with nose rings who wouldn't even look twice at me.

"Okay," Mr. Desiderio shouted, keeping his eyes fixed on his wristwatch. "Let's take a ten-minute hydration break, but *please* stay in your seats."

We let out a collective groan. Sam shot me a pouty face from her spot in the wind section. I held up my hands in the shape of a heart. She tried to send one back, nearly dropping her piccolo.

"Dude, give me my freaking pick back."

"I don't have it."

"Then where the hell did it go?"

Someone let loose a wet, guttural burp.

"Oh my *freaking* God." I whipped my head around. "Can you three freaks act normal for fifteen seconds?"

Eddie, Jake, and Wiley stared back at me with wide eyes. Eddie was seated behind me, standing bass leaning against him, so he looked like just a pair of big brown eyes and a gray-blue beanie.

"Whoa." Jake smirked from his seat at the piano. "Someone's angry."

"She's mad she doesn't have a date to the dance." I couldn't see Eddie's mouth, but I could tell he was grinning.

"I don't *want* a date to the dance," I reminded him.

"Yeah, you do. You wanna take Jake."

"*Ew.* No offense, Jake."

He played a single, mournful chord. "None taken."

"No date?" I looked over at the voice. It was coming from Shoa, a cello player and a junior. There were many rules about who could and couldn't be hot in high school, but sometimes someone managed to escape the matrix. They dared to skirt the fragile ecosystem of Lisa Simpsons and Tully Martinos, and in doing so became legendary.

There were rumors about Shoa and his friends. They smoked cigarettes between class periods; they snuck out for lunch and paid the front office off with Taco Bell; they went to homecoming drunk and only danced with underclassmen.

Shoa was more than hot. He was devastating and gorgeous. He had jet-black hair that hung in a messy swoop over his oversize glasses. Sometimes he showed up to orchestra late, smelling like too much body spray, a smirk on his lips. We'd made eye contact five times. Not that I was keeping track.

"Uh, yeah." I pulled at my braid. Nervous habit. "No date."

He swiveled in his chair, a playful smile on his lips. He looked like a man next to Eddie. "You boys think she'd really want to take one of you? Lads, keep dreaming."

"Del's a total dork," Eddie piped up. "She just acts cool."

"It's called maturity, brother." He turned back around in his chair, looking at me. "Flying solo is really dope."

"Thanks," I croaked.

PRACTICE ENDED when Ryanne, second-chair clarinet, had an asthma attack and started crying about how chapped her lips were. We were ten minutes past our 5 P.M. end time and the percussion section had grown particularly impatient. Revolt was imminent. Steve Pham had started gonging his cymbals on the ones and threes in protest. We'd ultimately forced Mr. Desiderio's hand.

The gym cleared out almost immediately, everyone scurrying through the cold misting rain toward their rides. Tonight was one of my nights to stay with Roger. I only did this once—*max* twice—a month and only out of the kindness of my heart for Nan. Technically, she and Roger had joint custody of me and keeping tabs on him was a big part of the *I'll raise your daughter, but don't get up to any funny business* deal.

My Roger nights usually consisted of an awkward dinner at Pier Point Diner; Roger ordered the meatloaf platter and tried to act like he wasn't counting down the minutes until we left. I got pancakes and let them sweat on my plate till they were freezing cold. Then I'd take one wretched bite, remembering that Roger never had any snacks.

Tonight, I was starving and actually looking forward to my pancakes. I checked the big clock behind the basketball net. Quarter to six. *Where the fuck are you, Roger?* When the custodian began sweeping at the far end of the gym, I migrated to the front hall. Some upperclassmen were lingering by the double doors, spinning car keys on their fingers. Someone was fiddling with a lighter.

"Oh, hey." I turned toward the voice from where I was sitting on a bench near the front office. *Shoa.*

"Hey." I slid my backpack into my lap, now unbearably self-conscious of my own entirety.

"You need a ride?"

"Uh . . ." I chewed at my lip. "I'm kinda waiting for my dad."

He bobbed his head in a solemn nod, long and nimble fingers pulling at the front of his hair. "So, this is super awkward, but the school locks their doors in like, five. Aaaand it's raining pretty hard now."

"Oh." A horrified, strangled laugh echoed through me. "Well, that sucks."

"Yeah." He laughed, too. "But I can still . . ." He jabbed his thumb toward the parking lot.

I nodded. I'd never gotten in a car driven by a kid before, but what choice did I have? I stood up, swinging my bag over my shoulder. "Okay. Yeah."

Another smirk from him. "Dope."

Shoa waved goodbye to his friends, who eyed me with a wary irony that made my already anxious tummy kick up into actual, stabbing pain.

"Cool hoodie," Shoa said once we were outside, headed toward a beat-up station wagon. He reached over, fingers pulling gently at the drawstring. The rain wasn't nearly as heavy as I had expected, but it was already pitch black out.

"Oh, um, thanks." I tucked my hands into my sleeves so he couldn't see my fingers shaking.

I took a deep, steady breath. Shoa had picked up his pace, but I couldn't bring myself to move any faster. This went against Nan's golden rules: never get in a car with a stranger; never trust people who are nice for no reason; never make decisions without first eating a snack. I'd found a way to violate all three.

I'd basically stopped walking when the black sedan pulled up next to me.

"Yo," Eddie called out to me, head sticking out in the rain. "What the shit, Patty? Get in."

I sat in the back seat wedged between Eddie and his sister Mell. Eddie's mom, who introduced herself as Lani, was driving and beside her was Eddie's older sister, Yari. I knew Yari because she was uniformly regarded as beautiful and dangerous. Sort of like a local Angelina Jolie, minus some of the weird blood stuff.

I couldn't have cared less about Yari; I was mesmerized by Miss Rodriguez. Her hair was smoothed back into a tight bun at the nape of her neck, her broad lips glossed in an iridescent copper, and she had the most beautiful pale pink manicure I'd ever seen. She was my Platonic ideal of beauty—all clean lines and visibly well moisturized. The best part was that I could tell she was chubby, like me. *Beautiful and chubby.*

My shoulder rubbed against Eddie's as I buckled my seat belt; he smelled like wet concrete and clean clothes. His skin was warm against mine.

"We were *not* going to let you walk home, Delfina." Lani smiled at me in the rearview mirror. "Where do you live?"

"In the Bel Sol on Crestfallen. It's the old building with the creepy sun," I added with a nervous smile, hoping my self-awareness and keen observational humor would charm her. *Haha, oh my God! Eddie, did you hear that? Del, you are the funniest person I've ever met—literally and actually. Please, take my lip gloss.*

"Oh, I know the Bel Sol. We used to live in an apartment on Mulberry. Remember that, Eddie?"

He bounced his head against the headrest, as if causing some sort of brain damage would be more favorable than experiencing a car ride where our thighs touched. "It *suuuucked.*"

"Our new house is the bomb," Mell noted thoughtfully, watching raindrops slip down her window. "I have my own bedroom."

"Is someone waiting for you at home, sweetie?"

It was a normal question, though made complicated by the one major annoyance in my life. *Roger.*

"My grandma's home, I think. My dad was supposed to pick me up, but he's working late." It was a convincing lie that came easily. I'd gotten good at covering for Roger.

"Next time, just tell Eddie and we'll make sure you get home." Lani turned onto Main Street. "Are you excited for the dance?"

"*Mom*," Eddie hissed.

"What? It's just a question. Relax." Lani rolled her eyes and threw me a wink. Was there anything more gratifying than sharing a private joke with a woman like Lani? "Eddie's still looking for a date."

My stomach jumped inside my chest. *Hadn't he asked Rachel?* I didn't look over at Eddie; I could feel him straighten up in his seat, knuckles turning white as he tightened his grip on his backpack.

"Mom," he barked, hard this time. *End of discussion*.

"Ain't no one going with you if you don't cut that hair," Yari mumbled, fingers flying impressively over her cell phone keyboard. "No one."

WHEN I got home Nan was sitting in her corner of the couch, eating toast and reading a magazine. Is this what she did on her free night? God, *so boring*.

I dropped my keys into the glass bowl we kept by the door. "Hi, Mom."

"What're you doing here?" Nan demanded, wide-eyed. I stayed perfectly still, hand frozen mid-key toss. "Did Roger not show up?" She shifted to the edge of the couch, dropping her *Soap Opera Daily*. "How did you get home?"

I swallowed roughly. "Um, Edgardo Rodriguez's mom gave me a ride."

"*Sonuvabitch*." Nan slammed a hand down onto the arm of the couch, lips pulling back with rage. "That *motherlover*—" Then, she stood up, yanked the landline off the wall, and disappeared into her bedroom.

"Um, okay, so like . . ." I called out. "I'm gonna go get some pizza." I cleared my throat, adding anxiously: "Just a snack, we can still have dinner."

This happened sometimes. Roger made a promise he couldn't keep; Nan flipped out; Roger went MIA until the situation became a memory; we went back to eating meatloaf and pancakes.

The entire process took four to six months and seemed to hurt Nan more deeply than me. I knew to keep my expectations low whenever my dad was involved in anything; I'd learned that lesson after he'd promised to buy me a Calico Critters dollhouse for my eighth birthday, but instead went "on vacation" to Arizona for six weeks.

I put my headphones on and pulled up the hood of my sweatshirt, bracing myself against the freezing, humid winds coming off the beach as I wandered down the planks toward Genie's Pizzeria. I wanted to give Nan her space—to shout and yell and curse out Roger however she needed.

The rain had stopped completely now, but the moisture burrowed deep into everything. The planks were soft under my feet and the streetlights gave off a diffused white light. It was while I was staring at all the lights that I'd spotted the familiar blue beanie under Genie's red awning.

"Hey," I called out, waving at Eddie. "You live on Evergreen, too?"

Eddie's eyes darted up to mine from the MP3 player in his hand. "Bayside."

"Cool." I pulled my hood down and smoothed a hand along the length of my hair. "Um, can you not tell people about my dad forgetting I exist?"

Eddie pushed off the metal-shuttered door he was leaning against, eyes moving rapidly back and forth among my face, my shoes, and the pickup window. "And you won't tell people about what my mom said?"

I nodded. "Deal."

"Cool." He kicked at a rock, sending it rolling down toward the public restrooms. "Don't go to the dance with Shoa, okay?"

I furrowed my brow. "Why?"

"He's in my sister's class and . . ." Eddie shot a look over his shoulder, like he was making sure the coast was clear. "He's not a good guy. Trust me. He just wants sex. That's why he dates underclassmen."

I stood a little taller. "Maybe that's all I want, too."

Eddie slouched forward, as if suddenly and briefly exhausted. As if he hadn't even considered that. He stepped on a french fry, flattening it into a pale little pancake. "Whatever, Del. Just don't come crying to me when he breaks your heart."

I folded my arms over my chest. "I would never cry to you."

"That's not what I meant."

"Are you jealous?"

A woman in a red visor and a winter coat popped her head out of the pickup window. "One pep pizza and a Greek salad."

"That's me," Eddie replied, handing her exact change. This must have been their usual order. It felt incredibly personal to know exactly what Eddie was eating for dinner. I averted my eyes.

He turned back toward me, clutching his order, which was now throwing steam into the freezing-cold air. "I'm just trying to be nice."

"Okay. I won't go out with him."

His entire face relaxed. "Okay, then."

I pushed my fist into his shoulder. "See you tomorrow, Soft Serve."
Eddie nodded, pulling his mouth to the side. "I'll see you."

WHEN I got home, Nan was in the kitchen, furiously washing dishes—scrubbing so hard her bracelets were jangling. She didn't even look up when the door slammed behind me.

"Nan." I rushed to her, pizza be damned. It was already sauce-side down on the rug when I reached her side, desperately pulling her hands out of the soapy water. "What happened? Are you okay?"

She fought back feebly, keeping her eyes downcast. *She's been crying.* "Oh, don't look at me when I'm like this."

"Nan," I pleaded, turning off the sink and gripping her bony, wet hands in mine. Panic swirled in my chest. "What happened? What did he do?"

"Nothing, baby, nothing." She tried to smile, but her mascara betrayed her. Thick gray streams cut through the powder on her cheeks. She gave in to my embrace, letting me pull her to my chest. I buried my face in her rose-scented neck.

"I'm so angry," she said finally. "It wasn't supposed to be like this for you."

12

Jimmy's Boardwalk Pizza

I woke up the day after the open mic feeling like the last hot dog on a 7-Eleven heat rack—uncomfortably warm, moist, filled with shame.

Up until last night I'd convinced myself that my inability to rewrite my set was all everyone else's fault: Ingram, because he cheated; Nan, because she chewed louder than anyone else in America; Eddie, because he dared to exist. But after my emotional projectile vomit, it was impossible to keep lying to myself.

I was blinking awake to my life like a car crash victim coming to in a hospital room. All the pain and scars and fear and only a handful of memories to match.

When had I realized that I was the joke that got the most laughs? When had I perfected it? Was I always this drawn to bad decisions—or just once I realized how good of a story it all made? I was so tempted to blame Sam for all this introspection—wasn't she always pestering me to heal my inner child?

Or maybe it was Eddie, popping up where he didn't belong, causing issues where there didn't need to be any. I'd imagined a few times what I would do if I ever saw him again. In most of my daydreams I was wearing a shifty little black dress and ruby-red lipstick, doling out devastating one-liners.

I spent the entire day marinating in my own self-pity juices until six-thirty, when Nan texted me that she was going out after work with "the girls" and I was on my own for dinner. I was standing barefoot in the kitchen, a mug of coffee held limply in my hand as I stared at the only sentence I'd written all day:

Sexy grandpa Vietnam war memorial.

I dug through the fridge looking for dinner and discovered my only options were lettuce, a T-bone steak, or a first-edition Slim-Fast. Pizza it was, then.

I passed Alfonzo swimming laps in the pool as I thundered down the steps toward the parking lot. The sun sat midway to the horizon, falling in languid, lazy stripes of buttercup yellow across all the white and baby-blue clapboard houses.

The boardwalk was empty, not unusual for a Wednesday evening before the weekend crowd made it out. But there were a fair number of joggers and some milling couples, one pair even arguing outside Sundee's T-Shirt Shoppe. Typical beach behavior, really.

Jimmy's had replaced Genie's at some point, revising the old-fashioned light-up marquee to say, WORLD FAMOUS TO-MATO PIE.

I pushed open the door and a bell tinkled over my head. The walls were covered in alternating green and white subway tiles; the floor still stuck to the bottom of my shoes with every step; and the piz-zas, tucked behind a glass case like prized jewels, smelled like slow-roasted garlic and fresh basil.

A man roughly the same dimensions as a brick chimney stood

behind the counter in a stained white shirt and a matching apron poking at a cell phone. When he heard the bell, he straightened up immediately and tossed me one of those tight-lipped service-industry smiles. Something about his ruddy cheeks and solid brow was *so* familiar, I just couldn't—

"Delfina?" His voice was a lot higher pitched than I anticipated. The man's face cracked into a real smile, one that showed off the gap in his teeth. "It's me—Tully Martino."

"Oh my God," I said slowly. "*Tully.* I thought you looked familiar."

He blushed, pink clouds blossoming on the sides of his already splotchy neck. "Yeah, it's me. What're you doing here?"

"Um." I *needed* to get better at answering this question. "Ordering pizza, I guess."

"No." He laughed. "I mean in Evergreen. I thought you were like, an actress now."

"I'm just . . ." I pulled my sunglasses off my head and then put them right back. "Visiting my parents."

He nodded with grave appreciation, mouth twisting into a shy smile. "Cool. What can I get you?"

"Just a slice of cheese." The sunglasses were off again. This was why people smoked indoors for so long. What the hell was I supposed to do with my hands? "To go."

He rapped his knuckles on the counter and let that creepy smile linger. "To go. You got it."

A few minutes later Tully returned with a slice of pizza roughly the size of my face laid over two paper plates. It was already leaving behind a gorgeous grease angel, steam curling up.

"Here ya go. I, uh, got you the slice with the most cheese."

I reached for the plates, an awkward laugh rolling through me. "Thanks, Tully." And I swear to God, he winked at me.

I SLIPPED off my sandals and propped my legs up on the board-walk railing, enormous slice balanced on my knees. I leaned forward and took tiny bites, chewing as slowly as I could. Through the golden tint of my sunglasses, the sunset dripped between the clouds like a melting Creamsicle.

Pizza is best consumed while sitting on a bench facing the Atlantic as the lazy low tide crashes into the shoreline. The space around you isn't totally quiet, but you're close enough to what feels like the edge of the whole world while spicy-sweet olive oil settles on the back of your tongue, a thin slick of sand coating everything, down to the ridges of your fingertips.

Sure, pizza tastes good in other places—like in Italy or whatever—but *this* was my favorite. Last night, and everything that lived inside it like a matryoshka doll of trauma, felt far away even if just for a moment.

"Is there room for two?"

I snapped my eyes open.

I lifted them in the direction of that familiar raspy voice—a voice that, years ago, I thought I'd never hear again. But there it was, cutting through my sensory retreat, pulling me back down to earth.

Eddie was standing at the end of the bench, balancing identical paper plates with an identical slice of pizza—slightly less cheesy—on the open palm of his hand. The length of his hair was unfurled from his work ponytail and rippling in the ocean breeze, curls swimming across his forehead. He wore a rumpled, faded gray T-shirt that dipped low in the front, revealing the top of a green-black tattoo. Eddie could so easily fit into my little daydream, if he just stood there with that tiny quirk of a smile frozen on his lips. Silent.

I licked my lips, making sure I wasn't wearing a thin layer of pizza grease. "Legally, I cannot stop you."

Eddie let out a sigh as he lowered himself down next to me, stretching his long legs and propping his feet up onto the railing beside mine. "Tully seemed excited that you're back in town."

"Oh great." I tore off the corner of my crust. "Guess I'm not too tall for him anymore."

Eddie's shoulders bounced with quiet laughter as he took a bite of pizza. "Poor guy's clueless."

I smirked, flitting my eyes toward him. "Did you let him know I joined the convent?"

"You think you'd convince anyone?" He raised his brows at me before taking another massive bite.

"What are you implying? I look unholy?"

"You have an alien tattoo and baby bangs."

"Mother Teresa could have had both and we wouldn't have ever known."

Eddie spied me ripping at the corner of one of my paper plates. "So, last night . . ."

"I'm kind of . . . in a bad place." I worked steadily on folding my paper plates into the smallest square possible. "That's why I'm back here." I lifted my eyes to the ocean. "I'm totally fucked, actually."

Eddie shifted on the bench beside me before reaching over and trying to ease the crumpled-up paper plates from out of my fingers. When I looked at him, his eyebrows were drawn together, lips pushing to the side in a thoughtful purse. "Elaborate."

I released my paper plates to him. "My literal dream is about to come true, and I'm not being hyperbolic—which is surprising, I know. I'm booked on the biggest comedy showcase in the industry and I'm supposed to perform in a month and a half—"

"*Whoa*, Del. That's amazing."

"Hold your horses." I laughed, turning on the bench to face him, tucking one leg under the other. "It's not a good thing."

"Are you crazy?" His eyes nearly doubled. "*How?*"

"Because . . ." I started weakly, pressing my thumb into the side of my nose. *Do not cry in front of this man, Delfina.* "It feels pathetic to say it out loud."

His chest expanded with a deep inhale. At some point, he had extended his arm over the back of the bench. "Look, I've been in a bad place, too." His eyes skimmed past me. "As you could probably tell."

I narrowed my eyes at him. "Not particularly. Elaborate."

"That first night you came by? My ex had just blown through and it was a *mess*. She wanted to talk, but I was short-staffed. She said I didn't care about figuring things out, that I don't care about being a responsible adult."

"Yikes," I whispered.

"Then, I saw you and"—he exhaled sharply—"I overreacted."

"Believe me, I know ex-girlfriends can be difficult."

He kept his eyes fixed on that spot behind my shoulder. "Wife."

I choked on air. "*Wife?*"

Eddie flashed me a soft, knowing smile, like he'd had to explain this so many times it was almost a joke. "She's my ex-*wife*."

"Damn," I breathed. "It really has been ten years."

"You're telling me." He rubbed at the side of his neck. "Ten years ago, all I cared about was getting laid once. Now, I'm a goatee and a pair of camo cargo shorts away from being the worst man you've ever met."

Getting laid once. I pushed the mental image of teenage Eddie out of my mind. *I remember what that kid wanted.* "You can't think of it like that. I could say the same thing. Ten years ago, all I cared about was having fifty dollars and access to a Sephora. Now, I'm . . ." I stopped short.

Eddie pulled his legs down from off the railing and leaned forward, resting his arms on his legs. We were even closer together now, and I couldn't help but examine the details of his face. The permanent crinkle between his heavy brows; the sharp parallel lines of his cheekbones and his jaw; the way the short, clipped sides of his hair still revealed the delicate ridges of his curl pattern. It wasn't something I had ever allowed myself to do when we were younger. It felt, oddly, like a privilege to be this close to someone I'd once known intimately, to study the details of the person he'd become after so much time.

"What are you?" he asked finally, encouraging me to keep going. His eyes turned soft beneath his omnipresent furrow as he searched my face. *Not worth it,* I wanted to warn him. *I've got a mean poker face.*

"Unemployed. Then, I catch my boyfriend and roommate hooking up. So, yeah. Also, homeless."

"Damn."

It was my turn to smirk, like I was telling an old joke. "Yep. It's like I can never be too lucky. So, now I'm here trying to figure out what the hell I'm going to say onstage, in front of *thousands* of people. But I'm constantly distracted—by family shit, by the ocean, by bombing, by you."

"Me?" His eyebrows leapt toward his hairline.

"Yeah, *you,* Edgardo. Showing up at my house at seven o'clock in the morning on a Tuesday."

"Right, right." He readjusted like that wasn't exactly what he was expecting to hear. Like I'd be dumb enough to just come out and say that I couldn't stop thinking about the curve of his Cupid's bow and the way my mind went blank when I watched him count out his register or refill a drink, that last night I'd only told him one-sixteenth of how I was really feeling. "So, your ex is blond, huh?"

I snapped out of our momentary civility and returned to the glare I'd been delivering him for the last few days. "Seriously? *That's* what you took away from last night?"

The sunset danced in his eyes. "You've always had pretty bad taste in men."

"You really wanna go there, pal?"

"What?" He was grinning, the bastard. "It's true."

"Oh yeah?" I swiveled to face him full-on. "What about you? You only ever date petite princess types who want to take a single, brisk walk on the wild side. Then you're all, *oh brother, why didn't that work out for me?* Have you ever even dated another musician?"

He screwed his mouth up into a defensive knot. "No, I have not."

"Exactly. Comedians—musicians. You're all the same. Terrified of talented women." He was watching me closely and my breath hitched in my chest. We both knew what I said wasn't completely true. At least when it came to the people sitting on this bench together.

"Well, you nailed it. My ex was like that, like what you just described."

I let out a laugh that seemingly took five pounds of pressure off my chest. "I guess mine was, too. I'm a huge hypocrite. I have awful taste in men. You should push me into the ocean."

"To be fair . . ." Eddie finally gave in to a full smile as he bumped his shoulder into mine. "You have awful taste in a lot of things."

I screwed my face up into mock laughter. "*Sooo funny*. Asshole." But now a real smile was taking over because Eddie wouldn't stop bumping his shoulder into mine.

"Tell me all about this New Yorker I need to fight."

"Please, New York is innocent. The man's Canadian." I huffed. "I don't even care that he cheated, honestly. I'm more upset about the jokes."

Eddie stopped bumping and pressed his shoulder into mine. "I have a whole EP dedicated to my ex."

"How tragic of us."

"Hopeless romantics," he noted.

"Maybe just hopeless. I should quit now before I humiliate myself in front of America's biggest comedy nerds."

"You're joking, right?" he asked as he watched me intently. "How hard have you worked for this?"

"So hard," I admitted. "I put everything into getting here."

"There you go—you can't give up." He shrugged. "Look—the bar's empty all day. What if you came there to write? It's just me doing paperwork, and I can stay out of your way. You can use the stage if you need to."

I leaned away from him. "Really? You wouldn't mind being around me?"

He rolled his eyes until his gaze landed back on me, flashing another crackling smile that made my chest ache. "I don't know, are you going to yell at me again?"

I pulled my eyes away from his, focusing on my hands in my lap. "Thank you so much, Eddie. Seriously."

"Hey." He bumped his shoulder against mine one last time. "Don't thank me." Then, he stood, slinging a guitar case over his shoulder, leaving me with a lingering warmth that pooled in my stomach. "Only thing is, I can't do weekends. But I'll see you Monday morning, bright and early?"

"Sure," I said, nodding. "Totally."

Eddie dragged his fingers through his hair, pulling it back into his work ponytail. "Cool. Maybe you can help me write some music. I've been, uh . . ." He ran his tongue over his bottom lip, eyes flicking from me to the ocean and back again. "Looking for someone to write with. Someone good."

I cleared my throat—not because I had a tickle or needed to cough, but because I almost let out a horrible little *errrghhnnuff* sound.

"It's been nice talking, Del." He tapped his fingers against the back of the bench before walking away, before I had a chance to respond.

13

The Pier Point Diner

Friday night when Nan got home from work we decided to go to our favorite place—the Pier Point Diner.

As we strolled down the boardwalk arm in arm, surrounded by what felt like a million couples enjoying the most romantic date night of their lives, I was confronted head-on with just how much Evergreen had changed. Not just in the last ten years, but since last summer.

"Yeesh," Nan grunted as we passed two sunburned day-trippers splitting their mouths between sharing a twisted cone and a deeply upsetting kiss. "When did everyone lose their manners?"

"Whenever they started letting women wear pants," I replied, eyes grazing over the throng of people coming toward us in the direction of the arcade and the surf mall. "Were Fridays always this busy? Jeez."

"Ever heard of a digital nomad?" Nan didn't wait for me to respond—not that I was planning on it. My favorite things about my nan in no particular order were her commitment to day-time programming, the fact that she had never voted in a single election—presidential or otherwise—her love of sequins, and her rants. "Me either," she concurred with no one. "I thought Alfonzo was saying a slur when he first mentioned them. He points at a gal with blue hair and says, *digital nomad*. I said: *Al, I think you're supposed to call 'em Democrats*." She rolled her eyes. "Come to find out it's a funky way to say that young people are fed up with the big city and want to live somewhere nice and do their work from a personal computer." She pressed her elbow into my side, steering us out of a wayward surrey bike's path. "Of course, they gotta come here. Good thing I paid off the condo years ago, otherwise I'd be hooking in Atlantic City for a hot meal and a warm bed."

"Hooking in Atlantic City," I repeated slowly, stepping over an abandoned funnel cake.

"We have a Starbucks on *every* corner," Nan started again. "You can't spit without hitting one. You're at the beach, dammit. Lay off the cappuccinos. Have a beer. Eat some pizza. Thank God for people like Eddie." Nan jabbed a finger into the chest of an invisible digital nomad, confronting the rotten gentrifiers head-on. "He's what's keeping this place real."

"Eddie's your bestie now, I guess," I said, biting at the inside of my cheek to keep from grinning. I liked hearing what Nan had to say about Eddie; I liked his status as hometown hero. We crossed the boards, headed toward the diner's entrance.

Nan nodded, dislodging her arm from mine so she could push open one of the heavy doors. "Oh yeah. He's my pal. Handsome, young thing but he can't find a girlfriend to save his life, so he's stuck with the old farts like me. It started when I noticed him and his little girl at the grocery store and, gosh, she is just the cutest—"

I furrowed my brow, slipping into the frigid diner behind her. "Little girl?"

A sleepy-eyed teen in a bright blue polo greeted us with a monotone "How many?" then led us to a booth that overlooked the last jetty before the boardwalk met sand and officially ended.

We slid in across from each other. The waitress—Callie, according to her name tag—set down two overflowing glasses of ice water and a sticky menu for each of us.

"Little girl?" I repeated, smacking my hand down on Nan's menu so she couldn't open it until she answered me.

"Yes, dear." Nan rolled her eyes, swatting my hand away. "His *daughter.*"

"Daughter?" I repeated. Louder than I meant to. I tightened my grip on her menu. "He never told me he has a daughter."

"Well, did you ask?"

"Am I supposed to ask every man I meet if they have a kid?"

"At your age," Nan grumbled. "She's as cute as a button. Just turned two."

Two. *Wow.* A whole two-year-old. A little miniature Eddie who probably talked and walked and had his curly eyelashes. "I can't believe he didn't tell me."

"You're not very pleasant to speak to sometimes, sweetie," she remarked, flipping through the Deli Sandwich selection.

I frowned at the Breakfast Extravaganza, suddenly overcome with a heaviness. I'd naively thought Eddie and I had been moving toward a sort of friendship. He'd told me things—about his ex, even. *He'd chased me down.* "I can't believe you know more about Eddie than I do."

Nan lowered her menu to give me a pointed look. "I live here, Del. You just got back. Give it a little while, he'll warm up to you. You know, things really did *not* go well with his child's mother. He's been in mourning."

I sunk my teeth into my bottom lip. "Mourning, huh?"

"They were an odd couple. Her father is a pastor, and her mother has diabetes. And you know Eddie's a musician."

"The devil's profession. The opposite of having diabetes."

"What I mean is, they weren't into his whole rock and roll life-style." Nan reached across the table and took my hand in hers. "You're thinking about Ingram, aren't you?"

Ingram? She assumed that talk of Eddie's flop relationship might have reminded me of my own. But no. When it came to Eddie in a relationship, the only part I'd ever been capable of focusing on was Eddie. Suddenly, I was embarrassed I hadn't been thinking of Ingram at all. The waitress appeared again, saving me. "Ready to order?" Horrible service, excellent timing.

"I'll have a Diet Pepsi and the broiled scallops," Nan said, handing her menu over with a flourish.

I grimaced. "Scallops at a diner?"

The waitress looked at me like I'd just dribbled vomit down the front of my shirt. "They're literally our specialty."

"Noted." I forced a smile, handing her my menu. "I'll just take a black coffee and the breakfast thing in the picture, hold the bacon." Once the waitress was gone, I leaned close. "No, I'm not. It's actually . . . uh, Roger."

"Roger?"

"I know he's sort of off-limits, but . . . I haven't seen him in ten years. Every time I come back here, we're so busy having fun I just forget about him. Is it weird that I feel bad?"

"Kind of," she offered bluntly. "He's never really been Father of the Year."

"I know that. But he's still my father and he's . . . here, you know?" What I'd wanted to say was *alive*. "Maybe I just need to know what he's doing—whether it's good, bad, or ugly. *Still* ugly." I huffed, fidgeting with my napkin.

She made a small disapproving noise. "You always loved to take risks."

I reached across the table for her other hand. "He can't hurt me any more than he already has, I promise. I just think my brain is . . . working through some real subconscious shit."

Nan was watching me closely, her hazel eyes flitting between my nervous fingers entwined with hers and my face. "You know, he wasn't a mess when your mother met him."

"Really?"

She nodded slowly, pulling her hands away and unfolding her paper napkin, tucking it into the front of her shirt. "He was fixing cars down at a body shop in Surf City and taking classes at the community college for some specialty license so he could drive a truck. He played bass guitar in a band on the weekends. Of course, I still didn't approve." Nan rolled her eyes, dropping them on the streetlights that lined the boardwalk. "I thought if Michelle was hanging around with someone, he was probably trouble. She was *definitely* trouble." She let out a dry laugh. "I did what I could, but then she turned eighteen and . . . I think she brought him around drugs for the first time. I can never forgive myself for that. I have my issues with Roger, believe me, but . . ." She tapped her fingernails on the table. "He's got a mother, too."

I let the back of my head hit the vinyl booth. I wanted to ask her a million questions, but this wasn't just story time. This had been her life, her trauma. I was terrified that the wrong question might break her all over again. So, instead I just whispered, "Wow."

"Stupid kids, bless their hearts," she noted thoughtfully.

The waitress whizzed by, setting down our drinks. We thanked the dust cloud she left behind.

As I stirred a creamer into my coffee, Nan finally broke her silence. "He's doing okay now. He's sobered up. Lives in a trailer park across the bay called Oceanfront." She gave me a long look before plunging a straw into the icy depths of her Pepsi. "You have his number."

I HADN'T planned on rushing over to Roger's house after dinner, but as soon as I had the name of the trailer park from Nan, I entered a daddy-issue-fueled fugue state. I was opening Google Maps and punching in "Oceanfront Trailer Park." The official name was Oceanfront Presidential Park and it was a fifteen-minute drive away.

The map took me on a country road ride, snaking through thickets of overgrown sand grass and across narrow bridges that connected the disparate neighborhoods that made up most of Malaga County, separated by marsh, bay, and ocean. The map led me deeper inland, past the high school and the library and St. Agnes Catholic Church. I followed a two-lane highway perpendicular to the bay as it curved along the jagged shoreline. No other cars were on the road with me. I rolled down my window and breathed deeply as the salty air rushed in, trying to steady the thunking of my heart.

Eventually, the road straightened and connected to a bridge where I was instructed to turn left past a Wawa (of course) and keep going till I hit a set of train tracks.

Then, I saw it. A small community of identical mobile homes hidden between enormous pine and red cedar trees; modest matchbox homes lined up one after another, all painted various shades of pastel orange and cotton-candy pink on either side of a long, winding bike trail. As a community, they seemed to have a fondness for windmills; each house had one shoved into a potted plant or flower box outside.

It was adorable. The type of place a single man in his sixties might retire—or hell, live his entire life in beachside suburban bliss. At the end of the bike trail I spied a clearing—maybe a campground—with a firepit and picnic tables. I pulled up alongside the first set of homes and killed my engine. They were all various shades of well-loved pink, some in more need of a power washing than others, but none looked neglected.

A little girl with pigtails and in a pair of sparkly rain boots was dragging tree branches over to the firepit while a petite woman sat on one of the picnic benches, watching her as she talked on the phone. I could tell by her pajama pants that they must live in one of the homes right around the clearing. The little girl dropped a particularly large branch and let out a gleeful screech, running back to the woman.

This was the perfect place for a little girl to grow up.

A hollow knot grew in my stomach, pressing up into my throat.

Oceanfront was a far cry from Roger's litany of dingy studio apartments. Seemed like Roger had somehow magically managed to get his shit together, just in time for me to be a full-ass adult. And he didn't even have the courtesy to let me know.

I wondered where Eddie lived, what kind of bedroom he'd put together for his daughter. Did she have sparkly rain boots?

I clenched the steering wheel, eyes fixed on the little girl. I was gritting my teeth so tightly I wouldn't have been surprised if I'd sprained a muscle in my jaw.

I'd had a great childhood without Roger. Without Michelle. Without all their bullshit. I'd grown up in a perfectly nice apartment with my own bedroom. I'd spent every weekend of my childhood sitting on the shores of the Atlantic looking for seashells or skipping rocks on the bay. For my eleventh birthday Nan had bought me a ukulele, sparkly just like the little girl's boots, proof enough that I didn't need anyone other than her.

Some people are just like that. Big enough in their goodness to fill in all your empty spaces.

The woman in her pajama pants caught my eye and smiled without pulling the phone away from her ear. I smiled back, but I doubted the emotion reached my eyes. Once she turned away, I let myself slump forward against the steering wheel and let that hollow knot expand until the heat in my chest reached my eyes. Then, I drove away.

14

The Old House Between Brambleberry and Washington

Monday morning, I arrived at The Billiards's front door with my laptop before the mist had cleared, emerging from the fog and clutching my necessities like a pilgrim. The night before, I'd gotten a terse text from Misty asking if I had really moved out and if so, to please pick up my stuff by Tuesday.

She was *so* good at reading the room.

Instead of replying to Misty, I texted Ingram to let him know that he could tell Misty I'd be there on Tuesday. Ingram must have had some appreciation for the game I was playing, because he asked me to get coffee—so we "could talk."

I pressed my nose to The Billiards's door, too exhausted to push it open, leaving behind a nostril-shaped smear. Eddie was sitting at the farthest edge of the bar, squinting at a laptop as he palmed a mug, gray beanie pushed back on his head while he pulled absentmindedly at one of his curls, jaw set in deep contemplation. *That man is a father*, I thought over and over. *That man has a kid*. A kid that needed him just to survive. I hated that this fact somehow made him more attractive to me. Eddie was rapidly transforming into the type of person I'd want on my side if I ever, again, found myself in need of assistance. He was a little hot and cold—jumping too quickly from cold-shoulder wisecracker to being as comforting as a warm bowl of soup—but it would have been a lie to say that Eddie's emotional red light/green light hadn't been what drew me to him in the first place.

What drew me to him now.

Was I really going to spend eight hours alone with him, fighting back the constant barrage of conflicting Eddie-based thoughts? How had this ever seemed like a good idea?

Before I had a chance to harness all the energy in my soul to tuck and roll under his hedges, Eddie looked up from his laptop and noticed me. His eyes jumped up to meet mine—forehead still pressed against the door—and he smirked, crossing the room and yanking the door open.

"Did you forget how doors work?"

"No coffee," I croaked. "Arms won't work."

"Aha," he announced, gesturing for me to enter. "You're a fiend."

I dragged myself across the threshold, barely mustering enough strength to roll my eyes. "Why does it look like you're doing math at eight in the morning?"

"Just making sense of this month's inventory. I think one of my servers is stealing White Claws."

"Smart kid," I said, flinging my laptop up onto the bar.

"Absolute genius." He futzed behind the bar, rearranging some limes and eyeing me with the hesitance of a snake tamer. "Let me get you a coffee."

I shot him finger guns as a sign of gratitude. After an eternity, he returned with a ceramic diner mug filled to the top with pitch-black coffee.

"Gracias por el café," I said, doing a very flat and unimpressive imitation of Nan's precise, lingering Spanish.

He let out a snort, leaning back against the column that housed the cash register and shelves of bottles. "De nada. You always this quiet in the morning?"

I grunted. Truthfully, I was never this quiet, even when under-caffeinated. I was just *nervous.*

He nodded, spinning around and returning with the entire pot of coffee. He set it down gently in front of me. "All yours, Tim Allen."

I flashed him a grateful look as I opened my laptop. "I promise I'll be a beacon of charisma in like, thirteen minutes."

"Don't waste your time," he said as he circled the bar, returning to his workstation. "I appreciate the quiet."

I side-eyed him, wading carefully into the friendly banter category. "You're very alert and punchy, aren't you?"

He shrugged a shoulder as he eased himself back up onto his stool. "I'm used to waking up early these days."

I let the words hang between us for a moment, wondering if this was the moment he'd say: *because of my kid*. But he stayed quiet, just kept typing at his computer, humming under his breath.

"For any particular reason? Or you just freakishly into sunrises?" I asked, bringing my face mug-height and slurping.

Eddie paused mid-type. "Genuine question for you, Del. What time do you think the sun rises?"

"I don't know. Like, eight?" I muttered.

First order of business for today was to watch all of my old tapes. Write out the jokes that featured Ingram—or any man, for that matter. Once I had them all out on paper, I could start edit-ing. Picking through the pile and piecing together something that resembled a set. I popped in my headphones and got to work.

The morning passed in a haze of humiliation as I endured foot-age of myself performing between refills of coffee and the occa-sional glass of ice water, pushed in my direction by Eddie.

Around eleven-thirty, he slid a plate of toast down the bar toward me. It hit my laptop with a terrifying *thunk,* snapping me out of my haze. At some point I'd pulled the hood of my sweatshirt over my head and drawn the cords, so my world was confined to a strangled, scrunched peephole.

"Toast," I grunted like a caveman, shoving a triangle into my mouth then quickly returning to my all-you-can-eat buffet of shame.

My jokes were *technically* great. I was empirically funny. And with each tape, I got better and better at delivering them. The audience always laughed. But Jesus Christ, there wasn't a part of myself I hadn't totally eviscerated. I'd pillaged the most sacred details of my life for laughs, everything from the size and shape of my body to the theme of my third-grade birthday party. It was becoming clearer to me that there were only two parts of myself I'd left off-limits—Evergreen and my parents. There was no scar tissue to protect me there. It was all raw, bloody, soft.

After I drank all his coffee and hoovered his toast, Eddie disappeared into the kitchen before returning with a hammer and a toolbox. He came to a stop in front of me, waving the hammer until I pushed off my hood and pulled out my earbuds.

"Any particular reason you're flailing that thing around?"

"Flailing th—?" Eddie's eyes fell to the weight in his left hand. "Oh. Yeah. Um, you should probably give me your number."

I pulled a Sharpie from my purse, scribbling my number down on a napkin. "You can have my number, but I will be texting you my coffee order every Sunday night."

"You have to text me to remind me to get you a large black coffee, extra coffee?" he teased, tossing the hammer onto the stage and setting the toolbox down at his feet. He hiked his pants up before descending into a devastating squat, back muscles visibly working under his T-shirt as he balanced on his haunches. The edge of his sleeve slipped back, and I could make out the tattoo on the back of his triceps.

"Large black coffee, extra coffee *and* a pack of Marlboro Red 100s." I yanked my eyes away and went back to tapping at my mouse till my screen jumped back to life. A joke popped into my head: *You ever see a man do a full squat and wonder why being horny isn't a crime?*

Eddie tossed a dark look at me over his shoulder. "Please don't tell me you smoke."

Something in my belly twisted deliciously at that look   vaguely protective and completely focused on me. "Jeez, what if I did? What's it to you?"

He huffed, swiveling on his feet to face me, forearms flexing as he worked to keep his balance. He was pressing his fist into the palm of his other hand. Those stupid square knuckles. "I'm not going to lecture you—"

"But you're gonna lecture me?" I wanted to pick a fight, to keep that look burning in his eyes.

"Not only is it gross, smoking is—"

His personal essay was going to have to wait—a *tap-tap-tap* on the front door grabbed both of our attention, cutting Eddie off. The source? A mostly toothless, very small human.

"Eddie, I don't know how to tell you this but there's a child stuck to your front door."

"Not this again," he muttered, taking off toward the goofy face staring back at us—a skinny mess of freckles with one enormous front tooth and a pair of pool goggles shoved into his red-brown hair. Eddie crossed the room in approximately seven long steps, propping the door open with the tip of his shoe. "Go home, Chip."

"Um, Mr. Eddie?" the kid squeaked, completely unfazed by the instant and unwarranted aggression. Despite his tone, Eddie was looking down at the kid pretty warmly.

"This is a bar, Chip, I can't let you in."

"My mom said you'd say that but she said it's okay for me."

"Oh, it's okay for you? Well, then . . ." Eddie rolled his eyes as Chip flew under his outstretched arm and beelined directly to a two-top, tossing a decoupage box with a little sign, secured with Popsicle sticks, that read EVERGREEN TRINITY EPISCOPAL CHURCH FUN-RAISER onto the table. Then, he began mercilessly scratching at his eye.

"I'm, um, selling tickets to a roller-skate night to help raise money for the, um, elevator."

"I know why you're raising money, bud," Eddie replied, flicking the sign before heading back to the stage. "I already told your mom I can't donate. I don't go to your church anymore."

"You went to church? Did they have to drive you to the burn ward after?" I mused, unhelpful as ever.

Eddie shot me a warning look as he leaned back against the stage, folding his arms over his chest. It was a real dad move, and if I weren't holding Nan's revelation about Eddie's daughter close to my chest like something precious, I would have told him so. Instead, I tried not to grin, thoroughly amused with my *excellent* joke.

"'Cause you sinned?" Chip asked. *Sick burn.*

"Because I'm not Episcopalian," Eddie corrected him.

"Then what are you?"

"I don't know." Eddie shrugged. "Nothing?"

Poor little Chip was having a hard time wrapping his head around this news. His faint russet brows pulled together as he shoved his tongue in and out of the place where his front tooth had once been.

I interjected before Chip's head exploded. "He's Catholic, buddy."

"Either way." Eddie held his hands out to Chip, palms up. The international symbol for *I ain't got nothin', chief.* "I'm cutting you off. I already gave two hundred dollars to help fix the roof *and* I sponsored the winter bocci league. Remind your mom about the bocci league."

"Oh, okay." Chip's eyes had gone completely unfocused somewhere between *two hundred* and *winter bocci league.* "Can I use your restroom, please?"

Eddie scrubbed at his brow before turning back to his tools. "You know where it is. If you can't reach the sink this time, yell."

The kid abandoned his box and broke into a sprint down the hall. "Thanks, Mr. Eddie!"

I waited until he was out of earshot before I said, "Cute kid. He a regular?"

Eddie shook his head and pushed off the stage, making his way back behind the bar. "Chip's adorable. His mother, Celeste? A nightmare."

"They've really shaken you down over the years."

Eddie let out a belly laugh, pointing the soda gun into my glass and refilling it with water. "I'm one of ten locals that still does all the community bullshit."

"Very noble," I said. "They must have heard about your world-famous customer service."

"Believe it or not, Miller," he said as he unscrewed a jar of maraschino cherries and popped one into his mouth, "I am frequently too nice to say no."

"Oh, I believe." I held out my hand for a cherry. "There's a six-year-old spray-painting your tiles right now because you can't say no."

Eddie placed a cherry in the palm of my hand, but not before carefully pulling out the stem. I tried not to think too hard about how *damn* thoughtful that tiny action was. "Ever since I bought this place, they're always asking for something."

"How'd you do that, by the way?" I tossed my cherry back. "Afford the bar, I mean."

"My uncle Ignacio passed away a few years back, and he left me some money. The building was a wreck. The damage from Hurricane Sandy had been massive and the owners couldn't afford to keep up." He ran a hand over the top of the bar like he was smoothing back the mane on a beloved horse. "I wanted to run a concert venue, but people prefer chicken wings to live music."

I gave in to the soft smile playing at my lips, leaning forward to rest my head in my hand. "I don't eat chicken, but your wings do smell really good."

He tilted his head, mirroring my smile, the warmth in his eyes drawing me in, like dark pools I could have swum in for hours. His warmth was singular in that way. "Thanks. It's not exactly what I had in mind, but between all the Taylor Swift dance nights, we manage to play some music."

"Taylor's fun. The best part is it's your place. You can perform whenever you want, and you never have to ask permission or kiss ass. Do you know what I'd do for that?" I shook my head and picked up my Sharpie, pushing the cap in and out of place.

He chucked a dish towel over his shoulder, eyes still fixed on me. "I figured you were running shit up there."

"Oh no. Doesn't work like that." I shook my head. "I'm just one of thousands of comedians who all want the same thing."

"Well . . ." Eddie jabbed his thumb toward the stage. "Any time you want, she's all yours."

"I appreciate that."

Eddie nodded curtly, pressing his hands into his hips. "I'm gonna make us lunch. You like tacos?"

I tried not to think about the fact that no one had ever offered to make me tacos before. How maybe it was better when Eddie hated me, because otherwise, I could get used to sitting on the other side of his bar, watching him interact with every local weirdo that came through his doors. Because Eddie was maybe the type of person with a halo effect—that warmed your insides, all the way down to your knees.

I took a sip of water. "Love 'em."

Chip barreled back down the hall, hair flapping over his forehead, the front of his shirt soaked. "Thank you, Eddie!" he shouted, scooping up his box and disappearing through the front door.

EDDIE SAT on the edge of the stage, plucking out a few self-conscious chords. He was working through something, tongue pressed to the ridge between his nose and lips. I kept my headphones in but music off, listening to each note, as his hands moved slowly up and down the neck of his electric guitar. I knew he hadn't noticed my eyes on him, and I relished a moment to catch him off guard. The curve of his brow, the way he pressed his lips together in concentration . . . He still had that deadly serious look in his eyes, fingers moving deftly, eyebrows rising and falling with each note.

If I focused hard enough, I could still see the sixteen-year-old boy with the Iron Maiden sticker on his binder. But there was something else there, too. A hardness in the angle of his cheekbones, the taut energy trapped in his jaw. As he played his song, discovering each note one after the other, that hardness began to fall away. His gaze softened at the edges—dark, full lashes casting a shadow over his cheeks.

Suddenly, he changed key.

"No."

My own voice shocked me. It came out scratchy, from the back of my throat.

Eddie looked up at me, holding me there with that softness.

I cleared my throat and pulled out my earbuds, sitting up straight. "I liked it better before."

He replicated the first chord progression. "Like this?" His voice was soft, too. Different.

I nodded. "I can hear the words when you play it like that."

His mouth flickered into a smile. "What're the words?" he asked, playing the notes again, this time smoothly, with confidence.

"*I'm so sorry I called you Soft Serve all those years ago,*" I hummed to the notes.

He gave his nose a little scratch, trying and failing to hide a smile. "Walked right into that one."

I slid off my stool and crossed the room, folding my arms over my chest. "You need to add a little spice at the end."

He raised a brow, playing the chords over and over as I made my way toward him. He still had that bar towel over his shoulder. "Spice?"

"You know . . ." I pantomimed pressing the heel of my hand into a whammy bar. "A little *wee-wow.*"

I paused in front of him, hands on my hips. His eyes slid over me, from the top of my ponytail down to the cuffs of my jean shorts, giving me a look that was both deeply suspicious and playful, eyes shining like garnet in a crystal-clear creek—a brown so deep and rich they almost glowed red.

I raised my eyebrows. "Just try it."

So, he did. The first time, it came out a little clunky. But the second time? He paused and looked up at me. "That was dope."

I smirked. "Told ya."

He played the entire progression through again. This time I imagined the song fully formed, the words coming to me in bits and pieces. It would be a light country-rock song—a song about lips tasting like cherries. Champagne being sticky. *Taste you on my tongue, all summer long. Something, something, when you call me baby*

"Nailed it," I said once he finished.

"Thanks, Del." His voice was little more than a whisper, eyes trained on me as he handed over the guitar. "Your turn."

"I don't know." I still played all the time, only for myself—for my sanity. The last time I'd played in front of Eddie, things had gone poorly. I strummed the strings before letting my fingers fall into the song I always played when I needed to clear my mind. It was a song most people knew, and it wasn't long before Eddie started humming along.

I faded to a stop, pulling my eyes up to meet his. He was leaning forward, arms resting on his thighs, eyes locked on mine.

"You should play here, at our next show."

I dragged my eyes away as I handed the instrument back. "I haven't played in public in years. I'd probably choke."

"No way." He reached for the guitar, fingers grazing mine before he pulled it away and set it down gently on the stage. "You're a natural."

A nervous laugh rippled through me. "Even naturals should practice."

He let out a low, humming laugh before he stood and slowly closed the space between us with a languid step. I wasn't sure what he was doing—if I should slink away, recoil. I didn't want to. I never wanted there to be any distance between Eddie and me; the space I'd put between us, in the form of ten years and all of New Jersey, had been out of necessity. Eddie had the ability to take my entire mood and shift it in a nanosecond. This had always been true—would probably always be true.

Now, with our chests nearly touching, he lifted a hand until it was even with my face, then, hesitance vibrating in his fingertips, grazed the curve of my cheek.

"You," he started quietly, "had a hair."

My eyes involuntarily fluttered shut as his fingers connected with my skin and I felt his heavy-lidded gaze resting on my lips.

"Well," I said, my voice hoarse. "I think I've done enough writing for today."

Eddie nodded, taking a step back and immediately bringing his hands to his neck. "I'll see you again tomorrow?"

"Definitely, in the afternoon. I just need to take care of something in the morning."

He nodded, massaging the muscles in his neck. "Life shit."

Eddie knew about life shit. Real life shit. He knew about babies and divorce and owning a small business and helping his community.

I was just picking up my clown lamp.

"Exactly," I said, scurrying to collect my laptop. "Lots of life shit."

THE NEXT morning, I left town before Evergreen had rubbed the sleep from its eyes, setting out into the misty early morning air armed with Windex and a heavy gut.

As I sat in traffic in the Holland Tunnel, all I could think about was Eddie.

Eddie playing his guitar on the edge of the stage.

Eddie rubbing the back of his neck as he poured me another cup of coffee.

Eddie yawning and stretching, his shirt pulling up to reveal a patch of perfectly tan stomach.

Eddie and his kid. His daughter. A little girl he still hadn't yet mentioned to me. Not even in a roundabout way, not even after an entire day in the same room together. She was old enough to sit on his shoulders; to toddle across the room into his arms; to pick a flower just for him.

TUCKER AND Cyrus met me in front of a CVS two blocks from my old place, and I forced them to engage in a group hug.

"My *babies*," I crowed, tightening my arms around their very moist backs, laying my head against Tucker's big, soft chest. "I missed you *so* much."

Cyrus patted the top of my head while wiggling his other arm free. "Dislodge, woman."

"I can't." I squeezed tighter, and they let out a harmonic series of grunts.

"Okay," Tucker said, expanding his arms and breaking us apart. "Enough."

I hiked my bags up onto my shoulder and started down the block toward my old place. "You two can say whatever you want, but the only reason to meet someone at eight in the morning on a Tuesday is *love*."

"I miss ya, Fina," Cyrus said, knocking his shoulder into mine. "Gimbley's is so boring without you."

"How much have you two been hanging out without me? Be honest, I won't cry."

They traded an anxious look over my head, though Cyrus wasn't quite tall enough to not get caught. "Um. Well, here's the thing," Cyrus started slowly, eyes flickering to mine. "We've both been . . . kind of busy."

"With shows and stuff?" I adjusted my bags, taking special care to not whack Tucker with the handle of the broom shoved in one of them.

"Cyrus has a girlfriend," Tucker blurted out.

Cyrus reared back and sputtered, "Tucker got a real job!"

"*What?*" I came to a halt on the sidewalk. I didn't even know where to begin. I hadn't even been gone two weeks. I turned to Tucker first. "You quit Gimbley's?"

"I found a way better gig managing a cafeteria in Brooklyn. It's salaried and everything."

I spun my head in Cyrus's direction. "You're in a committed relationship?"

He nodded. "With the girl from the night you came by." That was a very mild way of explaining the night in question.

"Jeez." I paused to survey the two of them, shifting awkwardly beside each other. Tucker in a wrinkled T-shirt, practically casting a shadow over lithe Cyrus, tote bag death-gripped under his arm. We'd been a strange trio—Cyrus too New York for us transplants; Tucker too corn-fed for us East Coasters; and me too extroverted and melodramatic for two gentle dorks. But we'd been inseparable for so long, bonded by our batshit work schedules and from the moment I'd told them all about my dad and Tucker had replied, "My dad sucks, too."

"Have you guys hung out *at all* since I left?"

They traded a look and slowly shook their heads.

"It's great to see you, brother," Cyrus muttered.

"Same here, king," Tucker replied, pulling him into a half hug.

TUCKER AND Cyrus were lying beside each other horizontally on my bed while I carefully folded and bagged my clothes. They were playing some game that made the most infuriating series of dings, whoops, and *yee-haw* sounds.

"Such help you both are," I said as I crawled over Tucker's head to yank down my tapestry.

"You can do it," Cyrus said flatly without looking up from his phone. "Believe in yourself."

"Through Christ all things are possible," Tucker added blandly.

"I was hoping for actual, physical support," I grunted, emptying a dresser drawer into a trash bag. After a solid attempt at packing up everything, I found myself also lying horizontally on my bed, playing the stupid game on my phone.

"Ugh, I lost." I clicked my phone screen off. "Okay, I need official best friend advice from the Adult Children of Assholes, New York City contingent."

"We talking dad stuff or mom stuff?" Cyrus asked without looking up.

"Dad." I gnawed at my lip for a moment, before coming clean: "I drove to my dad's house the other day. I didn't go in or anything. I didn't even text him. I just sat there—*staring*."

Tucker made a small *yeesh*, air hissing through his teeth. "Very spooky of you."

"*Why* can't I stop thinking about him? Ever since I got back in town, he's constantly on my mind. I haven't seen the guy in years and now I'm mouth-breathing at his window."

"No contact is hard," Tucker offered simply, shrugging a

shoulder. "My parents are crazy evangelical assholes and even I go home for Christmas."

Cyrus let out a huff. "I have dinner with my parents every Friday night."

Tucker nodded sympathetically. "It's hard to deny how much you love your parents even if the version of them you love is maybe one you made up."

"Whoa, hold up." I kicked into an upright position. "I do not love my dad; I don't know my dad. He was barely around when I was a kid. And when he was, he was always fucking up or being unbearably selfish."

Tucker and Cyrus traded a conspiratorial glance before Tucker rested a loving hand on my knee. "Are you sure about that?"

"I'm telling you guys. I called my dad Steve for six months just to piss him off, to see if he would care enough to correct me. And guess what? He didn't."

"You don't have to spend every Sunday with the guy, but maybe just . . ." Cyrus shrugged. "Text him. Maybe you can't stop thinking about him because you're finally ready."

"I don't know. I'm already meeting Ingram for lunch. How many assholes can I fit into my life?"

Cyrus stared at me like I'd just slapped him with a rubber chicken. "You're meeting up with Ingram, but you won't give the guy who *made you* a second chance?"

"Ingram owes me an apology," I countered.

"Ingram's a piece of shit you've known for sixty-seven days. Your dad is a piece of shit who you are biologically engineered to care about. Text him, even if it's just to help you think about him less."

I scoffed at Tucker and his very sound, rational advice. "What is this? You two find the loves of your lives and real jobs, and suddenly I'm the dodo who can't do anything right?"

Cyrus slid off the bed and headed toward the bathroom, calling over his shoulder, "Were you ever not the dodo? I feel like you've always been a dodo."

Tucker reached across the bed and took my hand in his. "Cancel on Ingram." He gave me a squeeze. "You deserve it."

15

Home

When Cyrus, Tucker, and I said goodbye, we engaged in a *real* embrace. One where we bent our heads close together and said nothing at all. When I pulled away, Cyrus told me to keep his car for as long as I needed. Then, I made them promise to text more often.

There was weight in my words this time; I was really gone. Until Brainwave and depending on how it went, maybe forever. Either way, we all knew, standing on the corner of Thirty-First Avenue, that we would never get the Gimbley's days back again. We would never again be three nobodies in a rotten bar, with our eyes pointed at our futures, somewhere far off.

My heart sat heavier in my chest as I merged onto the turnpike and headed toward Evergreen—toward home. But when the road flattened out and the highway turned wide, that heaviness was replaced one mile at a time with a buzzing, not unlike the frizzing feeling of being backstage five minutes before you go on.

I PULLED up to The Billiards right as he was leaving, waving goodbye to someone, his work T-shirt tossed over his shoulder. I beeped my horn to grab his attention, and rolled down my window.

"I'm *so* sorry," I shouted across the lawn.

Eddie's shoulders relaxed when he saw me. "Del."

"I am so sorry," I repeated as he crossed the gravel path and leaned against my car. "I know I said I would show up, but I went and moved out of my old place today, then I got caught up in traffic and all of my stuff was in these awful bags and I just started sobbing in the Roy Rogers' bathroom—"

"Hey." He leaned down, resting his palms on the window ledge. "It's okay."

"But I told you I'd be by."

He shrugged, smiling softly. "Shit happens."

Relief rippled through me and I fell forward onto the steering wheel, releasing a sigh big enough to cover the last six hours. "Today sucked so bad. I really need to clear my head. Wanna go for a ride?"

He threw a concerned glance back at the bar. "I don't know . . ."

"No worries." I leaned my head back against the seat. "I can't even think straight, let alone drive more." But when I opened my eyes, Eddie's were flickering over my face and down my neck as he chewed his lip. I was too tired to fight the eye contact, and I let myself feel liquid under his gaze.

He threw a final glance over his shoulder at the bar before saying, "Let me drive, then."

I straightened up. "Really?"

He flicked his chin toward the passenger seat. "Move over before I change my mind."

I grinned at him before unbuckling myself and getting out of the car.

"Chop, chop," he yelled out the open driver's window. The man had gotten in and buckled up before I'd even made it halfway around the car.

"I'm chopping," I retorted, flopping into the passenger seat and slamming my door shut. "Where to?"

Eddie sent a wayward glance at the mountain of trash bags in the back seat. "The dump?"

I blinked at him. "Oh God. No. That's my stuff."

"Yikes."

"Yikes yourself. I spent three hours bagging up my whole life then hauled it across state lines."

Eddie tutted, releasing the emergency brake and making a U-turn toward the road. "You and your taste in men. Should have just married Jake."

"Jake?" I yelled, turning sideways in my seat, glowering at Eddie's perfect profile, illuminated by the reflection of the headlights off the road. "I never had a thing with Jake. I was just being nice to Jake because Jake was nice *to me*."

Eddie screwed up his face in a gorgeous, hilarious look of contempt. "The man was harboring a crush on you the size of Texas."

"Really?"

"Try not to sound so satisfied."

"That's why you didn't want me in your little band, huh?"

"No," Eddie scoffed with a definitive shake of his head. "I was just super jealous."

Something deep inside me relaxed. A tension I'd been holding for years, released with this nugget of truth. "You know, that's what Nan thought."

"Your voice . . ." He flexed his hands around the steering wheel a few times. "Is gorgeous. You should sing more often."

"Thanks," I said softly. His compliment hung around us in the air. "So, Jake liked me, huh?"

Eddie narrowed his eyes at the horizon and blew out a breath between his lips. "Oh yeah. *Big*-time."

WE TALKED the entire car ride in a sort of uninterruptible word-vomit while the sun set around us in big, bold streaks of corn-flower blue and honey gold. I kept waiting for him to bring up his daughter each time the conversation momentarily stalled or veered violently close to our own childhoods. It wasn't like Eddie and I avoided the deep end; we'd met each other in the deep end.

I did find out he wasn't in a band with Jake and Wiley any-more; he hadn't seen them since our freshman year of college. Eddie had chosen to stay local and got his degree from a small satellite campus of a big state school. When he told me he'd been mostly focused on touring and making music, I couldn't help but smile.

"My grades were total shit," he said, vaguely proud of himself. "Barely graduated, to be honest."

"What was your major?"

"Hospitality management," he said. "What about you?"

"Well, here's the thing . . ." I scrubbed at my nose and rolled my eyes around the car.

"Don't tell me you flunked out?"

"No! I dropped out. Nan never told you?"

"How many times do I have to tell you that we don't talk about you?" He said this through laughter.

"Feels impossible."

"Man, I can't believe you dropped out." He shot me a quick look. "Not that it matters. You're still the most impressive one out of all of us."

"Really?" I scrunched up my nose. "What about Sam? She's literally a doctor."

He shrugged. "I don't know, she was always on that track. She was never totally a kid. It's different with you."

I bit my lip and slid my eyes toward the road rushing by so he couldn't see how poorly I was hiding a grin. "Same with you, Ed. Your bar is cool. It's very impressive."

"Put my whole heart and soul into her." There was something about the way he said those words; they made me feel like my chest was gently caving in.

"What about your new band?" I asked. "Do you perform at the bar a lot?"

"I hate to say it, but we're really just a cover band." He was doing that thing again—where he drove with just the tips of his fingers, his left arm draped over the windowsill. With his right hand, he fussed with his hair, frowning slightly into the rearview mirror as he pushed his curls into a perfectly styled fluff. I tried to keep my eyes from wandering over his forearms when he scratched at his triceps under his shirt sleeve.

"It's easy to get gigs when you're doing the hits—Incubus, blink-182, even some good old Dave."

"No Dream Theater?"

He let out a big bark of a laugh. "No. No fifteen-minute prog rock solos."

I leaned forward in my seat, trying to peer through the heavy curtains of midnight-like darkness. "Where are we headed, anyway?"

"Patience. We're getting close—oh shit, Del." Eddie pressed the back of his hand into my arm, and I nearly vomited from the sudden contact. "Your 'check engine' light's on."

I flicked my eyes over toward the dash. *Shit.* "Just ignore it," I said, feigning casualness. "The light's broken. That's all."

Eddie met my gaze, eyes heavy with skepticism. "Ignore it? This car's older than God."

"And much like God . . ." I reached over and thunked the dash, a move I'd witnessed many times in my childhood. "She is very forgiving."

Eddie let out a rush of air. "That actually fuckin' worked!"

"Of course it did. I'm a witch." It was as good a reason as any and certainly more endearing than the truth. *This isn't my car! My friend had to lend it to me so he could have sex with a kind stranger and so I wouldn't be left stranded!*

From all the evidence I'd gathered so far, Eddie seemed beyond competent, and I didn't want to jeopardize what little respect he'd cultivated for me by telling him about Cyrus's dry spell.

We made a left at a busy intersection, then we were on a narrow bridge over a stretch of ink-black water. On the other side of the dark expanse, I could make out big white houses on stilts dotting the shoreline. Behind them, muted by a mix of ocean mist and light pollution, rose the candy-colored silhouette of an amusement park.

"We're in Ocean Harbor." I could barely hide the excitement in my voice.

"I figured you probably haven't been to this boardwalk in a few years."

I sat up straighter in my seat. "Can we ride rides? Will you go on the Ferris wheel with me?"

Eddie pressed his lips together, fighting mercilessly against a grin. "You're taking a literal approach to clearing your head?"

"Eddie." I pivoted in my chair to face him. "This was a *very* thoughtful idea."

"Yeah, yeah." He was losing the battle with his cheek muscles, one millimeter at a time.

"Eddie," I said again, shifting my voice up an octave. "You're being *so* nice to me."

"Okay." He flexed his hands around the wheel. "Miss Sarcasm. You're welcome."

"*Eddie*," I ratcheted my voice up again, "*you're sooo sweet.*"

"Don't," he growled, "make me regret this."

I let out my best evil cackle, flopping back in my seat. "I can't wait to see all thirty years of your life flash before your eyes after exactly one flip on the Zipper."

"First of all, I'm twenty-eight. And second of all, I will never get on the Zipper."

I narrowed my eyes at him. "You sure? I'm proving to be a very persuasive force in your life."

He returned my narrowed stare, beating me in intensity. "Oh yeah? Or is it the other way around?"

16

What's our game plan?" I rubbed my hands together as we climbed the steps toward South Jersey's Coney Island clapback, entering the throngs of people milling back and forth from storefronts to ice cream parlor to amusement park rides and back again. "Are we prioritizing funnel cake over Ferris wheel? More importantly, do you still identify as lactose intolerant?"

Eddie trailed behind me, laughter winking in his eyes alongside the flickering multicolor lights that surrounded us. "I do, but it's your night." He ducked his head down low, his voice close to my ear. "You're the one who had a bad day, remember?"

The hairs on the back of my neck stood on end, my breath catching behind my teeth. "Fine," I managed, spinning around to face him. I couldn't handle our bodies being so close. "Then I want one of those awful soda concoctions from Stevie's."

"Is this self-harm?" he quipped. "Should I be concerned?"

"I am simply reliving the joys of my youth," I replied. "Diarrhea et al."

"Well, in that case . . ." He jerked his head toward Stevie's Olde School Sodas. "Let's fuck it up, Miller."

"Actually?"

"Actually." He smirked, a rakish bounce in his step, like he really wanted to see me shit myself. "Come on, keep up."

"Wait!" I froze, holding up a finger. "I know you said no Zipper, but—"

He cocked his chin toward me. "No Zipper."

I raised an eyebrow. "What about the Cat and Mouse?"

WE CRAMMED into a roller-coaster car, Eddie's knees almost at his chin and my boobs nearly covering Mr. Mouse's eyes.

"Okay, so not really designed for a six-foot-four man," Eddie grumbled.

"Nope." I took seven deep breaths and then secured my safety belt. "Not built for adults with breasts, either."

He laughed, his shoulder shaking against mine, sending a gentle trill up my spine. I wondered briefly, dangerously, if anyone else had ever managed to make Eddie laugh this much.

"All limbs in the vehicle, please." This command came from a freckle-faced attendant, clearly drunk off the power that came with wearing a lanyard.

"We're trying," Eddie replied, fruitlessly pulling his shoulders toward each other in an attempt to tuck his elbows.

"Put your arm around me," I instructed him.

"You sure?"

"Stop being weird and put your arm around me."

"I'm just being *respectful*." He gingerly draped a long arm over my shoulders. Side by side it was slightly less terrifying to feel his lungs expanding against me, to feel his fingers glancing off my sticky skin. "Maybe the concept hasn't reached Canada yet."

"Joke's on you. I love talking shit about all my exes, past and present." I seemed to fit well under his arm. Had he noticed, too? Even if it meant nothing, I hoped he had.

"Thank you!" Freckles barked.

"You're welcome!" we shouted back.

Freckles sent the man operating the roller coaster a series of umpire-style hand signals. The cars jolted to life, every bolt and screw vibrating.

We lurched forward, tentatively, like the tracks and wheels were remembering an old dance.

"Oh *fuck*."

Then, we were clicking forward with confidence, the chill of ocean breeze pushing us backward into our seats. The sky angled into view, neon lines dragging past us as we gained momentum, taking the noise of the night with them.

Eddie tensed his grip on me, pulling my face into his chest. "How did I let you talk me into this?"

Laughter poured out of me as my face smashed into his chest. "Are you really that afraid? It's just a little—"

But it was too late. We were already flying down the first drop.

EDDIE DIDN'T scream on the ride, but he did sort of *shout*.

Oh, dear Lord.

Oh my God. Heaven help me.

Fucking hell. Oh my God.

After I stopped laughing long enough to stand up straight, we went directly to Stevie's and secured one of the tables outside, beneath strings of winking fairy lights and an enormous red-and-white-striped umbrella.

I ordered something called a Sea Foam Float while Eddie opted for a horrifyingly and unnaturally purple sorbet.

"Will this make it into your new set?" he asked, still pale and damp as he limply spooned radioactive ice shavings into his mouth. "Grown man nearly dies on a baby-coaster?"

"I'm not sure I should write about men anymore." I swirled my straw around my float, blending the Technicolor layers.

Eddie's smile faltered, eyes flickering over my face. "What happened today?"

"Well," I began. "I was supposed to meet my ex for coffee—"

Eddie sucked air in through his teeth. "Bad idea."

"I ended up canceling, don't worry." I took another bite of ice cream. "I stupidly thought I could maybe squeeze an apology out of him."

Eddie let out a small laugh, shaking his head. "Amateur move. You're his ex now. That's an entirely different category of human."

I watched him for a moment. "Does your ex-wife hate you?"

He nodded emphatically, nabbing the cherry off the top of my float. "She'd never admit it out loud—she's way too nice—but I think I'm definitely cracking her top ten biggest mistakes."

I couldn't help but laugh. "No way. You're basically the patron saint of Evergreen. You run a small business; you raise funds; you're a—" I almost blurted out *active father*, but I managed to catch myself. "You've always been a softie. Underneath all the cool guy bullshit."

He licked the tips of his fingers, sucking the sticky cherry juice off them slowly, his gaze fixed on mine, and for the first time I noticed how hard I was breathing in and out of my nostrils. "I appreciate that coming from you. Especially considering . . ." His voice trailed off completely.

"That we didn't leave things on the best terms?"

And I didn't think he expected it. Eddie's mouth jumped into an awkward smile, like it was connected by an invisible string to the tension in my stomach. He abandoned his sorbet and stuck his spoon directly in my ice cream. "Can I compliment you?"

"Sure? But not too much, or I'll start fanning myself and talking in a very thick Southern accent." I turned the cup so he could get a better spoonful—one with all the layers of green, yellow, and blue ice cream.

"You're a class act, Delfina."

"Five words never before spoken."

"I'm being serious." He laughed. "You could have told me to go fuck myself, but . . ." He shook his head, his eyes lingering on mine before flitting, just for a moment, down to my mouth. "It's nice to be around someone who gets me."

"Wow." I swallowed roughly. "I was hoping you were going to say something like, you have the greatest knockers I've ever seen in my life."

He snorted, keeping his eyes fixed on his overflowing spoon before it passed through his lips, sending my breathing into another bout of heaviness. "Come on," he said, gently pressing his knee against mine under the table. "Let's finish this ice cream so you can watch me shit bricks on a Ferris wheel."

We couldn't take fifteen steps without someone recognizing Eddie. The hundred-yard commute from Stevie's to the Ferris wheel was starting to feel like a cross-country trek. After a guy who went by Denim Rand finally released Eddie from a mind-numbing diatribe about horseshoe crab mating patterns, I made sure we stayed far away from crowds.

"How long did you live in Philly?" I asked, steering Eddie away from a man in a ragged camo trucker hat frothing at the mouth to say hello.

"Four years. Then, I, uh"—he screwed up his face in a rush of disgust—"fell in love?"

"Hot."

"Right," he drawled. "When I got back, things were so different.

My mom's house sold for triple what she bought it for. There were all these new shops and tourists. Downtown Evergreen became a whole thing. They fixed the carousel." He counted off the changes on his fingers, shaking his head with each one. "I thought, damn. If Evergreen becomes the type of place where a kid like me"—he looked down at me—"or a kid like you couldn't have a great childhood, I would be really pissed. If a place like The Billiards got bought up by some real estate company and turned into condos? I wouldn't be able to take it." Eddie came to an abrupt stop, pointing off into the distance toward a warmly lit restaurant situated on the very end of the pier, overlooking the ocean. Through the windows, I could make out diners in cocktail attire laughing over seafood towers and martini glasses.

"See? Look." He rested his hands gently on my shoulders and shifted me in the direction of a private boat that had just pulled up to the end of the pier. "There are places for rich people everywhere. The beach is part of nature, it's public, but we built all this shit around it and now it's a luxury. *They* get the best view."

I eyed him, trying to keep my face relaxed, like the gentle weight of his fingers against my skin wasn't one of the most transformative sensations of my life. "You sound like Denim Rand."

"You joke, but you know I'm right," he said slowly, lifting his eyebrows, taking a step closer to me.

I did. I got it. Growing up in Evergreen had meant, despite our parents' economic situations, we had seen the ocean; we'd ridden roller coasters; we'd taken the train to New York City and Philadelphia; we went to a quaint high school filled with kids whose parents' greatest crimes were laundering money and posting in all caps on Facebook. It felt impossible to be so lucky when I looked at it that way. I hated the idea that Evergreen could become inaccessible; it filled my stomach with a needling anxiety, two steps away from rage.

I watched a woman—probably my age—take a shaky stilettoed step off the boat and onto the pier.

"They paved paradise and put up a Giovanni's Seafood Bar & Grille."

"Yum," Eddie deadpanned.

I shot my gaze over to him, my finger following, pressing firmly into the center of his chest. His eyebrows arched as I wiggled into the taut skin across his sternum, his gaze falling to my hand. "You need to use your special Evergreen celebrity status and get that church lady to clean up the dog beach. It's a mess. The road's all overgrown, I almost didn't find it. It's one of the only totally free beaches."

"Okay," Eddie agreed.

I raised my eyebrows, snatching my finger back. "*Okay?* Really? That's it?"

"Yeah." He laughed. "What do you want me to say?"

"I-I don't know. I was expecting at least a *little* pushback. Maybe a *get in line, Miller.*"

He clicked his tongue. "Your ex really did a number, huh?"

My mouth fell open. *Flabbergasted.* This comment left me flabbergasted—but I didn't even have time to respond. Eddie was already pointing over my shoulder and walking away.

"There's Limpy Tim. I gotta say hi."

I found out, directly from the source, that Limpy Tim was a self-inflicted nickname. An auto-baptism, if you will, as Timothy Joseph Wojcik had injured his leg many years ago in Vietnam and since then had walked with a bit of a sloping limp. But he was still fast as hell, rest assured. After we said goodbye, Eddie and I continued our weaving path through the crowd toward the Ferris wheel while we argued over our own octogenarian nicknames.

"I wanna be Big Eddie."

"That is *so* hack. What about Lanky Ed?"

"Lanky Ed sounds like a pirate. You can be Flirty Del."

"*Flirty* Del? Seriously? I'm just being nice to people. What about Big Del?"

"Because that's not confusing. 'Anyone seen Big Del? Oh yeah, there she is—that perfectly normal-size woman, right over there.'"

"Mmm, I love it when you call me *perfectly normal-size*."

"That—" Eddie froze to point a finger gun at me. "That's flirting."

We kept going, even as we boarded our pill-shaped carrier and held on tight as the wheel jerked to life, transporting us slowly into the sky.

Then, the Ferris wheel came to a stop, leaving us perfectly positioned between the yellow lights of the boardwalk and the expansive star-filled sky. The ocean twisted and lapped at the sand, a bolt of indigo satin rippling in the wind. The air was brisk and clear up here—moving across my face, pushing back my bangs and passing through the tightest corners of my brain.

"You okay?" Eddie leaned forward from where he sat across from me, his hands falling gently around my knees. His touch was warm against my skin. It was the first time he'd officially bridged the gap between our bodies without any encouragement, though our legs had been interlocked for the entire ride. It felt right to have his hands on me. I guess I'd been silently, subconsciously hoping for it the entire time.

I nodded. "Just thinking about what you said."

Eddie shifted his gaze back to the ocean. "The thing about your ex or the thing about growing up in Evergreen?"

"All of it. Even a broken clock is right twice a day," I teased, bumping my knee against his. He tightened his fingers on my skin in response and a warmth blossomed deep between my hips. "I used to hate coming back here to see Nan."

He nodded, dragging his bottom lip up between his teeth. "You went through a lot here."

"I wanted so badly for New York to feel like home, but now . . ." I shook my head, cutting myself off with a self-conscious laugh. "I can't even think about what I'm going to do next. I just need to write my jokes."

Eddie's thumb swiped at the top of my kneecap before he pulled back, bringing his hands to a fold that hung between our legs. "Maybe you could write about this. About coming home."

I chewed my lip. "About Evergreen."

Eddie's eyes fell to mine, holding me still with his liquid amber gaze as we swung in the night breeze. After a moment, he said, "Do you know why it's called Evergreen?"

"Because of the trees?"

"You'd think, but actually there were no evergreen pines until the sixties. It was named by the first lighthouse attendant. He wrote all these letters to his wife, who was living in Maine. At first, he hated Jersey—the weather was finicky, the seasons made no sense. Winter was too long, summer was too hot, and the water was a weird color. Not the color the Atlantic should be. But by the time his stint was done, he'd grown to love it. Because—"

"Because of the smell of the bay," I cut in, my voice soft.

"Exactly," he agreed, mouth twisting into a smile. "The smell of the bay; the long summers; the salt marshes. He left for a while, went to Philadelphia or something, and he actually missed it. Right before he returned to Maine, he wrote his wife a letter: *I'll love you forever, unendingly. With no end and no beginning and as much as I've grown to love this place. I'll love you for as long as the waves reach the shore, for as long as this indelible stretch of ocean is ever green.*"

His eyes were locked on mine, his gaze soft and rich. It was happening again—the molecular things that happened when Eddie and I found ourselves alone, with nothing to hold us back but our pride. *My pride.*

But if Eddie Rodriguez was going to break my heart again, it would be on my terms. I slid forward, leaning my body into his, angling my chin toward the moonlight.

"No fucking way, Romeo."

"What?" he said innocently, shifting toward me and unwinding his hands. "It's true."

"Oh yeah? They let you read his diary?"

"Letters to his wife," he corrected me. "And yeah. They're on display at the Lighthouse Museum."

"Amazing." I smirked. "In the last ten years you got cute *and* learned how to read."

His hands were back on my knees, the rough planes of his palms curving around my legs, pulling me just a millimeter closer as he gave me that look. That madcap, devilish gaze through the thickets of his lashes. "You think I'm cute?"

I leaned forward. "And funny, unfortunately."

17

I think Sean and I are gonna do it."

We were sitting in plush chairs in the back corner of the library. It was the last day of our sophomore year, finals officially done.

What I wanted to say: *Gross.*

What I actually said: "Really?" My eyes were wider than I wanted to admit. I was a little bit of a prude—not by choice, but AOL chat rooms could only get a girl so far. "When?"

"Soon." Sam leaned forward, pulling her European History binder to her chest. "The guys are gonna throw a party but it's going to be like, super low-key." She lowered her voice to something barely above a whisper. "Eddie and Rachel broke up."

I rolled my eyes. "Shocking." I scribbled at the corner of my notebook, over and over in the same spot until the page was scarred.

"He said he's going to put a band together and wants a female vocalist."

My skin goose pimpled. *A band.* The only thing I wanted more than to not be a prude was to be in a band. "Why? He, Jake, and Wiley have their whole thing going on."

Sam shrugged. "Who cares? You *have* to audition."

"Forget it," I huffed. "Eddie hates me."

"It's like, a pretend hate. He's acting."

I scrunched up my nose in response. Sam reached over and started drawing on my notebook, too. I looked down.

Just F***ing Do It!! Written in purple ink.

THE AUDITIONS took place in Jake's garage. He lived in a rancher right across the bridge, and his parents were barely ever home. The garage had turned into a bit of a hang spot, with futons and love seats, a TV set, and the permanent rank smell of skunky weed. The guys had set up the back corner with amps, a drum set, and a Sublime poster.

I could only play two songs well on the guitar, so my choices were limited, but I'd prepared a medley and performed for Nan as she lounged on the couch sipping white wine.

"'Heart of Glass,'" she said definitively. "But slow like the other song."

"So, Blondie lyrics with 'Zombie' energy?"

She lifted her glass in the air. "They'll love it."

So, that was what I played. My voice was strong, even though I could feel my hands trembling each time they connected with the guitar strings. The words came as effortlessly as sucking in air and pushing it out again. When I finished, Jake was clapping. Wiley was on his feet, grinning at me. But Eddie wouldn't meet my eye.

"That was dope," Wiley said.

"Sick," Jake added.

I let a smile play out on my lips. "Yeah? I can sing something faster, too. If you want."

"It's not our sound," Eddie announced without looking up. He was sitting at the drum set, eyes digging into the snare, cheeks red.

"That's dumb," I pointed out. "You guys just started playing. You don't have a sound."

"She's right, bro."

"We're a rock band," Eddie rebuked.

"Yeah, and I just sang Blondie."

"Your voice isn't rock. Your voice is like, soul or something."

"And what's your voice, Eddie? Dying goat begging for mercy?"

"Haha, you're *so* funny." He swiveled away from me in his chair, snatching up his phone and heading for the front lawn. Probably to call Rachel. *Hey, babe. Sorry, I had to listen to some stupid cow. It was like torture. Wahhhh. When can I come over and rub your shoulders until I feel better?*

"What crawled up your ass and died?" I shouted after him. I gritted my teeth. "I don't even wanna be in your tiny-dick trio."

Wiley looked viscerally hurt. "Man, what's the problem?"

"Just forget it," Eddie grumbled. "Thanks, but no thanks, Pat," he called over his shoulder, ducking under the garage door and wandering off somewhere.

I slammed my guitar case shut. "Fine," I yelled after him. I hefted it back up onto my back. "Your bass is out of key, by the way. I could hear it down the block. Good luck with your band, Mr. Can't-even-tune-my-bass! Oh, and *fuck you!*"

That night I got an AOL instant message from Jake.

Ed is sooooooo jelly of ur skillz

I smirked.

Lawl, I replied.

JAKE INVITED Sam and me over to his garage to smoke "dank reefer" and I knew immediately this was part of a larger scheme for Sam and Sean to have someplace to consummate their relationship.

I don't know why it was so hard for my friends to get that I was single, not stupid. Regardless, I accepted the invite. I'd burned through my backlog of *Twilight* fanfic and had no real reason to say no.

The garage was already cloaked in a thin cloud of smoke, everyone in their awkward little clusters—Rachel and Dani on a love seat, giggling and chatting; Sam and Sean in the corner, heads bent low. Jake and Eddie on the futon.

I plopped down on the end without asking Eddie's permission if I could be honored by his presence. He flitted his eyes over to me, uncertainty pulling his gaze.

"Hey." I ignored him. He cleared his throat and tried again. "Hey, Del."

"What, Soft Serve?"

He was twirling a rubber band between his fingers, nervously working the material. He made a slipknot, forming it into a bow tie. Then, he held it out to me. "I made this for you."

I smiled, despite myself. "If this is your way of saying sorry . . ." I took the bow tie. "I do not forgive you."

He smiled, too. "Why do you always smell like vanilla?"

"It's my perfume, dumbass."

He sat back against the futon, his shoulder meeting mine. He pressed into me, warmth traveling down my arm and across my belly, spreading into my thighs. Another little apology. He leaned over and sniffed loudly at my hair. "And bananas, too. You smell like vanilla and bananas."

I swatted at him. "Stop sniffing me, freak. You're high."

Wiley shushed us as he flopped down onto a concave beanbag chair. "Everyone, shut up. I'm starting *Wayne's World*." He sucked at a lumpy joint until the end glowed red. "Remember everyone: it's puff, puff, pass."

Eddie leaned close to me. "Remember," he whispered. "Puff, *puff*, pass."

His voice was warm and low against my ear. "Got it," I whispered back, biting down hard on the inside of my cheek.

THE CREDITS for *Wayne's World* rolled just as Sam came storming out of the laundry room, red-faced. "You're a pig, Sean Alexander."

"Come on, Sam. Please, I'm sorry!"

He took off running after her, but she was already down the driveway and was climbing into the front seat of her dad's car, tearing out down the block with Sean hanging on to the passenger window.

I groaned, my limbs too leaden for me to chase after her. "There goes my ride home."

Jake had turned off the movie, and now he and Wiley were staring like zombies at the TV screen, smashing buttons on their controllers, seemingly without blinking. Rachel and Dani were passed out under a fleece blanket on the love seat, snoring.

Weed is so boring, I thought, shifting my eyes (which felt like strange, slick marbles in my face) from person to person. *Why does my dad love this so much?*

Eddie yawned, pulling off his baseball cap and running his fingers through his hair before placing the hat back on his head backward. He'd changed a lot over the last year. His face had slimmed out, the baby fat melting away to reveal the delicate lines of razorsharp cheekbones. The planes of his face were higher, his jaw strong and rectangular. His cheeks were pocked with little acne scars that turned a cool shade of mauve in the sun. They looked like little freckles, detailing the curvature of his bone structure.

"I can take you home, Del." His voice had gotten deep, too. *What the hell?*

I was pretty high, so I just said it out loud: "Eddie, what the hell? Did you get hot?"

Jake and Wiley snapped out of their trance, staring at me in disbelief. Then, they turned to each other and dissolved into a pile of slapping and giggling.

Eddie screwed up his features at me, yanking a pillow to his chest. "What are you even saying, weirdo?"

I was giggling, too. "Your face is all strong and manly." I stuck out my jaw and narrowed my eyes into my best impression of his newfound rugged brood. Wiley and Jake started shrieking.

Eddie was rapidly turning brick red. "Yo, shut up." He swatted the pillow at my head, messing up my ponytail. "You're grossing me out."

"Oh yeah, I'm so gross." I rolled my eyes and smacked the pillow back toward him. "Jake, your dank reefer is giving me a headache."

"Come on." Eddie flicked his head toward the half-open garage door. "I gotta be home by eleven and I need to air out my car from your weed stink."

"Ooooh," Jake cooed. "Lani's striiiict."

Eddie rolled his eyes, jumping to smack a hand against the garage door before heading toward his car. "Let's not talk about moms, boys."

I grabbed my purse. "Are they okay?" I pointed at Rachel and Dani, who were now spooning.

Jake leaned back, eyeing them. "Yeah, this always happens. I'll wake them up soon."

"Delfina," Eddie shouted from across the lawn. "Ticktock."

I rolled my eyes, slipping under the garage door and making my way to the passenger side of his car—his mom's car, actually. I recognized it. "Patience, Rodriguez."

For most of the ride back to Evergreen we sat in silence. Usually this wouldn't have bothered me, especially because I kept intermittently remembering how shitty Eddie had been during my audition, but my high was rapidly fading and leaving a restlessness in its place. I felt awake, buzzing.

I fiddled with the radio knobs and AC, until Eddie shot me a sideways look. "Hyper much?"

"What's the deal with you and Rachel?" I asked.

He rolled his eyes. "There is no deal. She doesn't want anything to do with me." He looked kind of hurt, but I knew if I pressed, he'd shut me down.

"That sucks," I said plainly, pulling a ChapStick out of my purse and applying it slowly. "You guys have always kinda been a thing."

"Nah." He shook his head, putting on a blinker and turning onto a dark road that ran alongside the bay. "I think she was just bored."

For some reason this revelation hit me in the center of my chest like a searing knife. I was mostly not involved in the guy-girl part of high school; I was a wary observer on the sidelines, warming the bench. I figured that if Jake or Wiley ever got desperate enough, I might get asked to prom.

I turned to look out the window, watching the bay whizz by. "Must be nice to be tiny, thin, and blond. I wish I could make out with someone just because I'm bored."

Eddie let out a half laugh, flitting his eyes toward me as he worried his lip. "What're you talking about? You could."

"No way." I shook my head, running my fingers through my hair, gently pulling apart a knot. "All the guys just see me as like, one of them."

He shifted in his seat, tightening his grip on the steering

wheel. "Maybe a little bit, but that's kind of . . ." He eyed me nervously.

"What?" I narrowed my eyes at him. "And do not say *gross*."

"No. It's hot." He cleared his throat. "You are hot," he repeated, more confident.

The air between us suddenly felt like it was filled with static, with lightning, in the last plumes of Eddie's breath, snapping and crackling. The AC was pumping steadily against my neck, blowing wiry loose hairs around, but the moment felt as sticky and languid as the air outside.

Lately, Eddie had been spending less time teasing me and more time avoiding me. I'd assumed it had something to do with Rachel. I'd assumed it was because he was embarrassed by me, my loud voice, my big jokes, even my big body.

But then he said . . . *this*.

"Eddie?"

"Yeah?" His voice came out low and strained.

"Do you want to, um . . ." I pulled at a thread on the edge of my sundress. "Make out because we're bored?"

Eddie snapped upright in his seat like I'd pressed a hot iron to the middle of his back. "What?"

"Jesus." I dropped my face into my hands. "I'm being so weird. Just ignore me, please."

But Eddie was already slowing down to a complete stop. We were in the middle of a country road between high reeds and marsh with no streetlights. In the distance I could make out the hazy lights on the bayside houses, but between us and there it was only darkness. No other cars for miles.

He put the car in park and twisted in his seat to face me. "Do you mean that?"

"Yeah," I whispered. "Is that bad?"

"You promise this isn't a trick?"

I nodded.

Eddie lifted an accusing brow. "And you won't tell Sam some weird shit like I have too many teeth or something?"

I laughed. "No weird shit. I promise, I won't tell anyone."

"Okay. Same," he said softly, eyes traveling from his hand on the gearshift over to my crossed thighs. I'd barely noticed the way my dress was bunched up around my thighs. Suddenly self-conscious, I yanked the material down.

Eddie leaned in toward me. I was sitting tall, stiff as a board, head against the seat. He laughed a little, his breath dancing over my lips. "Can you relax?"

"I am relaxed," I whispered, shimmying my shoulders to prove my point. He was close now. He was so close I could smell his T-shirt—clean laundry, a hint of lavender. I could see the thin gold chain around his neck. I could spot the place on his nose where he had a few deep brown freckles from too much sun. And his lips. They were perfectly symmetrical.

Eddie *did* get hot. Almost overnight. He wasn't the dorky kid with the ponytail anymore. He was taller and his chest was broad and wide. His hands were big, and when his fingers grazed the side of my neck, his touch was like a satin scarf slipping over me.

There wasn't anything left to think about—what Eddie and I should and shouldn't be doing, according to the ever-changing, too-delicate rules of high school. All I wanted was to know what Eddie tasted like.

Our eyes fell shut and when our mouths connected, a swarm of anxious butterflies broke loose in my stomach. I relaxed against the seat as his lips parted against mine; he pushed off the center console, bringing his body over mine, his fingers moving up my arm, tucking into my hair. There was a riptide in my stomach the moment his fingers pressed into the back of my head and my mouth tilted deeper into his. Eddie tasted sweet like spearmint and honey. I'd kissed guys before but those kisses had been too much—too wet, too open, too rushed.

Not like this. Not like Eddie leaning back into his seat and taking me with him. Not like me fumbling to undo my seat belt, to keep up with the way his mouth worked fast while his hands moved slow, gripping me tight.

I pulled away, panting. "Oh my God."

"What?" he whispered, his face close to mine. "You okay?"

"I'm . . ." I paused because I wanted to say a million things. I wanted to demand that Eddie explain what was happening. Why he kissed me like that. Like he wanted it so badly. Instead, I just said: "Great."

I could see his teeth glinting in the dark as he smirked. "Then why stop?"

The butterflies were back, and they were rising through my stomach all the way into my throat, the beating of their wings sending ripples of heat down my abdomen, through my thighs. Eddie reached for the radio, raising the volume without ever pulling his mouth off mine.

It was a song I'd heard a million times. The lyrics were bizarre—nonsensical and silly, even. But now, with the lingering and hypnotic bass line, I knew it'd been written for moments like this, moments when touch turned flesh from iron to liquid fire.

I smell sex and candy here.

Who's that lounging in my chair?

Who's that casting devious stares in my direction?

I was melting. Melting into Eddie's hands and mouth, melting into the smell of July on his neck, the roughness of his hands lost in my hair. And just as the singer purred the chorus, I slid my hands over his, our hands twisting in a sticky, sweaty tangle as I brought his fingers to my neck, then down my chest. When his fingers connected with the exposed skin right near the collar of my dress, I shuddered in his arms. I forgot about everything outside of what was happening right now, between us on this country road.

18

Bethlehem Inn

Cyrus's car refused to start.

After the Ferris wheel we had walked all the way down to the end of Ocean Harbor's boardwalk in search of french fries, shoulders bumping together and fingers accidentally tangling every few steps.

Then, we'd split a greasy bag of curly fries that left us both feeling bloated and woozy and ready for bed.

"You drunk?" Eddie had asked, steadying me with a hand flat against the small of my back.

"Too much potato," I'd moaned in response, letting my head fall against his shoulder for a brief moment. Then I stumbled away, resetting us at the distance that made sense for friends to keep between their bodies.

Now, Eddie emerged from beneath the hood, looking like he'd just done open heart surgery as I sat gnawing at my thumbnail, seated on the curb.

"What's the prognosis, doc?"

"Fucked," he said, rubbing grease off his hands and down the front of his pants. He looked tired, the soft skin under his eyes more hollow than usual. It'd been a long-ass day, and it seemed to be only getting longer.

"Don't do that. Hold on." I jumped up and ran to the back seat, yanking out a T-shirt. I tossed it to him.

Eddie caught it deftly with a single hand. "I don't wanna ruin this."

I shrugged. "It's an Ingram shirt. Do whatever you want. So, what's our plan?"

"Call a tow truck. Uber back to Evergreen."

Panic surged in my chest. I couldn't have Cyrus's car towed in the middle of the night with almost all of my earthly possessions in the back seat. I couldn't afford a tow—and what if something *else* happened to the car? I was already out of my financial depths.

"I don't know," I said. "Can't we push it?"

"Push a car twenty miles?" Eddie tossed the shirt back to me. "After curly fries?"

"Or I can just wait here till morning?" I caught it, working the fabric between my fingers. "Then I can call a mechanic and make sure nothing happens to my . . ." I gestured at all my trash bags and poor Buster, still grinning. I leaned back against the car. "God, I just can't deal with another *thing* today. You can head home."

"No way," Eddie said. "If someone murders you, my Tuesday-morning aquarobics car pool is gonna be real awkward."

"You have the bar to think about and everything else."

Eddie moved toward me. Closer and closer, until he took up my entire vision. It was about as close as we'd been on the Ferris wheel, our knees even bumping together again. No matter how much we tried, it was like we'd always end up back like this—fingers tangled, knees bumping, pulling us together, closer and closer until . . .

"Delfina." His mouth wrapped around my name so perfectly. He ducked his head low, watching me through his full lashes. "If you're sleeping in a weird motor lodge off of the highway, then I am also sleeping in a weird motor lodge off of the highway."

As FATE would have it, we didn't need to travel far—the last motel with any vacancies in all of Ocean Harbor was close enough that I could have chucked my shoe at the Open sign to stop it from flickering.

"What are the absolute fucking chances?" Eddie asked, leaning back against Cyrus's car as we stared into the lobby.

"High. This place looks like a dump."

He pointed at a sign in the window. "But they have five stars on Yelp."

The sign read, in all caps: WE HAVE FIVE STARS ON YELP.

The Bethlehem Inn was a low-slung beige stucco building with plastic palm fronds framing the front door and a vaguely appropriative ceramic camel collection traversing the concierge desk. The ceiling was painted to look like a star-filled night sky; gem-toned throw pillows littered the bench by the front door and worn-out chairs were positioned around a rattan coffee table. It all looked as if Pier 1 had sponsored the birth of Christ.

"This is a weird Bible thing, right?"

Eddie grimaced. "Who cares?"

"Me." I yanked open the front door. "I care."

"Salam, shalom, and howdy!" the concierge chirped. She was a petite woman with a bob just long enough to pull into two teeny-tiny pigtails that stuck out behind her ears in sprays of mousy brown. "How can I help yinz?"

"Two rooms for tonight, please," I said, handing my credit card over. Eddie snaked an arm around my neck and quickly snatched it out of my hand.

"You are not paying for my room," Eddie hissed. I could feel his chest pressing against my arm, his breath on my ear. My skin reacted immediately, cropping up into a humiliating little pattern of goose bumps.

"Hush," I whispered back.

When I lifted my eyes, the woman was smiling at us with a gummy smile, index fingers pressed together. "Love is patient," she trilled.

I forced a smile and a laugh. "Right. Corinthians ten or whatever. We're not together, actually."

She ignored me, ignored the possibility that a man and a woman could exist together in space and not be in a romantic, God-honoring relationship. Instead, she took those index fingers and went to town on her keyboard, clipping and clopping while making little *hmmm* and *huh* sounds. "Okay . . . okay," she whispered. She looked up at us. "I am so sorry, folks. I have some really awful news. Ugh! It's just so rotten!"

We leaned forward.

"I only have one room left and it is part of our Wilderness Adventure Experience."

"And that's bad?" I asked, uneasy.

Eddie correctly identified this as his moment to act, bumping me out of the way with his hip and handing over a credit card. "We'll take it, uh . . ." He scanned her chest until his eyes fell onto her name tag. "Jean."

I recovered from the hip check and leaned back into Jean's line of sight. "Hey, Jean, do you have any extra toothbrushes?"

As soon as I opened the door to our Wilderness Adventure Experience room, I understood everything.

"Oh *wow*."

The entire room was wallpapered with a psychosis-inducing birch tree pattern. It was as if we were standing in the middle of a dense-forest clearing, complete with a buck peering at us with beady, flat eyes. A rustic pine desk was situated under a faux window and one of those talking-fish wall mounts, the kind that were advertised as *sassy*. The desk was equipped with a landline shaped like a set of antlers and a lamp made to look like a kerosene lantern. A dark green shag rug rose up around our feet, and in the center of the room stood a bunk bed.

Inexplicably, a bunk bed.

We were crammed into the doorway together, shoulder to shoulder, staring down our fate. "Huh." Eddie clicked his tongue. "Better than a trundle, I guess."

"Are we on a hidden camera show?" I stepped forward, turning slowly to take in what appeared to be three totally windowless and doorless walls. Then, I paused. Above the bed a set of elk antlers was mounted on a placard: *In Memory of Big Johnny*. "Oh great." I pointed up at the memorial. "This room is commemorative. We're part of someone's legacy."

Eddie was still leaning against the doorframe, arms folded over his chest. He was so tall he could have leaned forward and rested against the top of the doorjamb comfortably. His eyes were fixed on me, a shadow of a smile teasing at the corner of his mouth, pulling into a dimple that threatened, once again, to ruin my life.

My eyes caught his eyes. "What?"

Eddie cleared his throat, eyes dropping from mine. "Nothing, I just remembered something." He slapped a hand against the top of the doorframe and ducked into the room.

I pulled my eyes away and eased down onto the bottom bunk. "I'm really sorry, by the way. I know this is not how you want to be spending a night off—what are you doing?"

Eddie was splayed out completely flattened against the wall, hands running up and down the wallpaper. "There has got to be a bathroom here, right?"

"Oh God. Bathroom stuff. You're gonna hear me pee."

"I have a distinct memory of you and Sam peeing off the docks in Abby Bishop's backyard into the bay." He pantomimed holding an invisible wood beam, ass sticking out. "Pissing into the breeze, bay water rushing beneath you."

I let out a shocked cackle, my hand flying to my mouth. *We had done that, hadn't we?* "That is so dangerous. Why did you let us do that?"

He quirked an eyebrow at me. "I was supposed to stop you?"

Finally, he found a conspicuously designed doorknob, fashioned out of birchwood, and disappeared into the restroom while I plugged my phone in. Thank God I was forward-thinking enough to always travel with the essentials: a phone charger, a red lip tint, mini deodorant, and a receipt for one ticket to *Second Act*, Jennifer Lopez's finest work. I quickly sent two texts. One to Nan, explaining the entire situation in vivid detail. And another to Sam that simply said: Remember when we peed off the dock in Abby Bishop's backyard?

Eddie emerged from the bathroom, toothbrush shoved into the side of his mouth, a fresh look of horror on his face. "*Who* is this room for?"

I shifted up onto my side, propping my head on my hand. "Those two boys stacked in a trench coat pretending to be a man."

He smirked. "Bert and Ernie, honeymooning."

"Bert and Ernie, contemplating divorce," I countered, applying my lip tint.

"You're taking the bottom bunk?"

I frowned at him. "Duh."

"Doesn't it feel like . . . the lady should be on top?" We stared at each other for a moment. "That came out wrong," Eddie said finally.

"It *really* did." I rolled out of the bed, being extra careful to not bonk my head on the bed frame, and made my way into the bathroom.

"Wait, Del." I paused in front of him. In one fell swoop, Eddie pulled his T-shirt over his head, black curls slipping through the opening and bouncing back into place. He smoothed a rogue corkscrew away from his face. "Here—sleep in this."

"O-oh no, you don't—" I stammered.

"I know you don't want to sleep in a tight dress." He was offering me a soft smile, but I could not even look at him—because that look would have confirmed what I had already suspected: Eddie had learned a thing or two about chest exercises. Through the thin fabric of a T-shirt, one could easily—accidentally, really—observe Eddie's solid forearms and broad shoulders. But now, like this, I could feel and smell and see him—all of him. The heat from his skin; the smell of cologne and summer from his neck; the width of his chest and the taut, smooth flesh below his belly button.

His tattoos were beautiful, artful. Across his left pec was a mermaid free-falling through a seascape. Her tail curved upward along with her hair in an arch of blue, green, and purple. The seascape traveled over his shoulder and down his left biceps; an octopus, a koi fish, and the unmistakable swirl of the shoreline all kaleidoscoped together, barely contained by quick, fine black lines. On his right pec was a pair of lips. Feathered pink strokes that made up the undeniable purse of a woman's mouth.

"It's only kind of sweaty, I promise," he said, snapping me back into the moment.

"I-I . . ." I reached for the shirt and at the last moment, flicked my eyes up to his. "Are those lips on your boob?"

Eddie frowned, then shifted his gaze down his chest—which he was now flexing and puffing out. "Oh yeah." He let out a laugh. "Yeah, forgot about those. What a stupid idea."

I yanked the shirt out of his hands, murmured thanks, and

slipped into the bathroom only to be greeted by the largest tub I had ever seen.

"What in the world?"

"What?" Eddie called from behind me. "Everything okay?"

"This tub is built for like . . ."

"An orgy?" He was right behind me. I flicked my eyes to the huge mirror over two forest-green sinks built into a laminate countertop.

"Um, *yeah*."

He was grinning. I hadn't seen myself in hours. My chin-length black waves were wind-tousled and twisted. At some point, the tip of my nose and top of my forehead had burned, then tanned to the color of a toasted bagel. I noticed his eyes fixed on my lips—full and pink, *like they would match the tattoo on his chest perfectly.*

What was happening? Eddie and I had gone from gentle flirting to being trapped in a *Twilight Zone* sex prison.

I faced him full-on. The air between us had turned as heavy as laughing gas.

"Get out. I have to shit."

He held up his hands and took a solid step back. "Enjoy."

I slammed the door and immediately dropped my face into my hands.

Flirting on a Ferris wheel was one thing, but sharing bunk beds? Was I emotionally and psychologically prepared to spend an entire night sleeping in the same room as the only guy who had ever thoroughly gutted me?

Eddie was gorgeous—he was kind and respectful. But he was still Eddie.

I leaned forward onto the sink and splashed my face with cold water.

Things could be different. Hell, I wasn't the same Del as ten years ago. I was a different person now. I could handle whatever roller coaster Eddie Rodriguez put me on.

I SLIPPED out of the bathroom in Eddie's shirt and my socks. He was lying on the top bunk, phone held over his face. I paused, holding my arms out for him.

"How was your shit?" he asked casually. I could see he was wearing his boxers and had also kept his socks on. The rug simply could not be trusted. Suddenly, I was overwhelmed with the desire to climb the ladder and slip into bed next to him, tucking my knees back in between his.

"What do you think?" I said. His shirt barely came past my crotch. I wiggled my fingers and my eyebrows.

He propped himself up onto his elbows, taking a shallow breath, one that lodged in his throat and left his chest suspended in an inhale. "Fits perfectly."

I laughed. "Not exactly, but thanks." I settled into my bunk, pulling the sheets up around my chin. They were rough and starchy, but I was tired enough that, somehow, this goofy bed felt like heaven.

"Now what?" I sighed, flipping around until I found a comfy position. "Are we supposed to just fall asleep?"

He let out a low chuckle. "Aren't you exhausted?"

"Nah." I punched my pillows into a less shameful shape. "I'm like an overly tired toddler."

The slats over my head squeaked as Eddie rolled onto his side. "We can keep talking, if you want."

"Cool. So, who are you asking to prom?"

He sighed. "Good night, Del."

"I'm kidding, jeez." The quiet hung over us. *Now is my chance.*

"Nan told me something."

"Is it about Alfonzo's gambling?"

"Uh, no, but remind me to come back to that." I squeezed my eyes shut. "It's about you, actually."

Silence.

"I bet I can guess," he said eventually, quietly. "She told you about Valerie."

Valerie. A burst of softness from between his lips. Suddenly I wanted to hear him say my name, my full name. Not Del, not Miller. "Your daughter?" I asked, just as quiet.

"Yeah."

The room felt hot and still. The sheets were itchy, and I'd said too much. "We don't have to—" I hurried to backtrack.

"No, no. I'm just—God, I'm embarrassed." Eddie let out a hard laugh. "I should have told you. I-I don't want you to think I'm ashamed. I was afraid you might . . ."

"Eddie. It's *me*. My entire life is one big humiliation. How could I ever judge you?"

Above me, he shifted between his sheets. His voice was closer now. "What did Annie tell you?"

"That you have an adorable daughter who's *so* cute. That she saw you two together and that's how your freaky little friendship started."

"She is a very humble woman. Annie saw me at the grocery store having a panic attack in the baby food aisle with an eighteen-month-old strapped to my chest. It was pathetic. I had no idea how to take care of a baby alone." Another quiet laugh. A rueful, self-conscious chuckle. "When my ex and I split, she got everything. Our house, our car, our support system. I have my mom and my sisters, but it's not the same."

"Oh, Eddie . . ."

"After that, Annetta showed up at my house every Sunday with a lasagna."

"She's the best," I whispered.

"Any time she'd see me with Valerie—on one of my days— she'd give me little pieces of advice. Dad pointers. Like she knew exactly what I needed."

"She could tell it wasn't easy for you." I'd always imagined Nan as a gentle witch, sent here to guide us all in her own quirky way.

"No," he said softly. "It's hard as hell."

"I bet you're a great dad."

"Thank you." After a beat, he added: "Meghan let me name her." I smiled softly. "After your favorite song?"

"Of course," he said, his voice soft and low, settled in the back of his throat.

I reached my hand out and up. The slats groaned again and suddenly my hand was engulfed in his, warm and rough. An amber warmth exploded in my stomach as his thumb grazed slowly back and forth over mine.

Then, I did something that Del ten years ago would have never done.

I tugged on his hand.

His thumb froze. Terrified he might have missed it—or thought he imagined what I'd just done—I tugged on his arm again and whispered, "Come down here."

"How the hell are we going to fit?"

"We'll make it work."

Eddie clambered down in the dark, hair hanging over his face. The muscles in his stomach and chest effortlessly stretched as he pushed handfuls of hair out of his eyes. I tried to focus on anything, *anything*, other than his crotch—now almost at eye level.

We couldn't stop laughing as he attempted to roll into the twin bed next to me; it was ridiculous for us to try and cram ourselves into such a small space together, but neither of us even got close to suggesting we give up.

"Is this okay?" he asked, stuffing the pillow under our heads.

"It's perfect," I said. No matter which way I relaxed, I felt myself rolling into his chest, slipping under his arm.

"This is perfect?" he asked dryly.

"You know what I mean, dummy."

I hadn't been this close to Eddie in a very long time, long enough that the stirring in my stomach had me feeling like it was the very first time.

I'd dreamed many times of the first time we kissed; the way his hands fell sweetly from my chin to my shoulder; the way his fingers slid down the back of my arm and then up again. The way he smelled like a freshly line-dried shirt. He still smelled like that. I'd always considered those dreams a very inventive way for my brain to torture me, never acknowledging how badly I craved the feeling of his lips—full and soft—snagging between my teeth.

Eddie's eyes flitted over mine and his mouth made an inscrutable shape—not quite a smile, not quite a sound. He was lying on his side, head resting in his hand. I could make out the green veins under his wrist, beneath the soft cursive ink that wrapped around it. The tattoo I'd spotted at the pool. I was close enough to read it now: *Valerie Valerie Valerie.* Continuously connected in a looping script. He was watching my eyes travel up his arm when he lifted a hand and gently pushed my bangs away from my forehead, sending a Morse code of firecrackers through me. An atomic reaction to Eddie's skin on mine. My eyes fell shut as his fingertips connected with my skin.

"Remember when we kissed?" I asked softly. My voice was heavy.

I blinked my eyes open, and he was smiling. A soft tug at his lips, but it mostly lived in his eyes.

His fingertips traced the curve of my cheek. "Damn good kiss."

My throat constricted. "Yeah?"

He brushed the pad of his thumb over my lips, a tiny motion that set off even more devastating shifts inside my abdomen. "Thought about it for years."

"Stop lying."

"I totally did." He chuckled. "How often does the hottest girl you know ask you to kiss her?"

We were inches away from each other and the last words from his lips were a brush of warm air over my lips. And then I was shifting myself into the curvature of his body. His hand found my waist, slipping in perfectly like it'd always been meant to rest there. Our mouths connected once, briefly and softly. We pulled away, like the kiss had been an electric shock. Eddie's eyes danced over my face.

Are we doing this? Is this happening?

I nodded.

Then we met again, his lips connecting to mine with certainty. I inhaled deeply, pulling in the taste and scent of him. Ten years ago, kissing Eddie had felt cataclysmic. I thought maybe that was because I'd never kissed anyone I liked before. Now, ten years of kissing later, I knew *this* was special.

Eddie's entire body reacted to my eagerness; his hand slid around my jaw to the back of my neck as he pulled my lip between his teeth, his tongue moving gently against mine. I let out a soft gasp that twisted into a moan as his hips rolled against mine.

Then, he was over me, hands connecting firmly with my thighs as he pressed himself against my soft center, and we gave in to the deeper, rawer kiss that I desperately wanted. My hands were in his hair and then dragging down his back as his fingers worked at the thickness of my thighs, moving upward one inch at a time. I groaned again—half in pleasure, half in shock—as his fingers worked up under the hem of my shirt, then up over the softest, palest part of my thighs. Everything felt just as explosive as ten years ago. And I was left with the same question: *How long have you wanted this?*

My body fell open to his, like a flower blossoming, stretching in every direction to take in as much sun as possible. I palmed a fistful of sheet as one of his hands traveled over the planes of my stomach toward my breasts, the other slipping beneath the hem of my underwear.

Eddie broke away, just long enough to growl, *"Damn."*

Was he shocked to feel how badly I wanted him?

He pressed his forehead to mine, his erection throbbing against the inside of my thigh, our breathing synced and ragged.

Head dipped low, he pressed his lips to my ear. "Maybe," he managed, dragging in air in shallow gulps, "we shouldn't."

All of me, every molecule, crashed back to reality.

I squeezed my eyes shut. "Right."

Was it possible that I'd read this situation all wrong?

It didn't matter because I didn't need to read between the lines. It was all right here.

Whatever we had was years ago. And just how it ended—abruptly—it was ending again.

We were different people.

He was a father, and I owned a clown lamp.

19

The Parking Lot

If mixed signals were a sport, Edgardo Rodriguez would be a two-time Olympic gold medalist.

His alarm went off at some unlawfully early hour and I was jolted awake out of a deep slumber. Evidently, I'd fallen asleep on my back, locked into position by Eddie's limbs, strewn over me in a gangly, sweaty heap. His head was burrowed into my neck, the gentle whistle of air from his nose tickling my collarbones, and one of his hands rested with great care over my thigh.

I refused to move. I refused to interrupt this moment. I'd stay here with his hand on my thigh until my skin grew into these sheets.

With the alarm blaring some foghorn ridiculousness, I closed my eyes and tried to memorize what this felt like before it ended. That was when I noticed his thumb.

That *damn* thumb. Moving slowly back and forth, stroking the place where my bone suddenly bloomed into dimpled flesh.

We're both pretending to be asleep. It was a realization that nearly killed me. I shifted my eyes around, keeping my head perfectly still, but all I could make out was the top of his curly head and the knotted mess of sheets and legs and the terrifying birchwood wallpaper. If I moved anything more than my eyes, I risked losing this moment, the last remnants of what we'd done the night before rapidly fading as the sky turned to day.

The alarm stopped on its own, and Eddie began to rustle, turning slowly until his nose and lips were almost flush against my neck. I was goose-bumping; I could feel it. I squeezed my eyes shut as he pulled himself up onto his side, his body peeling away from mine.

"Del." His voice was deep and rough with sleep, tucked into the back of his throat. "Wake up."

I blinked my eyes open and there he was. Hands pressing into the mattress, his face hanging over me. *Kiss me,* I begged internally. *Please kiss me.*

"It's quarter past seven." He pushed a handful of curls away from his face. "I have to take Val to the doctor."

"Okay," I whispered.

"Sorry," he said nervously, swinging his legs off the bed. "I know it's early."

"It's no problem." I dug the heels of my hands into my eyes. "I understand."

WE BRUSHED our teeth in the orgy bathroom and clumsily pulled on our day-old clothes before heading back toward the lobby.

"Good morning," Jean sang out. She was standing on top of a ladder with a purple bandanna tied around her head, dusting a Moroccan lantern with a feather duster. "How did you two chickens sleep?"

"Like dead elk," I joked.

She stared at me in horror before erupting into laughter. "Oh God. *Of course,* Big John's room." She blessed herself with the sign of the cross. "May the rat-bastard that killed him rot in hell."

Eddie and I exchanged looks of horror. It was the first time we'd made sustained eye contact since the previous night, and the force of his eyes landing on mine nearly knocked me backward.

Murder? Eddie mouthed.

In that room? I mouthed back.

His eyes widened. *In the tub.*

I pressed my lips together to keep from letting out a honk of a laugh.

"So," Jean grunted as she descended the ladder. "What do you want for your complimentary breakfast? I have Meemaw's Old World Biscuit or Chilean Sun-caked Oats."

THE MORNING was foggy and overcast as we meandered toward Cyrus's car. Eddie was gnawing at Meemaw's Biscuit while I nursed a coffee that tasted like an ashtray.

"I think this may just be a stale bagel." Eddie pointed it at me. "Want a bite?"

"No, thanks." I took a repugnant sip of coffee. "I don't have dental insurance right now."

"Fair enough." He tossed the starchy disc into the trash can and dusted his hands off. "Are you sure you're okay waiting for the tow alone? I feel awful—"

"Stop worrying. Go." I flicked my hands at him, shooing him away. "I can handle this."

Eddie hefted a sigh, placing a hand on my shoulder. It was an intimate act, but oddly friendly. *Am I being friend-zoned? Oh my God.* "Thank you."

I kept my eyes fixed on the Ferris wheel, behind Eddie's head. It was off for the day, frozen in place. "I should be thanking you for staying with me."

He gave me a squeeze; I could feel his eyes working over my features. "I owe you one," he said.

"Consider yourself indebted."

A small laugh bubbled up from him. "And hey, about last night, I should have—"

"Not stolen my pillow?" I cut in. I couldn't have this conversation right now. The *I shouldn't have, we shouldn't have, it's not that I didn't want to* awkward ping-pong of blame and confusion. Not while I was sitting in a parking lot with a garbage heap of a car, under-caffeinated and penniless. Nope. We could easily save that chat for a day when I had a quart of iced coffee sloshing around in my belly. A day when maybe I was a little less sensitive to rejection from someone as kind as Eddie.

"Exactly. Sorry about that." He dropped his hand from my shoulder, fingertips skating over the soft flesh of my arm, down past my elbow until he finally disconnected from me someplace around my wrist. I wouldn't know because I couldn't look at Eddie right now. It was bad enough that I could still imagine perfectly what his lips looked like hovering over my face, what he felt like pressed between my legs, how his eyes moved like maple syrup in a glass bottle, melting and shifting over me right before he rolled away.

"I was thinking," Eddie said, cutting through the chaos of my thoughts. "We need another act next Friday at the bar. Me and the guys are playing a late-night set, but we need an opener. I think you'd be incredible."

My proverbial bingo card was filling up fast but *play live music at Eddie's bar* wasn't even on the card. I pulled my lip into my mouth, worrying it until I finally worked myself up to looking directly at him.

We were standing so close, his chest was practically pressed

to mine. His hands were resting on his hips. More certified dad
behavior.

"Let me think about it."

I SAT in the parking lot as the morning haze cleared, knee jiggling.
I burned a hole in my phone screen, staring at the seven-digit number. Turning each number over in my mind, along with a reason
why I should never, ever even entertain the idea.

But for each reason, there was one big, fat rebuttal: I wanted to.
I wanted to hear his voice, whether it made sense or not. And how
often did I want things so plainly?

I could have blamed Tucker, Cyrus—even Eddie. But ultimately,
it was my finger that hit the call button.

By the time his truck came skidding into the lot, I was down to
one thumbnail. He pulled to a lopsided stop between two plastic
potted palm fronds and the ice machine. The door swung open,
and he lumbered out of the driver's seat—much taller than I
remembered—wearing a pair of clunky running shoes and a well-
worn bait and tackle shirt. His face was tanned deeply, pocked with
lines and creases, white whiskers growing sparsely on his cheeks.
His hair had turned white, too. Long white waves pushed back by
a pair of wraparound sunglasses.

"Hey," he called out, slamming the car door behind him.

I folded my arms over my chest. "Hey," I called back.

He grabbed a toolbox from the bed of his truck and headed toward me. "Stuck?"

I stood, making my way to meet him. "It's my friend's car. I
couldn't call a tow."

He lowered the toolbox to the ground and placed his hands on
his hips. "You look great."

I pushed my hair behind my ears. "Thanks, Dad."

"Welp," Roger declared, pulling his head out from under the hood. "Your radiator's leaking. You can't drive this thing till we get that fixed."

"Shit," I hissed. "I really can't pay for new parts right now."

Roger watched me as he cleaned his hands off on an old rag. "I got one for you."

I watched him carefully before flicking my eyes back down at my phone. "No, it's okay. I'll figure it out."

"Hey now, you're my kid. I'll get one of the guys from the shop to come tow it back to my place, and we'll get you fixed up by the end of the day."

"Really?" I had many reasons to seriously doubt Roger.

He nodded before pulling out an ancient-looking flip phone from his pocket. "Let me dial Jerry. Go wait in the car with the AC." He tossed me his car keys.

I called Nan from the front seat of his car.

"Hello?"

"Don't be pissed at me, please."

"Oh dear." Someone—a child or a seagull—squawked behind her. She must have been lying out by the pool. "What an opener."

"You have to promise you won't be mad."

"What the hell is going on, Del?"

"I called Roger," I said, the words all rushing out together, "only for car help. I remembered he was always working with cars, and I figured he would know what to do." The line went completely silent. "I had to! Eddie had to get back to Evergreen for Valerie and I couldn't call a mechanic because the car isn't—are you smiling?"

"He told you about her, huh?"

I was smiling, too. Just a little bit. "Yeah, he did."

Nan let loose a long, high-pitched sigh. "Oh, you. Be safe, okay? Will you be home for dinner?"

"Don't worry about me," I assured her. Roger was crossing the parking lot again, headed back toward me. "This may take a while."

We hung up just as Roger opened the driver's side door. "Sorry 'bout that. Jerry's tied up, but Jerry Junior's gonna head on over." He clicked his seat belt into place and kept his gaze straight ahead. "Back in town, then, huh?"

"Just for the next month or so."

He nodded slowly. "Then you goin' back to the Big Apple?"

I nodded, too, while fiddling with the hem of my dress. "I should have called you sooner."

"That's okay." He fanned his hands out in front of him, wrists resting on the top of the steering wheel. "You're a grown girl now. I don't expect it."

"You look really good. Really healthy."

"Oh, healthy, huh?" He chuckled, patting his stomach. "They don't tell you when you can't drink, all you wanna do is eat."

A smile flickered at my lips. "It's been a few years now?"

"Just got my ten-year chip." There was a flash of pride in his voice.

I shifted in my seat. "Is that Jerry Junior?"

Roger rolled down his window and leaned out of the car just as a tow made its way into the parking lot. "Looks like it. Let me go help 'im."

I watched him head toward Jerry Junior, calling out a greeting and waving his hand over his head. Here Roger was, helping me like a real dad. How many times had I dreamed about a moment like this?

I thought of Eddie, taking an Uber home, driving his car—permanently fixed with a car seat—to his ex's house. Thinking, always—ultimately—of nothing but her.

Jerry Junior hooked Cyrus's shit mobile up to his truck and, with a great deal of noise and lights, loaded it up onto the tow.

ROGER SPENT the whole morning working on the car without taking a break while I sat on his couch, flipping through channels on his old-school "big-screen TV."

Roger's double-wide was tucked between two large magnolias, a splash of bubblegum pink among all the foliage. Outside, it was well loved albeit a little cluttered, but the inside was . . . *clinical*.

The walls were totally bare; the windows framed by the ratty lace curtains that came with all the trailers; the furniture minimal, utilitarian. There was a couch and a coffee table, a coatrack, and a cat tree. Everything was covered in a soft layer of dust.

At some point my dad had adopted a petite orange cat named Jim. Jim was also a bit clinical; he didn't make any noise, barely yawning or stretching. Instead, he just sat on the coffee table, on top of a stack of *Trucks & Ducks* magazines, staring at me—tail curling lazily back and forth.

I tried to focus on the episode of *Family Feud* playing behind him, but Jim's gaze burrowed into me, silently demanding I leave.

"I love you, but go away," I whispered to him.

He simply narrowed his eyes in response.

Later that afternoon Dad came banging in through the back door with a grunt. "Almost done," he called, opening the fridge and pulling out a casserole dish and a can of soda. "Help yourself to whatever you want." He pressed some buttons on the stove and slid the dish into the oven. "Gonna make some dinner if you'd like to stay."

I pointed at the cat. "Is he okay?"

"Yeah, why?"

"He hasn't *moved*."

Roger looked at the cat with exhaustion. "Jim, get down from there and leave your sister alone."

Sister, eh? I gave the little guy a gentle scratch behind the ear. He lifted his chin in approval, letting out his first sound: a purr.

"I think he likes me." I flashed Roger a tense smile. "I can stay."

ROGER SET the casserole dish down on the table between us. "Little burnt around the edges, but I'm getting pretty good."

I shrugged, sliding into my chair. "It looks good to me."

He pierced the top layer with his serving spoon. "Not like anything Annetta makes, but it'll get the job done."

I let out an awkward laugh, hearing him reference her so casually. I had no idea how often Nan and Roger saw each other. They probably bumped into each other once a year at the grocery store or at the Fourth of July fireworks. Nan was the least awkward person on earth; I imagined she did a good job at not revealing that she held all the years of nonexistent parenting against him.

Dad tapped out a serving spoon of bean enchilada casserole onto my plate. "So." I picked up my fork. "How's the car coming along?"

He shot me an anxious look as he filled his own plate. It was kind of weird seeing Roger eat a full plate of food, and I kept my eyes on him as he took his first bite. "All done," he said, wiping his mouth with a napkin. "You should be good to drive home. No need to stay if you're anxious to hit the sticks."

I shook my head. "I'm not in a rush. I don't have any plans tonight."

We ate in silence for a moment, forks clanking against our plates. It was weirdly delicious. *Were cooking classes part of rehab?*

"Alright." I looked up at the sound of his voice to find Roger staring at me with a bewildered, wide-eyed gaze. "When are you going to let me have it, then?"

"What?" I let out yet another nervous, tense laugh, voice constricted by the pounding of my heart. "What are you talking about?"

"I can't sit around like this, Delfina. I-I'm not used to feeling like this. Anxious and tense. So, come on now." He gestured at the space between us. "Yell at me. Get it out."

"What? I'm not gonna *yell*. Why would you want me to yell?"

He raised an eyebrow. "You're not mad at me?"

"Not right now. Not about anything specific," I replied, rolling my eyes. What a loaded question.

"How's that? You've spent years pissed at me. Then, we stop talking for a damn decade. Aren't you pissed at me?"

"I don't know, Dad. Yes? I am pissed, but I guess . . . I don't know," I said. My heart had snagged in my chest. I didn't know what to do—where to look. *Since when does Roger care how I feel?* I scrolled my eyes around the room, over the sun-bleached curtain covering the window over his sink, the dish rack with a single cup, plate, and spoon dripping dry. "I just don't think about you like I used to."

Roger's eyes fell from my face and dropped to the casserole between us. "Hard to hear, those words. Not that I don't deserve them." I scraped at the last bit of food on my plate, refusing to fill the silence that followed, to let guilt take over. Finally, he said, "I never wanted to push too hard. Maybe that was a mistake."

I squeezed my eyes shut tight. I hated hearing him say that. I didn't want to hurt him. Wanting to hurt someone was the type of thing people like Roger did—not me. "I think about you. I worry about you."

He kept his eyes down. "You worry?"

"What, you don't worry about me?" I snapped.

He set his fork down. "Not really, Del Marie. You got your grandmother and about a million angels on your side."

"I have myself," I reminded him.

"You do, you have yourself. I'm not a good man, you know that. I figured it was best to stay away, wait for you to reach out." He cleared his throat. "I'm old enough now to know I need to be better. For you. With you."

I wasn't going to argue with that. I set my fork down, too. "I have a lot going on right now. I can't sit here and help you work through how you feel."

No way in *hell* was I going to make Roger feel better about the last twenty-eight years and eleven months that he had failed to be an active participant in my life. One leaky radiator fixed could never undo all the knots he'd helped create in my life. Sometimes, in the darkest moments, I imagined how things would have gone if Nan hadn't stepped up when my mom died. Foster care, group homes, a loneliness and sadness I couldn't bear to imagine.

But there were no alternate timelines. Nan had stepped up. Roger had been a shitty dad. I survived.

And now, Roger was making an effort. He had fixed my car. Invited me to his home. Made me dinner. He was sober and he was doing well. For the first time ever, maybe.

He licked his lips nervously. "Let's talk about something else."

I nodded slowly, picked up my fork again. "This casserole is actually pretty good."

"Good." A self-conscious smile flickered over his lips. "And vegetarian. I . . . I remembered."

Suddenly, eye contact felt impossible. "You have to remind Nan now, too."

That made him chuckle. "So, Annetta told me all about your place in Queens and your big show."

I swallowed roughly. "What?"

"She said it's a real big deal—a festival, right? But they broad-cast it on the TV?"

"On the internet, yeah." I shook my head. "But you talk to Nan?"

He shrugged, twisting his fork around. "On the phone. Some-times we grab a coffee. Dinner, if they don't have any coffee left. We only talk 'bout you, though."

"Me?"

A tired smile flickered at the corner of his mouth. "Yeah."

Suddenly, all the air was gone from my lungs, coherent thought lost on its way from my mind to my mouth. If I could have, I would have said something.

20

Home

I let the front door slam behind me. Nan was sitting at the table, thumbing through a magazine. She let it fall from her hands to the table. "Did you get taller?"

I dropped my bag by the door. "Something interesting happened tonight."

"What's that, sweets?" She picked up her magazine again, licked her index finger, and turned the page.

"Roger told me you two talk. Frequently. Even go out for coffee."

Her fingers froze between the glossy pages. "It's happened, yes."

"I've been icing my biological father out since I was eighteen and you're having coffee with him? That's pretty funny," I said. I was trembling, so angry I almost levitated out of my shoes and flew across the room at her.

"Oh, Del." Nan rolled her eyes, like *I* was the ridiculous one. "We've probably had coffee together three times in the last ten years."

"But you've never gone a single year without talking?"

"I don't know! I haven't been counting."

"He knew about the showcase. He knew I lived in Queens."

My anger, my righteous anger, ballooned in my chest, my voice increasing in volume as I ticked each point off on my fingers.

Nan pulled her eyeglasses off the top of her head. "When he reaches out, I respond. When he asks about you, I respond. What am I supposed to do? Lie?"

"You did lie, Nan. You lied to *me*." I jabbed a finger into my chest. "*I* haven't spoken to him in years because I thought *we* had agreed he sucks."

"He does suck! Of course he sucks." She tossed her glasses down on the table, a dismissive gesture I'd seen before. "I didn't want to bring it up—I thought you liked it when I protected you."

I gritted my teeth, matching her fire with fire: "First, you're friends with Eddie. Now, you're in cahoots with Roger. Anyone else I should know about? A third husband locked away somewhere?"

"You're being as nasty as cat piss right now."

"He's my dad, and I had to *beg* you for his address."

"You didn't beg! You could have asked me whenever."

I let out a big, dry laugh. "Jesus Christ, what kind of fucked up conversation is this?"

"You've always had his phone number, Delfina." She raised her voice, her lips pulling into an angry, taut rosette. "Don't act like I'm some monster who kept you from your father."

"Why would I call him when all I ever hear is how much you think he fucking sucks?" I yelled. "About how every bad thing I've ever done is from *his side*?"

"I can't have this conversation right now—"

"You have to!" I cut her off. "We have to."

Nan froze. I'd never raised my voice at her before. In all my years of being an angry, lonely kid I'd never shouted or caused a scene.

"He's the only one left who remembers Michelle the way I do." She began to slowly gather up her things—her glasses, her magazine, her cup of coffee. "There. Happy? I don't talk to my ex-husband. You only have a handful of memories. But I was her mother. What am I supposed to do? Just let myself forget?" She paused, like I could ever actually answer her.

"I didn't think—"

"I don't expect you to. You were a kid, you needed me. How could I put that on you?" Her lips trembled as she fought to keep her eyes steady and dry, trained on me. "Roger's doing fine now— but that man was a forest fire and, my God, did he burn you. I will never forgive him for that. But he loved your mom. He was there—the night she . . ." *Overdosed*. The word itself was poison. We never said it.

"You never told me how much he loved my mom." I tried desperately to hold on to my anger, to keep going. "I could have changed my mind—"

"*Enough*." She took a steadying breath, gripping the chair like the word had knocked the air out of her. "I didn't want to make you miss another parent that wasn't around."

A truth more painful than any insult. She was right. I missed Michelle, in a way. I missed what I thought life would have been like with her. I missed knowing exactly where I came from. I missed her as a person.

But I had a mom. I'd always had Nan.

"I . . . I miss my mom," I offered. But there was something in my voice—a crack, a warble—and Nan knew. Recognition darkened in her eyes as she tilted her head to the side.

Now, I had lied, too.

21

The She-Shed

The next morning, I made my way to the Persaud-Jenkins residence.

"Hiiiii," Sam trilled, her face immediately crumbling in that oh-no-you-fucked-up-your-life-again kind of way.

I gave her my most dignified yes-I-did-didn't-I? smile. "Thanks so much for letting me use the she-shed."

"No problem." Sam waved me in. Morning cartoons were playing on the flat-screen in their living room, DJ babbling in Devon's arms.

"Hey," Devon sung out, smirking at me. "There she is."

"What's up?" I rubbed the top of his big, bald head before giving DJ a noisy kiss on the forehead.

"I heard you almost got laid the other night."

I narrowed my eyes at Sam. "Seriously?"

Sorry, she mouthed, waving me toward the sliding doors. "I had to tell someone. Is that a guitar?"

"No, it's a dead body in a cello case. Why did you tell Devon?"

"Why'd you bring your guitar?"

"My question is way more important," I complained as I followed Sam through the backyard, past the dock, and toward what looked like a miniature beach house, complete with flower boxes under each window. "Jeez, this place is nicer than one hundred percent of the apartments I've lived in."

Sam grinned, shrugging a shoulder. "It's a perfect space to take virtual clients, clear my mind, and work on writing articles."

"Well, I'm just grateful for a quiet place to work that isn't wall-papered with teddy bears."

Sam unlocked the door and we stepped into a single room with a vaulted ceiling, furnished with the perfect mix-and-match of modern and beach cottage furniture. The walls were painted a shade of blue that felt like a cool washcloth over my eyes.

"This *is* perfect," I whispered.

"Right?" Sam flopped down onto an apartment-size couch. "So, fighting with Nan, huh?"

"Yup." I set down my guitar case and purse, sitting in her office chair. "Because I didn't have enough shit keeping me up at night. The worst part is, I know I'm not totally in the wrong. She's been making it clear for years that Roger was someone to avoid completely. She's always making little comments. Every time I'm messy—"

"Always."

"Or late—"

"Constantly."

"Or doing something that she thinks won't work out, it's all 'Roger's side.'" I picked at a loose thread in one of my jeans' knee holes.

"She's sat through all of it, Del. Every playdate he missed. Every time you came back from his house in two-day-old clothes. Every time he forgot to pay for something." Sam leaned forward and placed a hand on my knee. "She loves you a lot."

I hated when Sam made valid points. By *far* her worst quality. "We'll make up. Eventually."

She gave me a squeeze. "Good. Now, tell me all about Eddie."

I NEVER consciously decided I wanted to become a comedian. When I moved to New York I had wanted to be a musician, but every time I got onstage to perform at an open mic I'd get so nervous I just ended up rambling. The third or fourth time it happened, Cyrus had been in the audience.

"Nice prop." He smirked, pointing at the guitar. "It's a cool bit, making people think you're gonna sing. Very alt."

"What?" I looked down at the instrument, slung across my body. "Oh—no. Not a prop. I'm a musician."

Cyrus narrowed his eyes at me. "Riiiight. Cool bit. You should come to Off the Chain Comedy. It's a mic out in Brooklyn. They love that kind of stuff."

Eventually, I was confident enough onstage that I no longer needed the pretense of the guitar. I could just get up on my own, with nothing but my words, and get laughs.

I wasn't sure if I was funny or lucky. I think that's how every comedian feels. The extreme highs and lows are disorienting. Something that works today could fail tomorrow. Something hilarious could leave you feeling hollowed out or like a liar, wondering if it's worth it if the joke leaves you so raw. I was envious of comedians who had it in them to lay open the facts of their lives, to turn them over and inspect them so fully as to be able to write a joke that was true and right. I'd found the idea terrifying. So, I went for cheap shots.

Cheap shots were off the table now. All I had were the facts of my life, clouding my every thought. Memories of Eddie, Roger, and Nan in complete opposition to the last twenty-four hours.

As I attempted to write something, splayed out on the floor of Sam's she-shed, I couldn't think of anything but that.

I groaned and pulled myself up, reaching over onto the couch and grabbing my guitar.

I strummed lazily, playing a few familiar chords—an easy, poppy chord progression.

Roger had given me my first guitar for my tenth birthday. It was actually his guitar, but I think he'd forgotten to get me a gift and the sentimentality of it all was right there. What he didn't realize was how much I would love it. An unintentional slam dunk in the parenting department, one he'd completely tripped into. We sat on the edge of his couch for hours as he taught me how to hold the enormous instrument in my lap—how to stretch and manipulate my fingers to make something that would eventually sound like a song.

But after a few days, I hadn't needed Roger anymore.

I kept strumming, picking up my tempo until I was playing a tune that sounded like "Don't Look Back in Anger" by Oasis, one of the first songs he'd taught me. *How fitting*, I thought. I huffed and paused. "Another shitty Dad memory."

Wait.

I played a chord.

Then another.

Then again, all together. It sounded pretty good. I laughed out loud. "Holy shit."

I'D ONLY ever heard my mom sing once: a fuzzy audio track on a VHS from my second birthday. Nan's holding me over the cake. Michelle's behind the camera.

She sounds tired. *Be careful, Mom*, she snaps at Nan. It's easy to ignore the strain in her voice, the fatigue and weight of addiction. She's in her early twenties, innumerable lives lived already behind her.

But then she sings—*Happy birthday to you, Happy birthday to you*—and it all melts away. Her timbre becomes lighter, more melodic.

When she sings, she's free.

How BALLER had Michelangelo felt the moment the clay before him stopped looking like an insurmountable lump and started to look like David—the David he'd imagined a million times? Because I knew how baller I felt the moment my Brainwave set finally began to take its form in front of me.

As soon as I finished one song, I had the beginnings of another right there waiting for me. I kept the guitar in my lap, even when my notebook was closed, plucking at the strings, matching rhythm and tempo to the cadence of a joke. Building setups and punchlines alongside simple, memorable melodies. Easy chord progressions I'd played around with for years were tucked away for this, I guess. The sun set and I barely noticed. I ran out of water and didn't move. It wasn't until my coffeepot was empty and Sam was knocking at the door that I broke out of my trance.

She poked her head in. "Devon's grilling, do you want anything?"

I was about to say *no, thank you* when my stomach let out a rumble. "Your finest meatless foods, please."

She leaned farther into the she-shed, staring around at the papers strewn all over the floor. "You got a lot done."

"I figured it out, I think. I think I know what I'm going to perform."

"Stay the night. Stay as long as you need to."

"You sure?" I laughed.

Sam nodded. "The she-shed's yours until you feel ready."

That was how I spent the next few days: spread out on the floor with my notebook, guitar, and phone, stopping only to use the bathroom, dip my feet in the bay, or share a meal with Sam and her family on the back patio. One night while I was lying awake on the couch, staring at the ceiling and mentally rehearsing the song I'd just finished, ironing out a funky transition, my phone dinged. I slid my thumb across the screen until it flashed to life, pulling the message up and close to my face.

It was from Roger. It was long.

Dear Daughter,

It's your Dad and Jim. Thank you for having dinner with us. You are always welcome in my humble home. Not anything special, that's for sure, but I have a table and a seat with your name always on it. You're beautiful like your mom. Your voice is sweet like hers. Looking at you across the table I had to blink twice because I thought I was seeing Michelle. She would be so proud. You made your dream (her dream) come true. Alright that's enough sap from me. Old age makes a man soft. You're a good one.

Lots of love,
Dad and Jim

I stared at the message, reading it over and over until my eyes burned. Then, I grabbed my notebook and wrote four words down, four words to start something new:

Lately I've been thinking

"WHAT DAY is it?" I asked between bites of tempeh sofritas tacos. In true Devon fashion, my presence in the she-shed had not been taken as an annoyance, but rather a moment to get *really* good at making vegan Mexican food. We were sipping margaritas and taste-testing his latest recipe as the sun set and mosquitos buzzed around our ankles and ears.

"Seriously?" Devon quirked a faint brow at me as he spatula'd a stack of grilled eggplant slices onto my paper plate. "It's Thursday."

"*Already?*" I spun my head toward Sam, as if she were the master of all time.

"Haven't you been looking at your phone?" Sam asked.

As if on cue, my phone chirped from where it was lying in a hammock of sundress between my knees. My heart leapt when I saw his name.

Eddie. I flicked my thumb over the slick surface, bringing up his words. You're not mad at me, are you?

Crap. He had no idea what had happened after he left me in the parking lot underneath the Ferris wheel—a moment that now felt like it had happened in a different year. He didn't know anything about Roger, about Nan.

I replied immediately: Sorry, had some family drama. I've been staying with Sam.

Got it, he wrote back. The words felt like ice. Then, another message: Annie may have mentioned a fight.

My heart sunk. I wrote back: Lol I forgot about you two

Don't worry, he replied. I got no details. Btw, you in for tomorrow night?

His show at the bar was tomorrow night, wasn't it?

I had to set aside what had happened between us. I needed to stay focused on Brainwave, and this was the perfect opportunity to test out my new material.

I bit my top lip as I wrote back: Yeah I'm in

It took him two hours, but he finally responded. Just one word.
Awesome.

I WROTE one more song before reaching out to Nan. She made a
tepid agreement to meet at the Pier Point Diner for breakfast the
next morning—but only after I promised I'd eventually try the
scallops.

With some time to spare, I slipped into salt & sage. Meghan was
unpacking some boxes in the back of the shop.

"Hey," I called out.

"Oh, hi!" She popped out from behind a mannequin, ethereal
as ever.

"I didn't want to scare you."

"Oh, please. The only things that scare me are Vacation Bible
School and low-rise jeans." She pulled her hair back away from her
face. "How can I help ya?"

"I need a gift for my grandmother," I said, trying to not sound
as nervous as I felt.

"Okay . . . Is it her birthday? Are her ears pierced?"

"It's a long story—but I guess I'm sort of apologizing. I need
something that says *thank you* and *I love you* and maybe also, *please
don't bring this up again.*"

"Oh, I have something perfect for you." She disappeared to the
back of the shop, then returned with her arms full. "Okay, so I
have this apron that says 'NO BITCHIN' IN THE KITCHEN'
or I have this set of angel cards designed by an artist from Ocean
Harbor."

God, this would be my Sophie's Choice, wouldn't it? I'd have to
finally turn my back on a novelty houseware item in favor of being
earnest and *real.*

Meghan read me like an open book, setting the apron aside and passing the deck of cards my way. "I know some people can get freaked out by tarot cards, but angel cards are meant to provide gentle, positive guidance whenever you need it. I promise, there's nothing spooky about them."

I turned the box over in my hands. "I don't know, I'm kind of weird about stuff like this—"

"She can do a card pull for herself alone. Look." She took the box back, opened it, and flipped over the first card. "Ha! The Queen card. Must be fate."

The art was spectacular—too beautiful to be hidden away like this. A woman with deep golden skin and long, braided hair made of seagrass and kelp stood on the shoreline, eyes fixed outward on a purple-pink sunset, her arms overflowing with riches from the water: clams, oysters, strings of pearls, and sea glass that glowed off the paper. "What does it mean?"

"Well, the Queen is . . . the queen. She's self-possessed; she's confident; she looks after herself and her kingdom." Meghan dragged her finger over the iridescent etchings of the Queen's wings, at rest by her sides. "Her wings are relaxed; she's grounded. Exactly where she's meant to be."

A breath rushed forward from my lips. "Fuck, that is *so* Nan." Astrology would come for us all, eventually. "Fine. I'll do the cards. But *only* because they're very pretty."

Meghan threw me a wink as she punched at her iPad, ringing me up. "Don't worry—I'll set the apron aside for you."

NAN SLID into the booth across from me in a cerulean caftan and a pair of rhinestone gladiator sandals, tight-lipped and quiet. *I've missed you so much.*

Before she could say anything, I pulled the deck of cards from my purse and slid them across the table toward her.

She cocked a brow. "Are you bribing me?"

"I'd never do such a thing." I fought back a smile, already pulling at the corners of my mouth.

"Is it a gag gift—a trick?"

"Just open them, goofball."

Nan carefully pulled back the paper Meghan had wrapped them in just a few moments ago, shimmying the lid free. There, sitting on top of the deck, facing upward, was the Queen. "They're angel cards," I rushed to explain, absolutely butchering Meghan's elegant sales pitch. "So you can talk to your angels whenever you want."

"Del, they're beautiful," Nan whispered.

"I want to get to know Roger now. You don't need to protect me anymore." I tapped the card. "And maybe the angels agree."

"I shouldn't have lied," she said softly, carefully placing the lid back on the box, as if she were tucking her angels into bed. Then, she reached for my hands. "Breakfast's on me."

22

The Billiards

I feel like he knows exactly what he needs to do to change my mind about him," I yelled over the thump of the music, coming from a speaker directly behind my head.

Sam shrugged. "People can change. I mean, they usually don't but they can."

"God," I groaned, throwing my head back. "I can't *like* my *dad*."

"You need to open your mind to the concept of nuance," Sam chastised me. "You can like your dad without forgiving him. You can eat dinner with the guy and still hold him accountable. Now, drink." She pressed a spiked seltzer back into my hand.

I sipped immediately. "Well, damn, Dr. Persaud. How much will that cost me?"

"Sorry, I'm already buzzed." She craned her neck, trying to peer through the crowd and get the bartender's attention. When she finally caught his eye, she flashed him her one-hundred-kilowatt smile. "Refill, please!"

The guy literally dropped the glass he was refilling and scrambled to make her another margarita.

I shook my head. "What power you possess, Samantha."

She rolled her eyes at me. "Del, look at me. I'm wearing a cardigan and Supergas. I'm telling you, it's because I'm lactating. I swear I'm producing some sort of pheromone that makes every man within seventeen feet of me absolutely feral." Her face lit up suddenly. "Eddie!"

I spun around to see Eddie standing behind me, hands shoved into his pockets, a lazy smile playing at his lips. He quirked a brow. "Sorry, didn't mean to interrupt your lactation talk." I hadn't seen Eddie since Ocean Harbor and somehow my memory had already failed in capturing how gorgeous he was. It wasn't just his Gucci model face; it was the light behind his smile—warm and genuine—and the way his eyes danced over me, quietly betraying his outward chill.

Sam dismissed him with a grin and held her arms open for a hug. "You look *so great*."

I flashed Sam a bewildered look. "How drunk are you?"

He pulled her into a sideways hug, patting the top of her head with an enormous hand. "You, too—congratulations, by the way."

As Sam pulled away, she looked from me to Eddie and back to me, face falling into the most pained explosion of social anxiety.

I pressed my hand to my forehead. "Christ Almighty, Samantha." She was hemming and hawing more than a rusted chain saw. Eddie threw me a wide-eyed, sidelong glance until I intervened. "Fucking aye, Sam, he could have probably guessed that I told you."

"Oh, *thank God*. Congratulations to you, too. And I guess also, sorry about the divorce?"

If my face was to get any redder—any warmer—my head might explode off my body.

A belly laugh rolled through Eddie as he rubbed a hand back and forth over his chest. "Oh man, thanks. Really appreciate it."

He pulled his other hand out of his pocket, bringing with it a set of tickets. "I saved you some drink tickets. Not sure who's the DD tonight—"

"What!" Sam snatched the tickets out of his hand. "Thank you, Ed!" And just like that, she disappeared into the throng to grab her refill.

I flashed him a knowing look. "It's me. I'm the DD."

The corner of his mouth twitched. "We need you sober enough to perform."

"Yeah, especially in front of a sold-out audience. You *really* downplayed your live music night."

Eddie surveyed the packed room, his lips working overtime as he fought against a proud smile. "Just a bunch of shoobies. You'll do great."

I smoothed a hand down the front of my outfit—a white T-shirt tucked into the green satin skirt I'd bought from the boutique. I was going for a high-low type of situation, an attempt at looking effortlessly chic. Somewhere, someplace, a Frenchwoman was tutting into her cigarette. "I'll try my best to not embarrass you, but that's it."

He lifted a hand and worked the muscles in the side of his neck. "Speaking of embarrassed. About last week—"

"Hey, it's fine." I cut him off with a wave of my hand. "Let's just skip the awkward stuff." I took a sip of my drink. "Been there, done that anyway, right?" I joked feebly, even as my stomach met my throat.

"Got it." Eddie cleared his throat. "Well, I'm gonna go set up the stage for you. I'll see you out there."

I nodded, doing my best to channel my own inner tutting Frenchwoman. "See you out there."

As promised, I opened the show at nine-thirty. The lights went down, and the crowd immediately went wild as I pulled a stool up to the microphone stand and settled in with my guitar pressed into my lap.

"How y'all doing tonight?" I said into the mic. The stage lights shined into my eyes and all I could make out were the bobbing heads of tens of people—maybe even a hundred—stretching out in front of me like a sea full of buoys.

They let out a swell of *wooooh*'s in response.

"Good." I chuckled, excitement threading through my ribs as I strummed my guitar. My fingers were quaking ever so slightly, but the crowd's eagerness had me feeling steady. A strange, new feeling of power flickered in my chest. *I can do this.* I did do this. All the time. This was where I belonged. "I like this crowd. Eddie, this is a good crowd." They erupted into more hooting and hollering. "I'm gonna play some music to warm you up, but you all seem very warm already, is that right?"

"*Big boy Ed-day!*" someone shouted from the back of the room.

"Let's play some music. This first song I just wrote, and I have to apologize because I sort of stole the guitar riff from someone who is way more talented than me." I flicked my eyes anxiously to the side of the stage. I figured he'd be standing there.

Through the dark I could make out Eddie, leaning against the doorway to the kitchen, arms crossed low over his chest. I kept my eyes fixed in his direction. "He's a real musician. I'm just a fool with a guitar. Anyway, this song is called 'Second Kiss' . . ."

Summer salt on your lips
When we kiss it's like
French vanilla, cherry bliss
A sunset, disco fever dream

Hot pink, yellow, orange-cream
Ocean sounds trapped in a shell
When only time will tell
Is gonna be real-life thing or just a, just a
Summer fling?
You say my name and it's like a spell
You go first and then I'll tell
You all my secrets
Summer salt on your lips, it's
A sunset hour, disco fever dream
Your mouth on mine and I can hardly breathe
It's summer salt and French vanilla bliss
It's everything and nothing quite like this
It's how you left me standing there
And I'm still wondering
Can we kiss?

I lost myself in the song, in the country-pop, grungy riff. When I'd first heard Eddie work through the chords, I'd known these notes were meant to be a song about wanting someone at golden hour. On a bench. In a bar. After ten long years. About summer seeping so deeply into you it reaches your heart and your bones. A song written while I watched the sky turn black, my heart moored to the weightless bob of anticipation and fear and desire in my chest. All the *what if*s and knowing one of them would be true.

I'd said I wanted to do something different, and wasn't it different for me to give in to my feelings? I didn't care if Eddie could piece it together—that I'd written this song about him, about us, about our kiss. That's how art worked, didn't it?

Maybe this is about you. Maybe it isn't.

And it wasn't just my song now. It was all of ours—everyone

in the bar. Everyone who quickly picked up on the words and by the end could sing along with me. Could harmonize every time I trilled on *French vanilla, cherry bliss*.

I closed out the song, but I couldn't bring myself to look back his way. Anyway, the crowd was too loud. Screaming and clapping louder than any audience at Gimbley's ever had. I was too busy staring back at them in wonder.

"Thank you," I said. "Now how about a funny one?"

23

The Billiards

After my set, Sam greeted me at the bottom of the stage steps in an absolute drunken tizzy. She was squeezing my cheeks and screaming about how I was an idiot or maybe a genius or maybe something else entirely, her words lost in the noise and the pounding of my heart.

I didn't have enough time to think about what I had just done because Sam was already pulling me through the crowd and telling me I had to meet her new friends.

The crowd spit us out the front entrance and onto The Billiards's front lawn, where there was a drunken cornhole tournament taking place and the air hung heavy with cigarette smoke and '00s hip-hop.

Someone handed us tequila shots and asked where they could download my songs, then I kissed Sam on the cheek and pushed my way back into the bar and through the crowd until I was up front at the edge of the stage, right as the lighting shifted.

For some reason, I had assumed Eddie was the front man. But now I could see he was on the bass guitar, tucked behind an amp, wearing one of his Billiards shirts. This one, a bleach-stained black T-shirt that looked like it was made for him. I could see him perfectly, but I knew he was partially blinded by the stage lights, and I was little more than a purple head-shaped blob. He pulled his top lip into his mouth, eyebrows furrowed as he scanned the crowd. *Is he looking for me?* Just as I was getting ready to shout his name, the mic cut in.

"Yooooooo!" the lead guitarist—an impish man with a receding hairline and beard—shouted into the mic. "Welcome to The-motherfuckin'-Billiards!"

Behind the drums, on an elevated platform, a hulking man with a nose ring slammed his sticks down in a raucous, celebratory beat as the crowd went wild around me. Eddie lifted his eyes to meet the drummer's, flashing him a smirk. They exchanged a knowing look, and I felt that jealous pang again.

"I'm Gabe. That's Eddie on the bass. And on the drums, give it up for Marwan! Tonight, we're gonna play you some music. Y'all like music?"

The crowd lost their minds.

HALFWAY THROUGH the first song, the crowd started shouting—not heckling or roaring. Yelling words.

"*Switch!*" someone shouted from the back of the room. A roar of approval traveled through the audience in a wave until the sweaty bodies on either side of me were half heaved onto the stage, clambering in unison.

"Switch!" a woman with tomato-soup sunburns screamed. I had never seen anything like this before. Suddenly I was acutely aware of why rock and roll had such an association with the devil. This response? Terrifying. Sexual. Terrifyingly sexual. Or, as the kids would say, horny.

Gabe flashed us a bemused, sheepish smile. "Already?"

"*Switch!*" the crowd boomed.

Eddie shook his head, chewing at the corner of his mouth to hide a grin. He hadn't noticed me yet, front and center and staring at the fine angles of his face.

"You heard 'em, boys."

Then, Eddie and Gabe stopped playing. Marwan broke out in a pop-punk solo, deftly whirling his sticks around his hands between expert cymbal and pedal work. Gabe and Eddie unwound themselves from their instruments and *literally* switched.

He slid behind Gabe up to the front mic, pushing his sweat-slick curls away from his face as he secured the guitar around his neck. And just like that he became the front man I had imagined. A broody, inky sex symbol under the relentless heat of the limelight. Someone screamed his name, and he looked up, mouth quirking into a delicious half smile.

Then he tossed Marwan and then Gabe a nod, and they simultaneously shifted into a higher, quicker pitch. Eddie and Gabe moved seamlessly into a distinctly bachata rhythm, while Marwan accompanied them with his snare and kick drums.

"This next one is in Spanish," he crooned, his lips flush against the mic. "So don't even try to sing along." He dropped his eyes to the guitar, but his gaze caught mine, forcing a small double take. I grinned at him, hoping through the dark the lights would catch my teeth and the pride in my eyes.

I'm proud of you, I screamed in my mind, hoping it'd reach him telepathically.

THE CROWD yelled *switch* about three more times in the course of the band's thirty-minute set.

"Aight, final number," Eddie announced, adjusting the guitar strap over his shoulder. "And don't you fucking dare yell *switch* during this one."

He lifted his hat and pushed back a palmful of drenched hair. He strummed at the strings, sending a melodic jolt rippling directly through my body.

"This is a song I'm sure you know," he said, eyes downcast, fixed on mine. He tilted his head, shouting into the air: "Here we go!"

Then, he played his version of a song I would never forget.

24

I was wearing a sparkly black cocktail dress— the closest Nan let me get to punk rock for prom. I'd cut my hair months ago, going from long, thick waves to choppy layers that skimmed my chin and fell to just about my collarbone. The hairdresser had said it was "kinda like the Rachel" and then I'd cried.

For the occasion, I was wearing red lipstick. Bright red. A shade that reminded me of *Chicago*, that made me powerful and adult like Velma Kelly.

The dress, the lipstick, the haircut—it had all been at Nan's encouragement.

Now, I felt like I'd marched into the dimly lit gymnasium, alone, with a neon sign that read: LOOK HOW STUPID I AM.

Thirty seconds ago, the deejay had announced his obligatory "Okay, folks, now it's time to slow it down," and, like field mice, everyone scattered. I booked it as fast as I could off the dance floor before I was caught in the center of the room—alone—as everyone swayed around me. I was, as someone had put it once, *flying solo* tonight.

Sam was nuzzling into Sean's chest. Jake clung to Rachel,

his big head flat against her chest. Wiley, clearly high out of his mind, had parked it by the snack table and was robotically shoveling Bugles into his mouth. Eddie, of course, wasn't dancing. He was sitting on the other side of the gym, on the set of bleachers opposite me, whispering into Dani's ear.

They were working together to wage some sort of sexy psychological warfare against Rachel, who had, once again, dumped Eddie. It frequently dawned on me that we were maybe the only friend group united not by mutual admiration and common interests, but rather fettered by sexual tension.

Everyone looked so old. Jake basically had a full beard. Rachel could easily buy us all beer without getting carded. Eddie had grown about a foot and a half over the summer. Rumor had it he'd gotten a tattoo, too. But that was all I really had now—rumors. We didn't talk much—maybe a *yo, what's up?* in group settings, when absolutely necessary.

It hurt at first. That moment between us in his car was supposedly bound by a sacred pact. We would never talk about it again; we'd never let it impact our friendship. Everything was supposed to go back to exactly the way it had been.

I was surprised how much I missed Eddie's constant ribbing. Almost an entire school year had passed, though, and I was getting used to the idea that maybe we'd ruined our friendship forever.

I'd kept up my end of the bargain—I hadn't told anyone about the kiss. Not even Sam. But a few weeks into the school year—on a Thursday of all days—a rumor reached me via Wiley that apparently Eddie and I had made out on the beach. By lunch, I'd given Eddie a blow job in the back seat of his car. By dismissal, we'd dated for six weeks but broke up under mysterious and severe circumstances the week before school started. I spent the entire day in a freezing-cold sweat, despite the early September heat wave, attempting to track Eddie down and confront him. He'd told someone—someone who probably hated me, mocked me, wanted to destroy me.

Somehow, our paths never crossed that day. Then, on Friday it came out that Morgan Santis was pregnant. Everyone forgot about Eddie and me. Everyone, it seemed, except me.

Sometimes I felt insane. Had I imagined that moment in the car? Had I entirely made up how seismic that kiss had felt? Could it be that the thickness in the air had been something I'd made up out of desperation—loneliness?

That had to be it. I had to have imagined everything. How else was it possible that Eddie looked at me and didn't feel what I felt? How could you look at someone you'd once spent so much time with, confided in, and act like they didn't exist? If I hadn't imagined everything, then maybe Eddie was evil.

I pulled my eyes away from him, smirking into Dani's neck as their faces got closer and closer. I wished I was a witch so I could put a spell on him. *May no kiss you ever have be as good as the kiss we shared. May you never feel the way you felt that night ever again.*

I checked my watch. *You just have to survive forty-five more minutes.* My plan was to call Roger at exactly ten-thirty and tell him I had a stomachache. Nan would have never fallen for that, but Roger was an absolute sucker.

"I need air," I said to no one before hopping down off the bleachers and making my way past the chaperones, through the front hall, and out into the parking lot.

It was freezing for April and the air smelled like horseshoe crabs.

"Gross," I mumbled, shivering against the breeze as I folded my arms over my chest and sat down on the broad stone steps that overlooked the parking lot that led down to the football field.

The lot was totally empty, except for a few cars. Some seniors were stumbling around laughing their asses off, falling in and out of the bushes. So clearly drunk. Or maybe faking it.

"*Jason!*" a girl in a hot-pink dress squealed, running barefoot through the trees, into the darkness.

I reached into my clutch purse. Had I brought my iPod? *Please, God, please.*

"No dancing for you?"

I stiffened at the sound of his voice behind me. "Very funny."

"What do I know? Maybe someone asked you." Eddie took the steps two at a time until he was next to me, leaning against the railing.

I huffed, dropping my eyes to my shoes—sparkly, black, embarrassing. "You know already that no one asked me."

Eddie stayed quiet for a while, arms folded over his chest. He watched the girl in pink run out of the bushes and then back into them. Finally, he said, "They're playing 'Sex and Candy' in there."

The words hit me like a tidal wave, but I tried to stay as motionless as possible, willing even my flyaways to stay still. "Not very school appropriate."

Eddie laughed quietly, into his sleeve. "I'm not a slow dance guy, but if you wanted . . ."

My heart sputtered in my chest. "What?" I said, keeping my voice even. "Aren't you having fun sucking on Dani's ear?"

He shrugged a bony shoulder. "Yeah, but she's kinda boring. At least you and I could talk music."

I rolled my eyes despite the tumbling, growing wave of excitement in my stomach. "Is that all you think about? Music?"

He fiddled with one of the buttons on his vest. He was wearing all black, too. Even his tie was black. "I think about other things."

"Dani's ear?" I stretched my legs out in front of me.

He let out a snort of laughter and stayed quiet for a long time. I looked up at him, watched as his dark eyes flicked around the empty parking lot from spot to spot. Never settling. He wanted to say something. My heart was pounding. We hadn't talked in months—now this? *How is he so good at acting like it hasn't been months since we talked?*

Then, he said it. He said, "You."

My eyes widened. "Me?"

Eddie rubbed the back of his neck. "Yeah, you. A lot, actually."

"What do you mean?" I said so softly, my voice barely more than a whisper.

He opened and closed his mouth. "You—you're always around. It's like, not special or anything."

He can't say it. Whatever he wanted to say to me, he physically could not. My brain immediately jumped to one place.

He was so embarrassed by me—by my dress and my short hair and my big boobs—that he couldn't even bring himself to tell me how he felt when no one was around.

Maybe he thought about me—but he'd never let anyone know. *Shame.*

Suddenly, my eyes were burning. My sinuses were buzzing. I was too hot and too cold all at once. I jumped up and grabbed my purse, which almost fell out of my hands, almost sent my lipstick, iPod, and flip phone falling down the steps. But I saved it and sealed the bag, stumbling away from Eddie, back up the steps.

"I have to go," I stuttered. "My dad is waiting, or . . . or something."

"Wait, Del—"

I sent one final look back over my shoulder at him. He was still leaning against the rail. I threw my weight into the doors and ran through the dark, empty halls back into the gym. The music was back to a thumping, bass-filled beat. I pushed through the crowd until I found Sam.

I grabbed her by the shoulder.

"Sam," I yelled into her ear. "I'm leaving. My dad's here."

Before she could stop me, I booked it to the bathroom.

25

Eddie's Office

Outside the night was still going, but inside The Billiards had emptied out. The night had turned cool as the party raged on until it was the perfect temperature for a cigarette and a deep conversation. Sam had long ago Ubered home, after telling me and all the new friends she'd made in the bathroom that she loved us as much as her son.

I sat on the edge of the stage, waiting for Eddie to emerge from the kitchen.

When he did, my heart dipped low into my stomach. He'd changed into a clean shirt, his hands wrapped around the long neck of a push broom.

"Your band's a real sausage fest," I joked, catching his attention. I latched my guitar case shut and hefted it off the stage.

Eddie let out a small, terse laugh between his teeth, a splash of red blooming over his neck. "Ah, yeah. We could do with some diversity in that department." He licked his lips slowly, taking a step toward me. "Need help? A ride home?"

"Oh no. I'm all set . . ." I let my voice trail off, unable to look him directly in the eye. He wasn't drunk; in fact, he looked terrifyingly sober and I just knew he was going to say something,

something we couldn't undo by morning. "I just wanted to see you before I left. To say thank you for having me. It was really great. This place is special."

Eddie brought a hand to his neck, rubbing at the spot where his anxiety had betrayed him, a flicker of devastation—or sadness?—in his eyes.

"Was your first song about us?" he asked finally, keeping the grip on his neck like his head was at risk of falling off.

Immediately, I felt the pulsing prick of heat in my cheeks and neck. "W-what do you mean?"

"I mean . . ." He dropped his hand and shoved it into his pocket. "Are we doing this?"

I flinched, recoiling against the memory his words held. But this wasn't ten years ago, and I wasn't going to stay quiet.

"Why are you saying it like that? Like I'm in this alone? You're here, too. You got in bed with me. You kissed me." I threw a hard look at him. "You and your thumb."

"My what?" He let out a laugh, leaving the broom resting against the wall as he came closer to me. "I didn't mean it like that, Del. Not at all."

Hold on. It wasn't sadness in his eyes. It was desire—plain and clear and *fragile.* It was a look that reminded me of pumpkin flowers and crepe paper. Wind could tear right through him.

"Then what do you mean? What do you want, Eddie?" I crossed my arms over my chest, meeting his soft gaze. "Because you played *the song.* And don't say, *what song?* You know 'Sex and Candy' was playing the first time we kissed."

"I know, Del. I know what I did. And I know what I want," he fired back, voice firm. "I wanted to talk to you about everything that happened, but you went MIA. Then earlier, you brushed me off. Look, I know in the past I didn't handle my feelings well, but

I want to do things differently this time and I know it's hard to believe me—"

"Eddie—"

He held up his hands to cut me off. His next words came out slow, dark eyes burning into mine. "No games." He took another step toward me. Hands still up. "No mixed signals. That's why I didn't want to take things further in the weird elk room. I didn't want you to get the wrong idea or think I wasn't serious. It's you, Del. It's us. And I just—I can't wait another ten years, praying you lose your job or your boyfriend and end up back here."

My heart was racing. "You prayed for me?"

"Shit, just about." He sighed, pushing his fingers through his curls. "I don't know what happened between us ten years ago. If I knew—if I could just make it all make sense—I would have made it right years ago. Believe me, Del." He dragged his teeth over his bottom lip, pulling in a chestful of air. "I want you. I promise I want you." He paused. "Do you want me, too?"

"Goddamnit, Eddie." I set my guitar case down, a shallow, anxious laugh moving through me. "Of course I fucking want you."

"Good," he breathed. "Perfect."

Then, Eddie closed the last bit of space between us. In one smooth motion he slid his hands around my neck and into my hair, pulling my mouth against his as he leaned low to bring his body against mine, leaving me stunned. Frozen with my arms limp at my sides as the entire world fell away from around us. His hips pressed against mine as he tilted my mouth against his, catching my bottom lip with his teeth.

He kissed me tenderly; not with a ten-year-long urgency but with a slow, burning longing. A longing that lit a blue heat in the middle of my stomach and moved through my abdomen, dripping like lava, like mercury. I could smell his coconut shampoo, the spicy sweetness of his cologne and taste the last bit of orange from his drink on the edge of his lips as he brought his fingers to trace the angle of my jaw and his tongue slipped between my lips. His fingers found their way over my throat and down my back until he gripped me at my waist.

Was it possible that I hadn't realized how much I'd missed him until now? That even if I spent the rest of my life getting to know Eddie, I knew I'd always miss the time we hadn't spent together? That I'd always be jealous of whoever got him for the last ten years? That I'd hate anyone and anything that threatened to take him away? With trembling hands, I grabbed ahold of the fabric pulled taut across his back, crushing his full weight into me as we stumbled backward. He pressed his hips flush against mine, easing me toward the stage, hands moving deftly down the curve of my ass.

He broke our kiss, keeping his forehead against mine.

"You're beautiful when you sing," he said, his voice thick in the back of his throat. "When you make jokes. When you laugh. I want you to laugh every day."

I wrenched back in his hold. "Are you drunk?"

"Sorry," he said, a smile pulling at his mouth as he buried his face in my neck, dusting his lips over my collarbones. "I'm coming on too strong, aren't I?"

I tilted my head back. "You're supposed to play it cool."

"I get excited," he whispered, panting breath warm against my ear.

"You're lucky I don't get spooked easily."

"Oh yeah?" He moved his mouth across my neck, tracing the curve of my throat, hands skating down my legs, producing a shiver that worked up from the base of my spine until I was pressing fully against him.

Then, he yanked me up onto the edge of the stage, and I let out a yelp just as his lips curved into a familiar smile—devilish, coy.

"Shut up," I chastised him, pushing my fingers into his hair. Eddie hooked his hands under my knees, lips finding mine again as his hands skimmed the curve of my calves, palms working in gentle circles up the inside of my thighs until his hands were lost between the cotton of my underwear and my skirt. I tightened my grasp on him, closing my eyes, drinking in this deeper kiss. He let out a throaty hum, his mouth moving down my neck again, fingers skimming over the place my thighs creased, gently encouraging my legs to part. I leaned back, pushing my hands into the taut, muscular width of his lower back, tracing around to his belt buckle. And then we dissolved into a fumbling, breathless mess.

We freed ourselves of the most limiting pieces of clothing first. His shirt, my shirt, my bra, and, for some reason, my earrings. Eddie hooked his fingers on my underwear and slid them slowly down my legs, pulling them free from the tangle of my shoes and skirt.

He flicked back the material of my skirt, pulling me forward with a definitive yank that made his belt buckle clank. He looked down at me, chest rising and falling in big waves. I loved the way his eyes drank me in. His fingers found me, and he inhaled sharply when he felt how wet I was.

"Wait," I gasped, pushing myself up off my elbows. His gaze followed mine to the front lawn, where a few drunk stragglers were sipping the last of their drinks as they stumbled toward the street and into the night. "Can they see us?"

"Who cares?"

"Uh." I rolled my eyes. "Me."

He gave my thighs a squeeze. "Okay, yeah, you're right. Follow me."

I didn't dare disobey. Eddie tugged on my hand, and we stumbled behind the first door down the hallway into a room that had
to be his office. The room was completely dark but I could make
out the hard, metallic angles of a desk covered in stacks of papers,
some framed photos, and a mug filled with pens.

He flicked on a small desk light that sent a chain of orange
shadows up the painted concrete walls. Then, he pushed his crap
aside before turning back to me, hunger in his eyes as the pads of
his fingers pressed into my bare stomach, guiding me to the desk.
Cloaked in the soft warm light I admired the curve of his biceps;
the soft, puckered copper flesh of his nipples; the few stray chest
hairs connected to the fine, soft happy trail down the middle of his
chest. He was breathtaking. I reached out to trace a finger over the
lips on his chest, over his pounding heart.

I could barely hold back my grin. "Have you been planning this?"

He held up a framed photo of what looked like a very ill Chi-
huahua. "Hooking up in front of Pepper? No." He tossed the picture frame onto a recliner in the corner of the room. "Being here
with you?" He snaked his fingers back through my hair, cradling
my face in his hand as he brought his lips close to mine. "Fuck
yeah. From the minute you walked into this bar."

Our bodies connected again as his lips found my cheek and his
hands slipped under the curve of my ass, easing me up onto the
desk. I pushed his pants down the rest of the way and wrapped
my legs around his waist, pressing myself into the length of his
erection, straining against the soft fabric of his boxers. Then, he
dropped to his knees, bringing his lips to my ankles.

"What're you doing?" My voice shook; every part of me shook,
vibrated with anticipation. The pressure of his fingers on my ankles alone was enough to send me over the edge. *Almost.*

"What do you want?" he rasped, his voice muffled against my

quivering legs. His tongue traced the curve of my calf, his mouth pausing at the crook of my knee. "Say it." He was watching me through his eyelashes, lips flush against the inside of my thigh.

"You," I managed. "All of you."

That's all he needed to hear. He stood and pulled me to the edge of the desk, then he was back between my legs, breaking apart only to push away the fabric of his boxers. His mouth was on mine, and I moaned into his eager kiss as he hitched my legs around his hips.

Greediness overtook me. I begged him to give me everything as he slipped inside me inch by inch. His mouth traveled from the hollow of my throat to my jaw, nipping at my skin as he breathed my name. His voice was like hot water washing over my cold skin, keeping me warm with his words.

Eddie must have studied the exact places I was sewn together, because he had no problem pulling me apart, one thread at a time. I felt safe enough to lose myself in his arms, against his body. Even as he slid a hand up over my throat, his thumb pushing gently into my mouth as he created space between our bodies, it was only to see me better. Hear me better. Watch me with his dark, languid eyes—mouth pouting in deep pleasure, a growl trapped between his teeth—as I finally let go and said his name.

26

13 Baywatch Drive

We fell asleep on the old tweed recliner in his office, wrapped in an afghan he pulled off a dusty shelf, while talking. We didn't consciously decide to fall asleep; it just sort of happened. With his lips pressed to my ear and my leg slung over his.

"I'm sorry I never found a way to you sooner," he whispered, voice drawling sleepily. "I didn't know where to look."

I replied with a hum, already falling into my first dream. "It's okay—I moved a lot," I murmured, drifting in and out of sleep. "Queens, Brooklyn, Queens again, Long Island for a few months . . ."

I woke up to the gentle sway of a breeze on my cheek. Until I realized it wasn't a breeze. It was Eddie's fingers, moving slowly back and forth from my chin to my ear.

He'd been watching me sleep, his head resting lazily in the crook of his arm, coils hanging gently in his eyes.

We didn't say anything, not for a while. His fingers moved slowly, skating over my shoulders. I reached out and pulled at a curl, watching the hair accordion back and forth.

"I can make us coffee," he murmured against my skin. Instantly, I loved the way his voice sounded after just waking up. I decided it was my favorite sound in the world; I loved it more than laughter. More than music.

I lifted my eyes to the big clock over his desk—barely 7 A.M.

I snaked my arm around his waist and nestled my head into his shoulder. "Not yet."

It was Saturday—one of his days with Valerie. He'd have to get up soon, go out into the world, be present and good. I could find coffee anywhere but I wanted to keep him close to me, like this, for as long as I could. I needed his body near mine way more than I needed coffee.

FOR SOME reason, after I kissed Eddie goodbye, I went right to the boutique. I was carrying my shoes in one hand, hair a tussled mess, when I pulled open salt & sage's front door. Meghan sat behind the counter in a big sun hat and a long linen caftan.

She looked up from her phone and gasped. "The skirt!"

I held my arms out. "The skirt, baby."

She clasped her hands in front of her chest. "Did you get laid?"

"Mama got laid," I announced.

Of course, she squealed and clapped before jumping up and rounding the counter, pulling me into a hug. "That's *incredible*. But wow, you smell like dust and alcohol."

I laughed, placing my shoes down on her counter. "Is it weird that I came right here? I literally came from his place to your store."

She flapped a hand at me before disappearing into the back room. She emerged moments later with a mug filled with coffee. *Goddess*. "Hey, I told you I wanted to see you in the skirt."

I took an enormous sip. "I'm not even hungover. I feel . . ." A rush of air erupted from my lips.

"Amazing?"

"Kinda?" I pressed a hand to my forehead. "He's such a good

guy. A dreamy guy. Fuck, *who am I?* I've never called anyone dreamy. And I made up with my grandmother *and* I'm writing jokes I actually like."

She tapped her fingers against the counter, eyes drifting over my rumpled outfit. "How old are you?"

"I'll be twenty-nine in a few weeks."

"Thought so." She reached into her desk drawer and pulled out a little pamphlet. The cover was embossed with a ringed planet in indigo ink. "You're in your Saturn return—Saturn's passed through all twelve constellations and is now in the same position as when you were born." She twirled her fingers around in a circle. "It's a rebirth of sorts—painful, beautiful, and necessary. Everything has to fall apart so it can come together again. You're ready to be the best version of yourself."

I stared at her in awe. How many times was this woman going to pull out some sort of magic prop to wow me? Was I being *Touched by an Angel*'ed?

I slid the pamphlet off the counter and into my hands. It was a calling card of sorts, with the shop's name and address printed on the bottom. The front page read: *Spirituality & The Sky—Saturn Return*.

I was laughing again. I'd never believed in anything, really. Not true love. Not fate. Not stars. And yet, here I was. I looked up at her. "I guess I'm returning."

"Mmmhmm." She'd somehow produced two plastic flutes of bubbling wine. "We deserve champagne before ten."

I took the glass from her, my fingers trembling around the stem. "Returning's a good thing?"

She considered this deeply as she eased up onto her stool, fiddling with a long gold necklace around her neck. "It's a hard thing. An ego death. You have to put aside who you planned to be and become who you're supposed to be. It requires submission." Her lips flickered into a smile. "Which I have a feeling you aren't a fan of."

"No, I'm not." I took a hasty sip. "I'm stubborn and I hate asking for help. If someone says *go left*, all I want to do is go right. Suddenly, *right* is the greatest place on earth."

Meghan considered this, taking a protracted sip of champagne. "But if you go right long enough, don't you end up left?"

"Holy *shit*."

She clinked her glass against mine. "To Saturn."

SUNDAY MORNING Sam met me at the dog beach with DJ and a cooler stocked with drinks, snacks, and a bottle of formula. We set up our chairs in the low tide and slathered on SPF as I filled her in on everything. Not just what happened between Eddie and me on Friday night—but what had really happened ten years ago.

"I can't believe you guys did it on a desk." She pressed a hand to her chest. "After all these years."

I handed her a can of rosé. "I can't believe it, either."

She threw back her head and let out a deep groan of frustration. "God, what I wouldn't give!"

DJ clutched my knees with his tiny little Mike and Ike fingers, staring at his mother with a big, drooling grin and googly-eyed fascination.

"You hear that?" I plucked him up off the sand and held him to my chest. "Mommy wants Daddy to rail her."

"Rail. Bang. Blast. Whatever it is that a person does on top of a desk." She let out an earsplitting gasp and grabbed my arm. "Did he go down on you?"

"Jesus, Sam. Since when are you so pornographic?" I held DJ up as he kicked his little feet violently in the air, nailing me in the boob a few times. "I don't remember—everything happened so, so fast."

"I am *really* into you two. The way he looks at you?" She shimmied her shoulders. "Shivers through my vulva."

"Is this another side effect of lactating?"

"I just love seeing you experience romance." Sam tightened her grip on my arm and began swinging her head back and forth to the rhythm of her words. "Big, ugly waves of feeling that just sweep you away. The kind of love that's like eating chocolate cake with your hands. None of that cool guy cold-shoulder stuff."

I pulled my sunglasses out of DJ's moist titanium grip. "You're already planning our wedding, aren't you?"

"Well, you're not just sleeping together, are you?" She looked *so* disappointed.

"I don't know," I admitted. "I'm supposed to go back to New York—that was always the plan."

Sam frowned into her can. "I keep forgetting you're gonna leave me again."

She gave my arm another squeeze before dusting some sand off DJ's chin. His little legs had collected sand in their chubby folds, and I had to physically keep myself from putting one of his chunky thighs in my mouth. I lifted him off my lap and held him high until he squealed and kicked.

"I definitely do not want to leave you, you gorgeous little sausage roll," I assured him.

Sam caught some drool tumbling from his bottom lip before it could hit me in the mouth.

I DIDN'T expect to hear from Eddie until Monday, so when he texted me Sunday night, I was filled with immediate girlish joy that manifested as a little giggle-squeal noise. Nan looked at me like I'd just announced my undying devotion to the Catholic Church.

Just dropped off Valerie. Can we have dinner?

With a few small gestures, he'd managed to make his intentions crystal clear. Eddie wasn't messing around; Eddie didn't mess around.

Unlike Ingram and every other guy I'd become entangled with, he seemed forthcoming and generous with his attention—his time was divided and precious, and I loved that he wanted to spend it with me.

I wrote back immediately: Definitely, can I bring anything?

I was in the bathroom, sculpting my bangs to perfection with a round brush, when my phone dinged again. Come outside.

I applied a sticky coat of lip gloss before grabbing my purse and storming down the steps.

Alfonzo was leaning against Eddie's car talking to him through the window. As I approached the car, Alfonzo stepped aside—greeting me with a "Where *you* goin'?"—but I was focused on Eddie.

I was coming to terms with the fact that maybe Eddie had always taken my breath away, but today he looked particularly incredible with his curls shining in the sunset, a short-sleeved button-down clinging to the curvature of his biceps. His sunglasses were down on the tip of his nose and his honey gaze dripped over me.

"Hey, baby," he called out, tone sarcastic. *Fucking Eddie*. It took a special type of man to be able to pull off a *baby* this early on. He shook hands with Alfonzo as I rounded the car and climbed into the passenger seat. The Honda was also all dressed up; the back seat had been vacuumed and cleared of all the random junk. There was a half-empty bottle still resting in the car seat.

"You look incredible," he said, pulling his sunglasses down further to get a good look at me. "I like those jeans."

"Oh, thanks." I smoothed a hand over my waist. "Nice button-up, I like your palm fronds."

"Oh yeah?" He smirked, casting his gaze down his own chest. "They're not too pretty for me?"

"I hate to break it to you . . ." I reached over and picked a piece of thread off his shoulder. "But you are very pretty."

He sucked his teeth, shaking his head in faux disapproval. "Val's got me losing my edge."

I picked up a stuffed ladybug sitting in the cup holder between us. "You're about as edgy as this toy." I squeezed the toy, expecting it to make a squeak noise before I remembered that babies aren't dogs.

He threw the car into drive and pulled out onto the street. "How was your Saturday?"

"Very Evergreen," I said, clicking my seat belt into place. "Nan and I went to the drive-in in Delsy on Saturday night, then Sam and I brought the baby to the beach this morning." I was already smiling in that effortless, light way.

Eddie returned my look of easy happiness. "Annie loves that movie theater."

"The way she talks about their tea selection, you'd think she had personally invested. We did a double feature—*Moonstruck* and *Burlesque*. We were the only people there so it was a sort of dealer's choice situation."

"I've never seen either."

"You've *never* seen *Moonstruck*? Who *are* you?" I gripped my wrist in melodramatic agony and shook my limp hand at the sky. "*Johnny has his hand, Johnny has his bride!*"

"What the fuck happens in this movie? Isn't it a romantic comedy?" He was laughing, watching me with a mixture of what I decided was jealousy and awe. "Real quick—I, um, got you some-thing. Can you reach into the back seat?"

"You got me something?" My voice came out small and soft even though I was still clutching my wrist, in character.

Eddie tossed his head toward the seat behind me. "Under the jacket. Can you grab it?" I reached back and pushed a navy-blue raincoat aside to reveal a single Stargazer lily wrapped in cello-phane. "I saw it and I thought you probably like lilies," he said. "Because they're nontraditional. Is that corny? I hope not."

"Not at all," I said. *He really meant it.* This wasn't going to be like last time. With the lily between my fingers, I leaned over, pressing my lips to his cheek and savoring the sensation of his smooth, warm skin against my lips. "Thank you, Eddie." I buried my nose in the flower as he made a left onto a wide, unfamiliar street. "Where are we headed?"

"I wanted to take you somewhere I should've taken you about ten years ago."

"Oh yeah?" I laughed. "Are we going to see Evanescence live at the TLA?"

"Oh God, no. We are . . ." He made another turn, this time up a short gravel driveway. He pulled up behind a Cadillac, next to some pristinely cared for hydrangeas. "Going to hang out with my family."

I froze. "Your family?"

EDDIE SLIPPED his fingers through mine and led me around the side of the house to a screen door. Before pulling it open, he turned to face me, rubbing the side of his neck. "So, one thing real quick—"

I lifted my eyebrows. "Uh oh."

"I may need to call you my girlfriend." He ripped his hand away from his neck, extending it toward me in a *before you freak* motion. "And that's just because my mom is very protective of Valerie. She's always ten steps down the road, worrying about how everyone's going to react. We do not have to—you know, whatever—unless you want to . . . you know."

I watched him fret nervously, rocking back and forth on his feet. "I promise I won't start shrieking if you choose to use the g-word."

He breathed a sigh of relief as he pressed his thumb into the lock on the door and pushed it open, waving for me to go ahead. "Perfect. Thank you, Del."

I skimmed my hands over his waist as I passed by. "And don't worry, I'll slip in that we *are* using protection and that my uterus *is* hostile."

He eyed me, anxiety pulling at his gaze. "I know you're kidding, but I feel like I have to say—please, do not do that."

I leaned up on my toes, pressing my lips gently to his. "Okay, I won't."

The Rodriguez home was a cozy and cluttered beach rancher filled with eclectic paintings of Caribbean cityscapes and modern furniture made of perfectly shined glass and brass. The air was thick with the starchy, sweet smell of freshly made rice, cooking in a large pot in the center of the stove. Beside the simmering, steaming pot, the fridge was plastered with photos and magnets, so copious I couldn't make out the color of its finish.

The best part was the enormous framed JCPenney portrait of Lani, Eddie, and his sisters mounted between the landline and an archway that led into a brightly lit dining room. In the portrait, teenage Yari and Eddie sat back to back on a cube, a baby-faced Mell lying across the floor. Lani was behind them, arms draped over her kids. I took a step closer to the picture, staring into young Eddie's eyes. I could tell by his braids that this portrait was taken our senior year, when he'd briefly gone for a young Omarion look.

Eddie slid his arms around my waist, bringing his mouth close to my neck. "Admiring my outfit?" he murmured against my temple, pressing his lips into my hairline.

I hooked my fingers in his, leaning back into the warmth of his chest. "No one wears an oversize polo quite like you."

"What about my earring? Miss it?"

I made a low humming noise in the back of my throat, shimmying my derriere into his crotch. "*No one* wears a diamond stud like you."

"Hello?" A woman's voice came from behind the door next to the refrigerator, causing me to gasp and fling myself away from Eddie's chest.

"Calm down." He chuckled, pulling the door open to reveal a flustered Lani standing at the top of the basement steps, holding a gallon milk jug filled with . . . *sand?*

"You should send a text message before you break into my home," she chastised Eddie, glaring up at him. "You scared the crap out of me."

"Let me just—" He lifted the jug easily out of her arms. "Sorry about that, Mom. I was in a rush."

Lani still looked amazing, like a burst of sunshine—just as I remembered her. Her hair was slicked back into a ponytail, slightly gray at her temples, and her lips were still perfectly glossed. She was shorter than me, but not by much, and I noticed an engagement ring glittering on her left hand. She pointed at the jug with a manicured pinky finger as she slipped an apron over her head. "I ran out of the good garlic, so I had to finish with the dried stuff from Egan's market. If people complain about the taste, you tell them that's why."

"Thank you." He leaned forward and pressed his lips to her forehead. "No one will notice, I swear." Eddie turned back toward me, holding up the jug. "Our secret spice blend. *This* is why our chicken wings smell so good. Mom, do you remember Del? We went to high school together."

Lani smiled at me, all the annoyance evaporating from her face, as she closed the door behind her. "Of course I do. I see your grandmother at church all the time. How are you, sweetie? I'd hug you but I smell like paprika."

She remembers me. Warmth fanned in my chest, spreading through me. "I'm great, Miss Rodriguez. Your home is beautiful." I lifted my hands toward the jug. "And I'm a huge fan of the way your spices smell."

"Thanks, dear." She tapped Eddie gently on his hip, flicking her wrists and signaling for him to *move, please.* "Are you two staying for dinner?"

Before Eddie could reply, the front door banged open, and a voice reached us from the other room. "*I'm home!*"

A petite woman with a long swish of dark hair and wearing purple scrubs rounded the corner. She had Eddie's articulated, striking features, but downsized to fit on her small heart-shaped face.

"Mami, your car has a scratch," she announced, tossing a stack of mail onto the table. "I thought you were going to take it to the dealership to get that buffed out?"

"Mell, we have a guest." There was a tightness in Lani's voice—slight, but still a tonal shift I recognized immediately as the distinct, private way two women nonverbally communicated important information. Mell's eyes immediately flicked up to mine.

"Hi," I said, giving her a small wave. Eddie had crossed the room and was now pawing through the mail. "I'm Del—we went to high school together; I was a few years ahead."

"Oh yeah. Delfina Silva-Miller." She grinned and took a seat at the dining room table, pulling her hair into a low bun. "Great to see you." She looked up at Eddie, already moving on. I don't know why I'd thought my presence would be more shocking—he had made it seem like bringing a girl home was crossing a very specific line. "Where's my baby?"

"Back at her mom's," he mumbled, tearing open an envelope. "She's going to Sesame Place tomorrow."

"And she didn't invite you to go along?" Mell's voice had taken on a defensive edge, a well-honed knife.

He flashed a look of vague irritability down his nose at her. "I couldn't have gone anyway. I have to work tomorrow night."

Lani let out a harrumph in the back of her throat as she dropped freshly chopped onion and a palmful of garlic into a pan of sizzling oil. "Maybe I could have gone. Is she at least going to take pictures?"

"If I'd known before yesterday, I would have told you," Eddie pointed out, tucking the envelope into his back pocket.

"Wait." Mell held up a finger. "She didn't even tell you she was planning on crossing state lines with your child until yesterday?"

"Melosa, *basta*," Lani called from the kitchen, peering at her through the archway.

"Just saying," she grumbled, tossing him a loaded look.

"Your head," Eddie said, cupping his hands around her head while maintaining a fraction of distance, "is like a grape."

She smacked his wrist. "Shut *up*. Your head is like a *watermelon*. A big, huge—"

There was another bang but this time, the back door flew open. If I hadn't been previously familiar with Yari Rodriguez's legendary beauty, I would have thought a very flustered Adriana Lima had just blown into the kitchen. "Eddie, you parked like shit."

"Yari," Lani warned without looking up as she cubed a potato directly into the pan. "Language."

I took a step back, leaning against the archway, out of the line of fire as Yari charged past me in a cloud of perfume, to the tune of espadrilles clonking on the tile floor.

I watched as she snatched an envelope from Eddie's hands with enough violence to take a finger along with it. "That's my Nordstrom's bill—don't look."

"Why would I look?" Eddie flashed me a dry smile, mischief winking in the corners of his dark eyes. "We already know you're in debt."

Movies and TV always got it wrong; they made siblings overly affectionate, parents moronic and out of touch, children too precocious. *This*, I thought, *is what being a family is like*. It was arguing without any ill will; it was lunging like a python without dispensing any venom; it was lancing close to the jugular and pulling back at the last nanosecond, kissing your victim on the forehead as you slipped away. I was witty, sure, but *this*—this was an art form I wasn't sure I had the training for.

"Aye." Mell cut them off with a firm snap of her fingers. "Yari, are you gonna say hi to our guest?"

Yari flipped her head in my direction, then back to Eddie, then back again with her freshly threaded eyebrows pulled into a gorgeous furrow. "I know you. Vanessa, right?"

"So close," I replied. "Del. We went to high school together—you probably don't remember—"

"Oh my God." She grabbed hold of my arm with a firm—and shockingly clammy—grip. "*Yes,* you were in Eddie's little band, right? You had the long braid."

"Well, I wasn't technically in the band." I made pointed eye contact with Eddie, strong enough that he retreated into the kitchen.

"Eddie refused to let me join, actually. Something about my voice not being 'rock enough.'" I hit *rock enough* with heavy air quotes.

"I'm in a different room. I can't hear you," he yelled back, sipping from a wooden spoon Lani held up to his mouth. He smacked his lips thoughtfully. "More pepper."

I rolled my eyes, giving Yari and Mell one of the underhanded looks I'd seen Nan wield expertly before. "He was totally jealous."

"I was! I admitted it!" Eddie was back, struggling to tie a red apron trimmed with pink lace around his waist. "I already told you that."

And then he did something magical. Maybe not magical to someone else—someone who grew up in a big, loud family where public displays of affection were frequent.

But to me it was the loveliest sensation I'd ever experienced: he pressed his lips to my temple.

"Didn't I already apologize?" he asked, giving up his attempt to tie himself into the apron and offering his back to Mell.

But I couldn't say anything. My face was rapidly warming, sizzling. I was still *uhm*-ing and *uhh*-ing, but again: the Rodriguez siblings had already moved on.

"What does Valerie want for Christmas?"

"Season tickets to the Flyers," Eddie said, disappearing and reappearing with a pot of perfectly fluffed rice. "Move your mail, Mell. Yari, can you get some plates?"

"You could say please," she huffed, kicking off her shoes and strutting over to a curio cabinet in the corner of the room. "Guest plates or family plates?"

"Hot dish!" Lani shouted, bustling into the room. "Everyone, move! Hot dish!"

"Family," Eddie replied, pressing a hand into my lower back. "Can you help me get the silverware?"

I swallowed against what felt like a beam of sunshine pressing into the back of my teeth, threatening to shoot out of my mouth if I smiled any harder.

"I CAN'T believe none of my grandbabies are here," Lani lamented as she tapped a spoonful of rice onto her plate.

Eddie, Mell, and Yari let out a shudder of aggravated commentary, exchanging looks containing eons of annoyance.

"What about *your* babies? Aren't you happy we're here?" Mell asked, sipping expectantly at her glass of wine.

"Of course I'm happy you're all here. I just wish Del could have met everyone." Lani used this as her segue to pass me the bowl of vegetarian guisada.

"Thanks," I said breathlessly—like she was the Rodriguez sweeping me off my feet.

Yari made a little half-snort, half-click noise as she turned her heavy-lidded eyes to Eddie in a sardonic flutter. "How would *she* feel about that?"

"Can you not? God." Eddie wiped his mouth with a napkin. "I'm not trying to have heartburn until after I'm done eating."

"Is Yari wrong?" Mell pressed.

"Not the point," Eddie fired back.

"So," I said, slipping my hand under the table and feeling around until I found Eddie's. "Mell, you're a nurse?"

"Yeah, I do injections," she explained. "I call it flotation-device installation. Wait, actually—" She lifted her fork, pointing it somewhere between my nose and neck, her deep-set eyes zeroing in on me like I was some sort of freshly discovered macrobiotic specimen. "You should come in for your next touch-up."

"Touch-up?" I brought my fingers to my lips.

"They're her real lips, idiot."

"Really? Huh." Mell was grinning. "*Fascinating*."

The rest of the meal passed in an effervescent blur. I kept my fingers laced with Eddie's, and every time I heard the annoyance in his voice, pulling his tone out of that dry lilt that lived in the back of his throat, I squeezed his fingers till he squeezed back.

Eddie wasn't the baby, but Mell and Yari loved him with a fierceness that indicated to me that, at one point, he must have really needed them. Probably more than he'd let on, but they'd known well enough to rally. They were his emotional bodyguards. It was the persistence in their voices that made my heart ache with both fullness and jealousy. Nan had done a really good job trying to fill all the roles in my life——Mom, Dad, sister, math tutor, swim coach——but it was impossible to re-create *this* with just one person.

Eventually, the baby mother talk ended with Mell shaking her head and muttering, "It's her world, we're just living in it."

"*Mmmmm*," Lani murmured, forgetting her own warning. Then, she looked right at me. "I was always very nice to her; I don't know why she has to act like this. Welcomed her into our home with no problem."

"Can we talk about something, *anything*, else?" Eddie sang. His voice was ragged from hours of defensive sparring. Our plates had been cleared, and Yari made each of us an espresso; I kept my hand tucked in Eddie's as we drank.

"Sorry. Of course," Lani said, pushing a plate of almond cookies toward Eddie. Her peace offering. "Let's talk about you, Del." She turned to me, resting her head in her hands. "Do you want to give me any grandbabies?"

WE DROVE back toward downtown Evergreen in silence. Eddie kept one hand glued to his jaw, rubbing it back and forth until his clean-shaven chin was red. I kept my eyes mostly fixed ahead on the road, twirling my lily between my fingers. As far as first dates went, this was leaps and bounds away from anything *awkward* or *bad* I'd previously experienced.

As he turned up the block toward The Billiards I reached over, resting my hand on his forearm. The darkness in his mood and features had done little to tamper the buzzing inside me. His skin was warm and soft under my fingers, the newness of being able to touch him so freely like a bubbling sip of prosecco in my belly. I wanted to pull his hand away from his jaw and press my lips to his chin.

"You okay?" I asked.

He cleared his throat, shifting in his seat as he pulled around the brick building into a parking spot. I'd never been around the back of The Billiards before. There were two industrial-size dumpsters and a set of steps that led to a deck and a door. "Yeah, sorry. I just pictured that going differently."

"Eddie." I laughed, shaking my head. "Are you nuts? My dad is a former raging alcoholic. My mom is dead. My grandmother is lovely, bless her, but objectively weird as hell." I gave him a soft look, offering him my lily. "I dreamed of having a family like yours my entire life. Tonight was perfect."

He reached over and ran his thumb over the curve of the lily's petal, skimming his fingers down its powdery white flesh to my wrist, then over to my cheek. He drew a heavy, warm line from my earlobe to my bottom lip. Everything inside me turned warm and liquid at the feeling of his thumb against the corner of my mouth, instantly bringing back memories of the other night. I leaned my head back against the headrest, eyelids heavy with desire.

"I probably don't deserve you," he said slowly, building the sentence one word at a time, his voice raspy. "And I am sorry I waited ten years to take you to my mom's house."

"Because ten years ago they wouldn't have embarrassed you?" I turned my face into the open palm of his hand—rough and calloused. It was a dangerous game for us to play—I Should Have, I Could Have: Ten Years Ago Edition. There were a million ways we could rewrite our story, filling it with *if only*'s. But why?

There was only one regret I had held on to from ten years ago. I wasn't going to let the opportunity fly by me now. No matter what happened with Brainwave and whatever our emotional damage, I knew I was different from ten years ago. I was confident, sure of myself, and categorically brave. I was messy and complicated, but so was everything else.

I pressed my lips into his hand and finished the conversation he had started ten years ago. "They *love* you," I reminded him. "And I *love* you."

Eddie did not say *I love you* back. But he didn't need to. Instead, he wove his fingers into my hair and pulled me into a hungry kiss. With his other hand, he undid my seat belt and looped his arm around my waist.

He pressed his nose into my hair and said something about vanilla and bananas that made me laugh. Before we totally lost our minds, I forced him to take me up to his place.

Eddie's apartment was not the mecca of single-dad-dom that I had anticipated. There was no black leather couch with cup holders and USB charging ports, no visible George Foreman Grill, and no katana mounted over the TV. His place was fastidiously decorated—tidy beyond comprehension. It was a small but airy apartment, a living room followed directly by a kitchen. He had no table or chairs—just an island with a high chair pulled up to it.

Eddie did have a frightening amount of conch shell–based art. But I didn't have enough time to think about whether or not that was a red flag, if I had somehow fallen in love with a conch-collecting freak.

Before I could fully unpack that realization, he was backing me up against the couch, guiding me with his mouth against my chest and firm hands on my hips.

27

It was the night after the Class of 2009's graduation, and we were officially seniors. We'd taken the SATs; we'd passed our driving tests (well, most of us had—Jake was working on it); we were one year away from solid ground and *freedom*, and there was enough electricity in the air that we were liable to start a fire.

What was there to do but get drunk in the woods behind Dani's house?

"Fuck Sean," Sam slurred, taking a two-handed gulp from a Disney mug filled with red wine and Hawaiian Punch. All I could think about was how gnarly her barf was going to look. I took a sip of Genesee. The beer was hot and flat—more piss-like than usual.

The night had started off like every other party, all excitement and energy and possibility. It was easy to get swept up in the moment, but nights like this had a way of quickly turning rancid for me. A comment overheard, a look I wasn't supposed to see, a murmur shared when I was just out of earshot—nights like these had a way of highlighting my unspoken status as *side character*.

All around me the girls nodded along in solidarity, echoing Sam's newly proclaimed anti-Sean stance. I felt the white-hot grip of jealousy take hold of my gut. *Sam's my best friend.* Unlike everyone else, I didn't have a boyfriend or even a crush. I didn't have anyone to text late at night or divulge my secrets to. It was Sam or Nan, end of list.

I instinctively grabbed her hand, lacing my fingers with hers. "Total prick," I said, giving her a squeeze. She gave me a wet-eyed, drunken smile.

"Sleazeball!" Dani screamed, throwing the contents of her red Solo cup directly into the air. We all recoiled as the liquid came sailing down. It smelled like gin and Mountain Dew.

"Jesus, Dan, shut *up.*"

"My shirt!" someone moaned.

"*Ugh.*" I dropped Sam's hand and wiped some sticky droplet-shrapnel off my face.

"*Oooooh* my God," Rachel mewed while holding up her smartphone. She was the only one in the group who had one *with* internet. "Sean just tweeted that 'the bois' are by the pier near Eighty-Third Avenue. We should totally crash their party."

The group immediately erupted into a chorus of bone-chillingly gleeful shrieks, Sam included. She was on her feet, grabbing her purse. "Let's go!"

"Wait," I called out, scrambling up off the log I'd been sitting on. "Didn't we all just agree Sean sucks?"

Everyone ignored me for the most part. Sam turned to me with glassy and wild eyes. "Yeah, but it'll be *so* badass. I'll walk right up to him and be like, *hey you, fuck you!*"

"Yeah!" Dani shrieked again. "And I'll run up to Eddie and be like, *in your dreams, boner boy.*"

My skin prickled at the sound of his name. After prom, Eddie and I had slowly started to become something like friends again. We even sat next to each other in English class. But tonight, everything felt flammable, fragile. I didn't want to see him when I felt like this, at a moment when leaving this thicket of evergreen trees felt distinctly like a bad idea. I was sober and clear-headed; I knew I was. But I was alone in that. I couldn't cop out. I had to do what side characters did.

"I'll drive," I yelled loud enough to break through everyone's screaming and chanting. "Give me your keys, Sam." She listened, immediately handing over the key to her dad's Toyota SUV.

I PARKED by the last pier on the boardwalk, the one right before the dunes and across from the diner. As soon as the car came to a stop, the girls were undoing their seat belts, ready to bolt toward the sand with their shoes in hand, straight across the planks and down the wooden steps that led to the shoreline.

The car emptied, except for Sam and me. She looked my way. "You okay, sister girl?"

I tried my best to smile. "I'm perfect."

The guys were standing around a dwindling bonfire, passing around a bottle of Colt 45. I didn't recognize any of them except Sean and Eddie, but the rest of the girls had already interrupted their fun with shouting and screaming. Dani had found herself someone to make out with—he had both his hands down the back of her pants. I could feel Eddie's eyes on me, like he wanted to talk, but I didn't look his way.

Even Sam ran off, leaving me to awkwardly kick at the sand and idle by the fire.

"Hey, fuck you," she slurred at Sean, grinning like she'd just told the world's funniest joke. He rolled his eyes and pulled her into a headlock, bending her backward over his thigh and kissing her cheek. That's when I noticed *him* staring at me—some guy in a Steelers hat with a full mustache. The source of all the beer, no doubt. He definitely was not in high school. I tried to avoid his eyes, but they were glued to me. I stuck out my hands, warming them against the fire. He was creeping closer, one sloping step at a time.

"You with the girls?"

"Yep."

"What, they make you their driver?"

"No, I offered."

"You want some?" He tilted the bottle of Colt 45 toward me—it had a single, hot sip left in it. I shook my head. "Aw, come on—just have some."

"I just told you I'm driving."

"They wanna have all the fun and leave you to take care of 'em."

"I don't mind." I bristled. My eyes flicked up and caught Eddie's. His jaw was tight. He narrowed his gaze at me before turning away slowly, back toward his conversation. My chest hurt.

"Looks like everyone's got someone but you and me."

I stiffened, focusing all my attention on one of the glowing pieces of birchwood at the center of the fire. "I should go get my jacket from the car."

"I can keep you warm." I could smell his beer breath as he took a lazy step closer to me. *Disgusting*.

"No, thank you." I turned to leave, but he was fast. He took a big step in front of me, and I froze.

"Aw, come on. You're too sexy to be alone."

"I'm sixteen." I don't know why I said that. I wasn't. I was seventeen. I was one of the oldest in my class, but for some reason it just came to me.

He instantly backed away. "No way."

I glared at him. "Yeah. I'm sixteen. Why would I lie? We're all in high school."

"*Shit.*" He laughed, disgust thick as his lazy tongue worked around the word. He ran a hand over his mustache. "I thought you were at least twenty. What the hell are you gonna look like when you *are* twenty?" He sucked his teeth before turning away and shooting a slick, quick ball of spit into the sand. "You're not even that cute. Just another cocktease, big girl."

Before I even had time to verbally eviscerate him, a fist came out of nowhere, crashing into his jaw and sending him stumbling backward.

I gasped, hands flying to my mouth.

Eddie.

"You fucking motherfucker! *Jesus,*" the guy crowed, clutching his face. "Are you *kidding* me?"

The whole crowd went silent as the two scrambled toward each other. The guy swung and called Eddie a slur, but Eddie ducked and fired back. The guy swung again, and this time his knuckles clipped Eddie's brow.

"*Stop,*" I yelled. They ignored me so I rushed forward. "Ed, stop. *Stop!*" I grabbed him by the back of his T-shirt. Inertia was on my side and I was able to easily pull him away. Eddie's hand flew to my wrist, and he held on to me.

"Stop. Please," I begged. His grip on me tightened. *Am I crying?* If I was, it was an accident.

His eyebrow was bleeding. I lifted a trembling hand to wipe the blood away from his eye. His fingers flexed around my wrist. It must have hurt. The other guy was carted away by Sean and maybe Wiley, while everyone else just stood there. Staring at us.

I let go of his shirt. I felt the blood between my fingers. *I knew it. I knew it. I knew something bad was going to happen tonight.*

Legs shaking, I started to walk away.

"Move," I instructed Rachel. And she did.

"Del," Sam yelled after me.

At the sound of my name, I started running, away from the group and away from the car. The sand fought back, but I pumped my arms and pushed as hard as I could, my breath coming in horrible, ragged drags. Humiliation burned in my throat. I wanted to die.

"*Delfina.*" I heard him behind me as I reached the dunes. I'd never been to this part of the beach before. I scrambled over them and almost tumbled down the other side. Finally, I landed back on solid ground, back on my feet, doubled over and panting.

"*Go away.*" I was almost too tired to keep running, but I forced myself. I had to get home. I had to get away.

"Del, *wait.*" He was catching up with me. "*Wait.*" He sounded so desperate that I listened. Eddie skid to a stop behind me, our bodies almost crashing into each other.

"Whatever you're going to say, I don't want to hear it. I don't care. I don't care about you or him or anyone—"

"That guy is a *fucking* asshole. Will you just stop and listen to me?"

"Listen to you say what? I'm not gonna thank you," I yelled, but my voice didn't come out as strong as I wanted it to. I sounded like I was going to cry again.

Eddie shook his head hard. "I don't want that!"

"Then what do you want? What do you ever *fucking* want from me?"

"Can you just listen for once?" he yelled back. Then, softer: "I think you're beautiful."

I wasn't sure how I was supposed to react, but his words hit me with force, crushing and immobilizing me. "What I look like and what *he* said have nothing to do with each other."

"That's not what I'm saying." Eddie pushed a hand through his hair and tugged. His head must have been killing him because the motion made him wince. "I just mean . . . I think about how beautiful you are." He swallowed roughly. "You asked me what I think about when I think about you and the thing I think about is how beautiful you are."

My ears were ringing. "That was months ago."

"Yeah, I know," he continued. "I know I fucked up a-and I didn't know what to say back then, but I know now and I . . . I like you, Del."

"Why are you telling me this now?" I demanded, taking a step closer to him. I felt crazed, insane. "Why are you telling me this here?"

"I-I don't know."

"Are you *embarrassed* by me?"

"What? No!"

"Then why like *this*?" I didn't know what to say—I didn't know how to tell him any other way than to just say it. I let go of a breath and the words rushed out along with it. "You couldn't even say hi to me earlier and now you're doing this? You've never asked me to be your date to a dance. Or asked me out. You date Rachel. You date Dani. You bring them flowers a-and hold their hands. You bring them home to meet your sisters—your *mom*." I sucked down a freezing rush of air. "But you can't even tell me I'm beautiful?"

He was trying to say something, chest rising and falling as he licked his lips. "Because they're not like you. With them, I just pretend or something. It's easy t-to act. I can't pretend with you. You . . . you scare me."

My anger dimmed then extinguished, Eddie's words like wet fingers to a flame. "You scare me, too," I whispered.

"Yeah?" He sounded hopeful, soft.

Nodding, I used my sleeve to wipe my nose. "Promise you're not lying?"

"Promise." He took a step toward me in the dark, his lips pale with cold. A single curl was trapped in the blood, rapidly drying, on his brow.

I reached out and brought a trembling finger to his forehead, liberating the strands of hair. "He hurt you."

"I don't care."

"I'm sorry for tonight, for everything, for existing—"

"Shut up, okay?" he whispered, bringing his hand to mine, interlocking our fingers, and drawing me to him. "And please, don't run away again."

OUR FRIENDS took turns leaving town, going on lush family vacations to Jamaica and Mexico or sleepaway camp in the Poconos. Evergreen filled up with vacationers, and Eddie and I were left behind, alone together. No one to catch us; no one to observe us.

We started a new tradition. After dinner, I'd sit on our balcony with my iPod, watching day-trippers lug their equipment back toward their cars, sunburned and spent. Anticipation thrummed through my body, to the beat of whatever song I'd put on. Sometimes I put on *our* song—*the* song. The lyrics made sense to me now.

> *Hangin' round downtown by myself and I had too much caffeine.*

As the sun began to set, my pulse would quicken. The air would change, the stars turned on. Then, he'd appear on his bike, heading down the planks toward me.

> *Mama, this surely is a dream.*

I'd hop down from the balcony, he'd lock up his bike. Then, he'd say something perfect like, *hey, you.*

Every night we found the courage to press against the barriers that had always existed between us, and every night, I found something that made me feel like any other way of living would never, ever be enough. Eddie became real to me. I knew how he laughed when he really thought I'd said something funny, what hurt him and how deeply.

I memorized the feeling of our knees pressing together when we sat on the guardrails and watched the waves, the sweet smell of his sweat, the weight of his hand when it fell into mine. I replayed his words, again and again. *You scare me.* I'd close my eyes and feel my body reacting to Eddie—every molecule calling out for more of him.

Daytime passed in lumbering anticipation. Chores and sunbathing and long showers, imagining what might happen between us. How quickly would we find the courage to let our knuckles graze, our eyes linger?

When the sky went from tangerine to inky black and the ocean whispered against our bare feet, something eased between us and we talked about everything. At night, we were just two voices, our bodies unobservable and therefore free from humiliation, error. That's when he'd grab my wrist, tug me back, pull me to his chest. I'd find the courage to slide my hands up his back, to hold on tight.

We told each other everything. Sometimes, he'd bring a single, hot beer and we'd sit on top of the dunes passing it back and forth, trading questions. His mom had started dating again, and he'd been struggling—anxious in a way that startled me.

Eddie told me how he was suddenly afraid of crowds, of the old rickety boardwalk rides, of one of his sisters going missing or getting in a car accident. Sleep was the hardest, because it meant not being there if Mell or Yari needed something, so instead he'd just walk around Evergreen until the bakeries and coffee shops opened, a death grip on his cell phone in case it rang.

One night, I told him about my mom.

I never talked about her; it felt like a direct betrayal of Nan. Unlike Roger, a ghost on the fringes of my life, her passing didn't feel like *my* loss. I knew Nan missed her, because we couldn't talk about her. Every time I tried, she'd wave a hand over her face and say something like, "Not today. I have places to go."

I wanted to feel something more for my mom—anything. I wanted to know Nan's pain. I wanted to know what happened.

That was why I went looking, tearing through Nan's drawers when she wasn't home, pilfering her dresser. I found a bunch of old documents in a bin at the back of the hall closet. There, in a water-stained manila folder, was my mom's paperwork from her last stay at a rehab facility in Georgia.

They described her as *an active participant* in group therapy, *funny and engaging*, but *prone to unprompted emotional outbursts*. In her exit interview, the clinician noted Michelle was most excited about *working toward living in an apartment with her daughter (Delfina, 5)*. Under Reason(s) for Stay, they'd written *court-ordered drug rehabilitation* and *parenting classes*.

I'd kept digging in the bin, a desperate hunger for information awoken in me. There were a handful of photos I'd never seen before. Michelle with her big eighties hair and golden-brown tan, smoking on the beach. She was leaning into a man with broad shoulders and a soft stomach. He had a full head of jet-black hair and eyes that sparkled back at me.

Roger.

I threw the picture back into the bin and slammed the closet door shut.

"They looked so in love," I whispered into the air between Eddie and me. "And normal. It was weird. Like if they had just stayed that way, they'd both still be here, and we would be a regular family."

Eddie let me talk until my voice was hoarse, never interrupting. He just picked up handfuls of sand and let it trickle through his fingers onto the tops of my feet until my toes were buried.

Then, we grabbed our shoes and raced back to the jetty near the Bel Sol like we always did.

That night he let me win.

"My DAD wants me to visit him." He was sitting between my legs, reclining into me. His hair was smoothed back into neat braids, flyaways tickling my nose. The sun was rising, and we'd been talking for so long, Eddie could only manage a whisper. "In Puerto Rico."

"Really?" I pressed my chin to the top of his head, fighting back against the heaviness in my eyelids.

Eddie nodded, his thumb lazily tracing the underside of my foot. "For the last two weeks in August. He's getting married."

"Are you gonna go?"

"I have to. I don't think I'll be able to talk much when I'm there."

I pressed my nose to his hair. *Fuck.* "That makes sense."

As if he could feel my terror, my readiness to shrink away, Eddie grabbed ahold of my bare ankles and wrapped my legs around his middle. "Don't get all emo on me, Fina."

I let out a shriek at the sudden, electric contact. "Shut up." I laughed. "I hate when you call me that."

He rolled over in my arms, taking me with him, tumbling us

sideways into the sand, delirious and laughing. I found myself underneath him, breathless, our hips pressed against each other. "We'll spend every night out here until I leave."

"Yeah, yeah," I grunted, adjusting myself underneath his weight. Safe, solid. I could have fallen asleep just like that, letting him watch me through his eyelashes. My breath came in deep, ragged gulps.

He made a small noise in the back of his throat. "You're gonna forget about me, aren't you?"

"Oh yeah, because that's just like me."

"Del." When he said my name, he sang it, a sly smile pulling at his lips. He dug his fingers into my sides. "Promise you won't forget about me."

"*Edgardo,*" I gasped, seizing up underneath him. "If you tickle me, I swear to God, I'll—"

"You'll what?"

"Throw you in the ocean!"

He made another noise in the back of his throat, clicking his tongue against his teeth. "Fine." He bowed his head to meet mine, his lips glancing against the corner of my mouth. "You'd never hurt me anyway, right?" His voice was a growl against my skin.

"Right," I whispered back, drawing my hands up his back. "I promise."

28

Oceanfront Presidential Park Lot #69 (nice)

The following Saturday, while Eddie spent the day with Valerie, I made my way back to Oceanfront. As I pulled into the spot behind Roger's truck in the driveway, I spied him lounging on the porch, sipping a soda, and watching a pair of dueling kites flitting through the sky.

I stepped out of the car and circled it, leaning against the hood. "Hey."

"Hey-oh, kid." He grunted as he stood up from his chair—one of those foldable ones you'd take to a soccer game. "Whatcha doing here?" Roger sounded so happy.

Good question. "Thought I'd pop over and say hi."

"Well." He smacked a hand against the wooden railing. "That's a nice thing to hear."

"Can I . . ." I gestured awkwardly at the chairs on his porch. "Hang out?"

"Of course!" He waved me up onto the narrow porch. "It's hot inside. AC's gone to shit and I'm waiting on some parts from—"

"Jerry Junior?" I interrupted, easing myself down beside him.

He chuckled. "That's him. Here—" He reached into a cooler and pulled out a can of soda. "Sorry, I don't have anything better."

I didn't open the can. I wasn't really a soda person—but Roger didn't know that. I rolled the aluminum cylinder between my fingers. "That's okay, I'll give—uh, Mountain Hydration?—a try." I popped the tab. Roger kept fidgeting next to me, his mouth flexing in and out of a nervous smile, waiting for me to speak.

I took a sip of the soda. "Tastes mountainous."

He laughed softly. "How's your grandmother doing?"

I set the can down between us. "She's okay. We got into a little fight after I saw you last time."

He let out a grunt, wiry eyebrows shooting up above his wraparound sunglasses. "Oh, dang. I'm sorry."

"I didn't know you two talked," I explained, my voice careful and slow. "I thought she and I had a sort of pact"—I gave him a half-hearted look of apology before I continued—"to not talk to you."

"I see."

"I thought that was what she wanted. She's always making these comments about you—about how much I'm like you. And it's *always* negative. I just figured we were firmly Anti-Roger."

His mouth quirked into a smile. "I didn't wanna say it, but you are a little like me. You got my ankles."

"Your ankles?"

He nodded and lifted his jeans to reveal a set of shockingly slender and dainty ankles for such a beefy man. His tendons were articulated, his skin smooth and hairless.

"Oh *God*. I do have your ankles." We both laughed big, loud laughs. I gave my Mountain Hydration another sip. "Do I have anything of Mom's?" I asked this doing my best impression of someone casual.

He let out a rush of air, leaning his head back against the house.

"You're gentle like her. Loving animals and stuff. You still got a worm farm?"

I rolled my eyes. "Unfortunately, no. I wasn't allowed to bring any pets to college."

He let out a cluck of disapproval. "Don't tell me you don't eat dirt anymore, either."

"Oh no, of course I do. That's my trademark."

Roger let out a low, long chuckle that filled me with a weird sense of pride. *Since when did I care about making him laugh?*

The recent downpours had left the air cool but sticky. Luckily, the sun was starting to set, casting the sky in the perfect shade of indigo. Another kite had joined the original pair, slicing past each other elegantly.

"Look at them go," I observed.

Roger nodded with grave appreciation. "Great weather for a kite."

We sipped our Mountain Hydrations in unison.

"I was planning on grilling tonight," he said. "If you want to stay, I know you don't eat meat, but I have some corn from—"

"Jerry Junior?"

"How'd you know?"

I bit back a laugh. "Wild guess."

I AGREED to stay and even helped Roger fire up the grill. It was a small charcoal contraption next to the side of his house. Without the kites, we struggled to fill the space—until I realized Roger was some sort of neighborhood confidant. Then, I forced him to fill me in on all the Presidential Park drama.

Once Roger's hamburgers and my sweet corn were charred to perfection, we sat back on the porch, paper plates balancing on our laps. Jerry Junior's corn was incredible—perfectly sweet and juicy.

The kites returned and we decided they were racing and kept up our chatter by making bets on who would win each round.

"I like that tattoo you got." Roger pointed his pinky in the direction of the little alien head on my forearm. "Bet that's got a story."

"Yeah, my first roommate gave it to me. Her name was Cassandra but she insisted we call her Bleu—" And because it was Roger, I kept going. "She brought a bunch of weed back from Maryland after fall break. We got way too high and decided to try stick and poke."

He snorted. "I know that wasn't a good idea."

"No, it was terrible." I laughed. "I thought she was going to hit a vein and I'd bleed to death."

"Yeesh. I got something like that." He set down his plate and lifted up his T-shirt sleeve to reveal what looked like the haunted remnants of a Rottweiler. "I was zooted to the moon when I got it. Cried my eyes out in the chair like the world's biggest baby. Your mother was sitting across from me laughing her ass off." He let out a little self-conscious chuckle once he saw how hard I was laughing—that I wasn't calling Child Protective Services or writing a scathing diary entry in permanent ink.

I admired the atrocity on his arm before pulling back and giving Roger a long look. His eyes were wide and alert. "You never really talked about Mom at all."

"We were divorced by the time she . . ." I knew he wouldn't say it. He pulled his sleeve down and kept going. "And you'd been living with Annetta for a while, because I was such a freaking loser. Made a real mess, she and I—not you. You're not the mess." He let out a heavy sigh and straightened up, sitting his full height in his chair.

I pressed my lips together in a tight smile. "That's good to know."

He pointed at me. "You're the best Miller by a long shot."

"Really?" I huffed, dropping my eyes to my empty plate. "How low's that bar? I haven't even done anything."

"I mean it, kid." He scratched his arm, eyeing me nervously. "You know, I wasn't supposed to make it this long. Not the way I was living. I feel like this . . . all of this is on borrowed time. I wake up and I can't believe it—I'm a sixty-year-old man. I look down at my body and I think *damn, we made it.* Now you're here, sitting and talking to me . . ." His voice trailed off and he swatted a big hand at the night sky, batting back a mosquito. "Damn skeeters," he whispered, voice thick. I knew he was stopping himself so I didn't see him tear up. "Just grateful for today, you know?"

I quietly picked up his plate and headed back inside, giving him space to collect his emotions. I knew Roger didn't want to cry in front of me—he knew better. He thought there couldn't possibly be any sympathy left in my heart for him.

But he was wrong.

There was a reason I'd wanted to see Roger—why I called him when I needed help. Tucker and Cyrus were right—he was my only dad and, against all odds, he was *still* here.

Sure, Nan's words echoed through my mind. *He's like a forest fire.* I knew it, I knew it better than anyone how deeply Roger could hurt people. But if I still had it in me to forgive him one last time, why not? Blame Eddie—blame Valerie—but I couldn't stop thinking about how hard, how devastating, it would be to be locked into a love as fierce as parenthood when you completely were incapable of loving yourself.

Roger was a shit bag. He'd fucked up, yes. But I'd recently learned about something called nuance and wanted to give it a try.

I dumped my trash in the bin and just as I headed back outside, I spied Roger talking to the woman I'd seen the very first time I'd driven over to Presidential Park. She was holding hands with the same little girl who now pulled at her arm and whined about something I couldn't make out.

Roger reached out, snatched the little girl's cheek between his thumb and index finger. She let out a gleeful shriek, throwing herself forward at his legs.

When I settled back into my chair on the porch, the woman had returned home.

"Who was that?" I asked.

"Rosa." He pointed toward a faded single-wide on one of the shabbier-looking lots. "She's a young thing, always having issues with her plumbing. I help out when I can."

I handed him a can from the cooler. "That's some good karma."

He snorted. "I'm gonna need all I can get."

The sky was dark now and a choir of cicadas sang their same old song. The smell of the bay—briny and clear—filled my nose. I leaned my head back against his house and smiled softly. "I wish you'd lived here when I was a kid."

Roger turned his face toward me, green eyes soft. "I know you do."

For the first time all day I could see the years in his face, the regret etched into every wrinkle that yawned from his tired, sad eyes. He reached over and placed his hand on mine. "But it wouldn't have changed anything, Del."

We waved goodbye as I drove away. Roger stood at the end of his driveway, watching until I turned the corner. I made it past the train tracks before I had to pull over. The tears came slow and heavy. I turned off the car and let myself cry.

29

Sam's House

On the last day of September, when temperatures soared to decade highs and the sky stretched cerulean in every direction, Devon Persaud-Jenkins Junior turned one. The party theme was one-DEER-ful. Can you be-leaf how bad that pun is? Berry upsetting.

I drove with Nan to Sam's house in her Jeep, which she'd adorned with plastic foliage and fruit, as well as the antlers from a Christmas car decal. Without the red nose, the Jeep was perfectly on theme.

I angsted over my outfit, even going as far as buying a satin scarf and a pair of gold hoops from salt & sage. I twisted the floral scarf around my head like a headband that felt chic, pairing it with a simple black dress that skimmed my shins. I sort of looked like a sexy peasant, which, given the ambiguous and woodsy theme, felt right.

Eddie was going to be at the party—with Valerie. A thirty-pound celebrity with saucer-size eyes and a headful of chestnut-brown curls. She was shy and quiet, preferring soft toys and lullabies over cartoons and puzzles. Eddie said she cried easily, which had been hard on him, but now made for the perfect excuse to let her sleep in his bed.

Eddie was a master class in what a dad should be like. I'd always known Roger had failed me in a macro way—but there were millions of micro-failures that lived inside the broad strokes that painted a picture of my life with him, and the more I saw Eddie as a father, the more I thought about Baby Del.

Nan and I arrived to find DJ's wild bash already in full swing. The backyard was decorated with plastic deer and rabbits, streamers hanging from the willow tree. Some older kids were splashing around in the bay, smaller kids toddling from creature to creature. Devon manned the grill while Sam ran after DJ, both wearing deer onesies. A Bluetooth speaker was pumping out such hits as "Row, Row, Row Your Boat."

"I brought fruit!" I grinned as Sam pulled me into a bone-crushing hug.

"Valerie's *here*," she hissed against my ear. "She's *here*."

"I know," I whispered back. "You're crushing the fruit."

I moved through the party with Sam at my heels until I spotted Eddie standing under the willow tree, his back turned to me. He was standing very still, swaying slightly in place, a head of soft curls resting against his shoulder. He'd either heard Sam's strangled breathing or my sandals on the grass, because as I stepped under the shadow of the willow's branches, he turned around.

"Hey, you."

Valerie was fast asleep against his chest, wild curls pushed away from her face, tiny rubber glasses strapped to her head, arms hanging limply around his neck. Everything about her was tiny and precious; if I was her size, I would cry a lot, too.

Holding her, Eddie looked like he'd been lit up from the inside, joy radiating out of his pores, like candlelight through the panels of a lantern.

"Hi," I replied. I was still holding the fruit, so I held out the bowl and said, "I brought fruit."

His eyebrows shot up. "Val loves fruit. You hear that, Val? Del brought fruit."

Eventually Valerie woke up, leaving a pink-tinged drool mark on Eddie's shoulder. She sat quietly in his arms, wide-eyed and smiling. She talked in long, nonsensical sentences that switched word by word from English to Spanish that only Eddie could decipher. When Eddie needed to use the restroom, he handed her to me. For a few brief moments, she sat in my lap, staring up at me in cross-eyed wonderment. Then, she lay her head on my chest and suddenly I was a human fondue pot, a vessel for melted joy. When Eddie came back from the bathroom, I gave him *fuck off* eyes and let him watch as Valerie sucked her thumb and drooled on my cleavage.

She was all Eddie. From the shape of her eyes down to the way she furrowed her brow in disgust while everyone sang "Happy Birthday." She was pensive like him—but prone to big, gooey smiles when you least expected it. In a lot of ways, she reminded me of Mell and that also made me want to break down in big, throaty sobs. *No wonder everyone loves this baby.* Her face was a Rodriguez family portrait, as real and delightful as the one that hung in Lani's kitchen.

As the sun began to set over the bay, turning everything the color of lemon curd, I sat on the back steps of Sam's house, watching as Nan walked Val around the edge of the garden. Eddie joined me with two plastic cups filled with strawberry wine.

"So." He handed me one. "What do you think?"

"If you had told me she has glasses, I would not have let you wait this long to let me meet her."

"The glasses," he said darkly. "Don't even get me started on the glasses."

"What? They're *adorable*."

"She needs corrective eye surgery—a basic procedure—but my ex doesn't think we should do it right now," he said, his voice thick with sarcasm. "Thinks she's too young. It's a simple surgery, one that would benefit her for the rest of her life." He looked at me fiercely. "Learn from my mistakes. Never have a baby with someone without discussing how they feel about surgery first."

"Noted." I laughed. "Hey, can I tell you a secret?"

"Just this once," he joked, wrapping his arm around my shoulders and pulling me into his chest. I'd never been with someone so effortlessly affectionate before. I could smell the strawberry wine on his breath, cologne on the edge of his collar.

"I started talking to my dad again."

"Whaaat?" His voice came out in a singsong pitch. "I thought he was dead to you."

"Me, too." I pulled away from his chest and met his gaze. "You were kind of dead to me, too."

He tightened his hold on me, turning his lips to rest against my temple. Nan shrieked in faux surprise as Valerie triumphantly yanked a dandelion from the grass. "I can see it, you know? For the first time in a long time."

"See what?" I asked, my voice little more than a whisper. I pulled away from his chest.

His eyes were locked on Valerie, toddling around the flower bed, waving at a bumblebee that buzzed by. "A future. A real one. Not just working at the bar and worrying about how I'm going to pay child support and pay for dance lessons and make sure she has the best bedroom and coolest bike. I get embarrassed, you know? That one day she's going to realize that every Saturday she has to leave her family to spend time with her lonely, old dad." He tore his gaze away and looked into my eyes. "But if you were there? If Valerie had you around to teach her things?" Eddie let out a slow, low whistle. "That would be badass."

I could feel myself blushing—not in a cute way, either. Big red splotches overtook my nose and neck. "You think I'm a badass?"

"One hundred percent," he said. "You never let anything hold you back. You told me you loved me after meeting my sisters."

I tilted my head back and let out a laugh. "You told me you loved me after I told you to go away forever."

"Yeah, I'm a badass, too." He smirked, folding me into an embrace. "Bad to the bone in my Honda CR-V."

I couldn't stop laughing—giggling, really. A jovial percolation that wasn't like Adult Del. Maybe more like Baby Del. Maybe someone could get me a spoon to suck on.

"I have another secret," I said, closing my eyes as I tucked in close to him. "I feel like—like I'm finally getting something right. I'm happy, Eddie."

He tightened his arms around me and whispered back, "Me, too."

30

Somewhere I'd Never Forget

I began showing up at the bar every morning with my guitar and laptop, under-caffeinated and cursing myself for still not buying a better pillow. I spent the mornings practicing my songs, then I'd throw on an apron and help Eddie open. Working at The Billiards wasn't anything like Gimbley's. He started every shift with a family dinner, then he ran through the specials and asked everyone if they had anything they wanted to bring up with the group. Usually Chelsea, a bubbly server home from college, used the open forum to update everyone on her sex life.

All I had been able to think about before was Brainwave, getting back to New York, but every time Eddie slipped a hot mug of coffee into my hands and pressed his lips to my forehead, I felt a twisting pang at the idea of ever leaving.

Eddie didn't know. But I didn't know what he was thinking, either. Time had made him a more anxious person and the quick creeping of Brainwave did little to help. He never pushed me to talk about what I was going to do after the festival, but the future hung over us constantly.

I watched him count out the register while pretending to write from the other end of the bar. His frown never faltered. His jaw was permanently locked into a visible clench, lips moving in rhythm with his fingers.

"Hey," I called out, throwing a balled-up straw wrapper at him. "You're going to break a tooth if you keep clenching."

Eddie huffed loudly and slammed the register closed. "Still short." And then he walked away, grumbling to himself.

I jumped down from my stool and followed him into his office. Eddie was bent over, fishing around in one of the drawers.

I leaned against the doorjamb. "Whatcha looking for?"

"Bartending schedule," he grunted, shoving an arm so deep into the desk I was certain it would come out the other side.

"You don't do that on a computer?"

Eddie snorted. "Yeah, right. I can barely get them to use the digital punch-in machine."

Gimbley's had plenty of that, but—unlike Eddie—our manager never hesitated to fire the more headstrong employees. I sat down on a child-size wooden stool opposite the desk. "You need a day off."

Eddie pulled his arm out of the jaws of life, clutching a severely mangled legal pad. "Got it!"

"*Eddie.*" I kicked the metal desk, sending a thunderous noise echoing through the tiny room. That snapped him out of it. He finally looked at me. Fully. Really. "You need a fucking day off."

His shoulders relaxed and he took a deep, steadying breath. "Yeah, I'm cracking."

"Baby, you could change your name to Black Pepper."

He smirked. "Is that one of your new jokes?"

"Perhaps." I crossed the room and yanked the legal pad out of his hands, tossing it onto the mountain of similar legal pads on the desk. "Let's go to the beach."

"I . . . I don't know, Del."

"You don't open for another"—I checked the wall clock—"four hours. We've been so productive this week."

His eyes flitted over me, over my profile and toward my lips. Eddie slid a hand around my hips, bringing the other to the side of my face. "I owe you a real date."

I turned my face into his palm, breathing in the scent of his skin. "You do."

He brought his other hand to my face and squeezed gently at my cheeks. "Aight, Miller. You got me."

"'*mazing*," I mumbled through squished cheeks.

WE SHOVED a bottle of prosecco into my tote bag along with an old tablecloth and headed toward the beach. The Billiards was just a few short blocks from the touristy part of the beach, now mostly empty with Labor Day behind us. We kicked off our shoes and trekked onto the sand. We shook out the tablecloth and fought the wind until we managed to have something like a picnic blanket.

"Does Valerie love the beach?" I asked as I settled beside him.

"Oh yeah." Eddie was lounging on his side, head propped in a hand. "It's our special place. Her new stepdad isn't from around here—he just doesn't get it. I don't think they take her very often." He huffed a bit.

"I'm imagining a man named Dirk." I grabbed the bottle from my bag and began unwrapping the cork. "A sentient pair of khaki chinos with the emotional intrigue of a dentist's office."

Eddie laughed. "It's not in my favor to agree or disagree."

"I bet he works at a car dealership but doesn't even do sales."

He let out a low, humming *oooooooh*. "So close. He's a parole officer."

I raised a brow. "For Malaga County? Fascinating. I should see if he's a fan of my family's work."

"You're telling me. I almost gave him a fake name the first time we met."

I smirked, popping the cork from the bottle. "At least Valerie will always have one cool dad."

Eddie wrapped an arm around my waist, pulling me back toward him. "Don't you have a cool dad?"

I sloshed a bit as I poured some prosecco into red Solo cups for us. "There's an argument to be made that my dad is perhaps too cool for his own good." I shuddered at the thought of Roger with his nineties swag that had outlived both the nineties and any microscopic existence of actual swag. "I think I've spent my entire life being some combination of horrifyingly angry at and absolutely humiliated by Roger." I passed him a cup.

He sipped thoughtfully. "I get that. I mean, my dad wasn't really around so it was more of a one-sided thing for me."

I nodded. "I remember that. We should have talked about this stuff more."

He shoved his cup into the sand and draped his arms over his knees, staring out at the ocean. "I had no idea how to talk to you, Del. I barely do now. You're . . ."

I bumped my shoulder against his. "What?"

He turned his amber gaze on me. "You sparkle."

"Ugh, shut up." I fought hard to hide my smile. "*So* corny."

"You do. When you perform. When you smile." He laughed at me, pulling my hands away from my face, drawing me close to his chest. "Don't hide from me, Miller."

"You sparkle, too," I whispered, laying my head on his shoulder.

"Nah." He dusted a self-conscious hand through his hair. "Maybe I did before."

"Before?"

His throat moved as he swallowed a sip of prosecco. "Before I got married, I guess."

My skin bristled like an icy breeze had blown up my exposed arms. Except it hadn't. The air was still. "It was really that bad, huh?"

"I met her at a show," Eddie started slowly, his jaw muscle quivering like each word had to be chewed. "She was in the front row, at a bachelorette party. They were so fucking loud." He laughed self-consciously, cracking his jaw. "Sorry, this sucks. Who talks about their ex-wife on a date?"

I dug my fingers into the sand between us. "This again? It's *me*. I know you. I know your favorite color is navy blue. I know your favorite band is Imagine Dragons—"

"Okay." He rolled his eyes. "Watch it."

"But you tell people it's St. Vincent. I know all the outside stuff." I took a handful of sand and began pouring it over his ankle. "Tell me the inside stuff. Please."

"Well," he began with a dry, low laugh. "We got married because Meghan, my ex, was pregnant, which is so stupid—almost embarrassingly stupid. We'd only been dating for five months and even then, it wasn't working. But it was what she wanted. So, yeah, we got married, even though she hated that I was traveling to play shows; she hated that I kept an apartment in Philly; when I bought the bar, she hated that, too. I sort of realized that Philly, music, the bar—they all had one thing in common." He reached down and dragged his fingers through the sand. "I was so scared that if she hated me, she'd hate Valerie, too." He took an uneasy breath before looking up at me, his expression dark and expectant. "So, I left."

A shudder ran through me, trickling down my spine. "You left?"

He nodded slowly. "I made sure she had everything she needed. Made sure the crib was assembled and her car seat was installed. Then I wrote a long note and left it on the counter. I promised her I would do everything I could for them. At the bottom I put: *If you need me, just call.*"

"She never called?"

"Nope." He tossed a broken seashell toward the tide. "Next time I saw her, we were parents, and everything was different. I thought it couldn't get worse between us. The divorce was awful—a mess— but nothing hurt like the custody stuff. I would do anything for Valerie, but because I walked out on Meg, I was a piece of shit. I had the letter—I'd saved a copy. I begged my lawyer to let me read it, to show that the relationship had been toxic, but he said it would only make me look *unsympathetic*." Eddie raked his teeth over his bottom lip. "There was so much in that word. She's rich—I'm not. She's white—I'm not. I took whatever I could get. I didn't want to rock the boat. I just wanted Valerie, as much of her as I could get. I never wanted her to look back and wonder if I had walked out on her, too."

I reached out and pushed his hair to the side, dragging my thumb down the curve of his cheekbone.

He was flushed with emotion underneath his summer tan, I could tell. He tried to lift his shoulder to his cheek to scrub at that one spot that always turned red, always betrayed him. But I didn't let him. "You're an amazing dad, because you're an amazing friend and an amazing brother and son and boss. You're amazing to everyone in this community. Every day you wake up and live for other people. No one can take that away from you. I don't want you to . . ." I shook my head. "Be afraid."

Eddie kept his eyes fixed on the ocean when he finally responded. "But I am."

"Of what?"

"Losing the bar. Losing Valerie." He hesitated before continuing. "I'm afraid of waking up the day after you leave, when I have to act like I didn't fall in love with you all over again."

I bit down hard to keep my jaw from falling open. "You think I'm just going to disappear?"

"You should." He flashed me a pained smile. "You need to get back to your dream."

How could I fight back? Argue with him? Say *no* and *I promise* when in a week I would be getting on a flight, I would be leaving Evergreen, I would hopefully get enough money together to move back to New York? That had always been my plan.

Why did it feel like everything had changed when all the facts of my life were exactly the same?

All of them except one.

"Eddie . . ."

He shook his head. "Let's not talk about it." He reached his hand out and traced his thumb down the curve of my cheek. "Come on, I want to show you something."

We gathered our things and started toward the sand dunes that separated the main beach from where the sand went farther out into the ocean and the tide came in warm and shallow. I remembered this patch of land. The boardwalk planks sloped high enough that a teenager or two could stand underneath, nestled between the dunes and completely out of sight. More important, two teenagers could lie down underneath the planks, completely out of view.

Eddie grabbed my tote bag and scaled the dune before turning around, sticking his hand out to me. I grabbed ahold of his wrist, and he pulled me up with him. I let out a yelp, tumbling into his arms. He caught me, hands flying to my waist to steady us.

"Been a while since you scaled a dune?"

My feet were sinking and slipping, but I couldn't stop laughing. We slid down the dune on our butts. We stood in the shallow, warm water, the boardwalk to our backs, no houses for miles. Just sand and the sound of the wind. Even the sun had tucked itself behind a cloud, like she knew about this moment.

I turned in a circle slowly. Eddie kept his distance.

"Do you remember?" he called out to me.

I nodded slowly, turning to face him. "How could I forget?"

I felt the rain on my shoulders and hands before I saw it. I tilted my face away from Eddie's and opened my eyes to see the sky filled with low gray clouds. His hands were pressed against my lower back, holding my body against his. His eyes skated over my face and down my neck, his lips following the trail they left behind. He kissed the soft skin under my eyes, the side of my nose, my chin, and finally my neck. I traced my fingers along the back of his neck, savoring the steadiness of his breathing, every part of him washing through me.

"I'm going to take tonight off," he whispered, lips soft against my humid skin. "I can't spend a minute away from you."

I tightened my grip on him.

We scaled the dunes and made it to the boardwalk just as the sky opened up and started to pour. By the time we made it back to the bar, our clothes were soaked through, and my hair was plastered to the sides of my face. I couldn't take a step without creating a devastating raspberry sound with my shoes.

Instead of unlocking the first floor, Eddie grabbed my hand, and we darted through ankle-high puddles around to the back of the building, up the steps to his apartment, falling into each other as he unlocked the door.

"Jesus," he exhaled, pushing his curls away from his face, shaking out the water.

I slammed the door shut behind me, collapsing against it. "Next date, no running."

He laughed, leaning forward to rest his hands on either side of my head, his mouth melting against mine, the saturated fabric of his shirt dripping onto me. Eddie's mouth was warm like sunshine, his lips full and sweet like cherries as they worked against mine.

Eventually, I pulled away. "Third date, we take a vow of celibacy."

He grabbed us towels and left me to dry off and slip out of my wet clothes while he disappeared down the hallway. I peeled my wet shirt over my head and stepped out of my jeans before wrapping the towel around my chest and tiptoeing down the hall. "Eddie?"

"In here," he called back.

I followed his voice to the end of the hall and pushed open the door.

"Just checking to make sure her window isn't leaking." He shot me a rueful look. "Don't worry, it is."

I stared around at the bedroom—a nursery, I guess. The walls were painted lavender. There was a rocking chair and a little mobile made up of shooting stars and crescent moons that hung over the crib. There was even a changing table. I couldn't imagine Eddie changing diapers. Actually, I guess I couldn't imagine myself changing diapers. With my clown lamp and my Deadhead wall tapestry. If Eddie's ex couldn't stand *his* lifestyle, what the hell would she think of me?

"You okay?" Eddie watched me as he finished laying down towels underneath the windowsill.

All I could manage was a nod. "Do you have a dryer?"

He didn't say anything, just stood slowly and crossed the room, taking the wet clothes from me and pressing his lips to my forehead.

A stuffed elephant was propped up on the changing table. I reached out to touch it, but I stepped on something. A sock. More specifically, the world's tiniest sock. Perfectly white with tiny, delicate lace frills around the edges. I bent down and picked it up, turning the soft cotton over and over in my hands.

Eddie cleared his throat and when I turned around, he was leaning against the doorway. I could hear our jeans tumbling distantly in the dryer. "I texted my manager Jules and let him know I'm not coming in tonight."

I held it up. "Tiny sock."

He pressed his lips together—a compact, proud smile. "For a tiny foot."

I set it down on the changing table, but I couldn't pull my hand away.

"Dad stuff," he said in a soft voice.

I nodded, feeling the lace between my fingers. "You can't leave Evergreen."

Eddie inhaled sharply, like I'd pressed a knife to his diaphragm. "No, I can't." After a beat: "Is that okay with you?"

I furrowed my brow, finally meeting his eyes. "You're such a good dad—a great dad. Valerie's your world. It's probably my favorite thing about you."

A look blossomed on his face; an expectant one—like he was just waiting for me to keep going, to break his heart. "What about you?" he asked softly. "Could you leave again?"

I pushed back against the prickling in my eyes, forcing a smile. "I know how badly it would hurt you—"

"Hey, stop that." Eddie reached for me, wrapping his fingers around my wrist and pulling me toward him. "Don't worry about me."

"You don't have to do this." I shook my head, but didn't fight his embrace. I let him pull me to his chest, wrap his arms around me.

"Do what?" he asked, his lips warm against my temple.

"Put on a happy act. If you want me to stay, just say it."

A humorless laugh vibrated in his chest as he tightened his arms around me. "If I didn't give a shit, I would. I'd say fuck the festival. Fuck New York. Move in with me, work at the bar, never leave my side. But you've got that damn light in your eyes."

"But what if *I* say fuck it?" I murmured, turning my face into his chest.

He pressed his thumbs gently into the soft skin under my jaw, lifting my eyes to meet his gaze. "You would never."

31

Today, we're dissecting frogs."

The entire classroom let out a pained groan.

"But, Mr. Esposito, we already did that our sophomore year," Sam whined from her seat at a lab table in the front row.

"You did." Mr. Esposito raised his eyebrows high above his wire-frame glasses. "I remember, Samantha. I taught that class. You almost puked on yourself." Mr. Esposito was a young teacher, but not a cool teacher.

"Last time you dissected a frog you were learning about the process, not the frog's anatomy." He held up a long, crooked finger and shook it at the ceiling. "*Today*, folks, we are focusing on anatomy. You and your lab partner will extract all of the frog's vital organs; you will pin them to your dissection board; and then you will work together to write a full lab report on your frog's respiratory system. Due tomorrow by three P.M." He stopped in front of us, arms open wide and a grin on his lips. "Easy peasy. Right, seniors?"

I raised my hand, speaking up without being called on. "Can we pick our lab partners this time? Please?"

Mr. Esposito pointed a finger at me. "No. And do not ask again. We are halfway through the year, Miss Miller. Your partner is your partner."

From across the room, Eddie wriggled his eyebrows at me.

I'd gotten good at acting like nothing he did affected me. It had been absolutely necessary; an evolutionary must. Because without the beach, without summer, we'd slowly fallen apart. Without the nightfall to cover us, we shrank away from each other. It was easy to blame myself—I was shy, in my own way; I was skittish and easily spooked, prone to folding in on myself; I was marred by Roger.

But Eddie had changed, too.

When he'd come back from Puerto Rico, he rode by on his bike. We walked down the planks and scaled the dunes like we had just a few weeks before. But he struggled to meet my eyes. He never reached for my hand. His jokes had taken on an edge, defensive and cold.

I cried myself to sleep that night. Humiliated, I vowed to never feel that awful sunken-gut feeling ever again.

Eddie stopped riding down the boardwalk to Bel Sol; no more wide, bright grin beaming up at me. Now, when we hung out in a group, I avoided his eyes. We knew too much about each other; we held on to each other's secrets like loaded guns, cocked and aimed.

I'd thought I couldn't live without the smell of his cologne on the collar of my shirt or the feeling of his thumb brushing the underside of my hand, but each day I woke up and let him slip away. Could I lose someone I'd never even really had? It was easy to talk myself out of trying because I knew, deep down, it would have worked if he had wanted it to.

I'd seen him with other girls.

I crossed the room, slamming my backpack down between us on the table. "Ground rules: you cannot call me Pat."

Eddie twisted his mouth to the side, eyebrows tenting in faux sadness. "Thought nicknames were our thing, but fine."

"And you cannot bring up my musical theater phase."

"But I sing 'Defying Gravity' so well."

I handed him a pencil. The kid never had a pencil. "And you have to make *some* effort."

"Your wish is my command," Eddie said, offering a sideways grin that simultaneously enraged me and made my stomach ache. "I'm not so bad. Plus . . ." He stretched a glove between his hands until it snapped back against his wrist. "I know you're a vegetarian. So, sit back and lemme handle this."

I took notes while Eddie worked on the frog. We worked well together and by the time the bell rang, I'd written half our lab report.

"I'm busy all day tomorrow," I reminded him as I shoved my textbook back into my bag. "We have orchestra at lunch and double gym, no study halls."

"I'll call you tonight." He shrugged his backpack onto his shoulders. "We can work on it over the phone."

"*You* are going to call *me*?" I repeated, eyebrows raised. My heart was thrumming again in that unmistakable way. *Maybe he isn't too far gone.*

"Yeah, we'll spend thirty minutes on the lab report *aaaand* then maybe you can tell me about your latest mixtape."

I stared at him for a moment, waiting for the retraction, the joke, the barb.

"Okay," I finally gave in. "You call me."

"Cool." He stood, and ruffled the top of my head as he skated past. "See ya, Pat."

ANOTHER ROGER night. Another bus ride to Long Branch, watching the soggy winter wasteland speed by. I hated being away from my bedroom, from Nan, from my CDs, even the boardwalk. Maybe if I were pulling out of Evergreen and heading toward someplace better—someplace less tragic—I would have felt something other than preternatural dread.

Roger's apartment was on the ground floor of a puke-colored building with plastic overhangs and big water stains under every window. Door after door looked out at the gas station across the freeway. The only other people I ever saw coming and going were faded and curled over, like they were also water damaged.

Inside his apartment, the sink was filled with dishes, crusted with dried ketchup, sitting in sour-smelling soapy water turned green with rot. I pulled my shirt up over my nose and forced myself to wash them. Then, I dug through his cabinets until I found a single package of Top Ramen. I made it, adding in the last egg from the back of his fridge.

At five-fifty Roger came home, red-faced in his work boots. He looked shocked to see me. We talked. It sucked.

I went into my "bedroom"—the spare room where he kept all his vinyl records in crates next to a cot. I plugged my phone in, fell back onto the rock-hard mattress, and waited.

At seven-thirty I could hear Roger snoring. I tiptoed down the hallway into the living room and found him passed out, the recycling bin pulled up next to the couch. Filled with empty cans.

At eight I realized I'd forgotten my shampoo and a clean shirt for school tomorrow. I wanted to call Nan but what if Eddie called exactly the moment she picked up?

At nine I changed out of my clothes and crawled into bed with my English homework, shivering under the scratchy blanket in only my underwear. I read the last two chapters of *Frankenstein*. I tried to stay as still as possible, using the tip of my nose to turn each page, so I wouldn't miss it if my phone started to vibrate under my pillow.

At some point, I fell asleep.

I WOKE up at five in the morning, way before my alarm, to no missed calls.

Pulling on my day-old clothes in the cold darkness of the spare bedroom, I felt suddenly that I had aged beyond sadness. Sure as *hell* beyond caring, let alone caring about someone like Roger. Or someone like Eddie. Because even if he had called and we had stayed up all night talking, how could I ever explain *this* to him?

The smell of mold, the dirty dishes, the "father" I was supposed to love passed out in his dirty construction clothes.

I walked back to Evergreen. It was only two miles, but the air was heavy with moisture, and I was barely able to move my fingers as I pushed my key into our apartment door.

Nan tried milking me for information, following me from room to room in her robe and curlers, but I ignored her, taking a long, hot shower and changing into clothes that didn't smell like body odor and cigarettes.

I ate a sticky raisin roll at the bus stop, but my stomach felt burdened. Bubbling with the hot fuzz of hatred. Instead of getting on the bus, I started walking toward school. Halfway over the bridge to Malaga, I stopped to vomit into the bay. I watched fragments of Top Ramen sail through the freezing air toward the Atlantic, hot tears dragging down my cheeks. My nose burned with bile that tasted just like the way Roger's apartment smelled.

I felt it even stronger now—the hate. It was straining against the walls of my stomach.

I got to school early. I stank like rain and sweat; I was exhausted. My bones ached.

I glared at all the smooth-haired girls getting out of the front seats of their mom's Mercedes. I hated them.

I hated Roger.

I hated my mom for having a baby with Roger.

I hated Eddie more than all of them combined.

Then, I saw him. Sitting at one of the metal tables by the steps. *Laughing.*

"Hey, dick cheese," I called out to him, ice-cold fingers digging numb wounds into the palms of my hands. "Where's your half of the lab report?"

"Oh shit." Eddie's eyes went wide and dark when he saw me. He hopped down from his seat on top of the table, running a hand over his hair as he slid in to intercept my path. "I swear I'm gonna do it at lunch."

"Oh, you're gonna do it at lunch?" I skirted around him. "*Fuck you*, Eddie."

The guys let out a chorus of *ooooh shit*'s from behind him.

"Yo." Eddie jockeyed back into my way, *directly* into my way. "What's your problem?"

You hurt me. "My problem is I want an A on this easy-ass assignment and you're the worst lab partner ever." Then, I shoulder-checked him, heading toward the steps that led to the cage-like doors of the school entrance.

"You'll get your A," he shouted after me. "I told you—lunch."

I scoffed, swiveling on my heels to face him. "There's no way you're doing A material between eating Combos and drawing Hentai in your notebook." *Oh shit,* someone yelled. His friends were doubled over with the type of laughter that felt too loud for this early. *Get 'em, Del!*

Eddie's neck deepened in color, the muscle in his jaw jump-ing. "Man, I can't even talk to you right now. You're fucking crazy."

"Like crazy is the worst thing a person could be," I bit back. "At least when I say I'm going to do something, I actually do it."

"Since when do you care about school?"

"Since when do you act like a dick? Oh, wait. Since *always*."

We were shouting at each other on the steps—me at the top, Eddie at the bottom. A few wayward freshmen had bottlenecked behind Eddie, nervously pulling at their backpack straps.

"Shit happens, okay?" He began counting the *shit*'s off on his fingers: "I couldn't use the phone. I had plans. I was busy. My mom ate my homework. Pick whatever excuse works for you."

"You're a *dick*," I spat.

"Hey!" I turned to find Coach Bill staring at me through the open door from down the hallway, tiny hands on his wide hips. He was licking his mustache. "Aggression on the play, Miss Silva-Miller. That's a detention."

"Fuck," I hissed, gritting my teeth. I took off up the last few steps, down the hall. Coach Bill held out a pink slip between his index and middle finger; I snatched it out of his hand before slam-ming my shoulder into the girls' restroom door.

"Shit. Del, wai—"

I could hear his sneakers squeaking on the linoleum tiles be-hind me.

In the bathroom I dropped my book bag and looked at myself, reflected in the dingy mirrors above the sinks. I looked sick: my eyes were framed by purple-blue bags, my freckles were glowing red, my lips were dry and cracked. I splashed my face with ice-cold water and then swished some around in my mouth, trying to get rid of the awful, stale taste.

Then, the door slammed open. I spun around. "What the hell are you doing in here?"

Eddie was staring at me wildly. "Can you stop running away from me and just talk?"

"Talk?" I balked. "About *what*?"

"Look, I wanted to call—I did."

"But?"

He took a woozy breath, leaning back against the wall. "Rachel gets jealous. Really jealous. Of you."

My stomach dropped. I took a step back, bumping into the sink. "You're dating her again."

He pressed his lips together. "Or something, yeah."

I felt dizzy, injured. Like I might fall over and die. Every muscle in my body hummed with tightness. *How? Why? Why did you follow me? How could you forget about me so easily? I thought things were different. I thought we could make things be different. I thought you wouldn't.*

They all thrummed in my mind, symphonic, every instrument going at once. Building, building, building, then . . .

Nothing.

I couldn't speak.

"You okay?"

I stared down at the wet paper towel in my hands. My eyes burned. "I wanted to talk last night. I thought it could be like, like last summer. I guess Rachel would be pissed if she knew we were talking outside class."

He let out a little hiss of air between his teeth. "Big-time." He'd meant for that to make me feel better, but *every* part of me stung. Hurt, like it was all new. Like I hadn't aged overnight.

"And that matters to you?" I brought my eyes to his, driving my gaze through him like a stake. "Rachel matters to you more than me? Do you tell Rachel all the things you told me? That she's different, that she *scares* you?"

Heat, brick-red heat, was spreading up his neck, growing from the hem of his T-shirt like moss. He forced out a single word: "No."

"Great." I threw my paper towel into the trash. "I think I'd rather be dead than spend another second in this shithole around people like you. I can't wait to graduate and just fucking forget you even exist."

Eddie pushed off the wall, moving to try and block my way out. "You don't mean that," he said, voice tight.

I paused and forced myself to look at him. "You have no idea."

I turned to go, but Eddie's hand found my arm and he grabbed ahold of me, fingers pressing into my buzzing flesh. "Take it back." His voice broke. "You promised."

I didn't turn around. "So did you."

"Del." His voice was small, strangled. "I love you, okay?"

I ripped my arm away from him. "Too fucking late."

32

salt & sage

The next morning, I stomped down the boardwalk in my Crocs to the boutique, pamphlet clutched in my hand and mania glowing in my eyes. After spending the night with Eddie, wrapped up in his body and his words, I was on the brink of something. A breakdown or a breakthrough. Either way, my world was cracking—yet again—around me.

"You know," I started, basically kicking open the door and causing Meghan to jolt and curse under her breath. "I used to hate this town so much I tried to put a curse on it."

"*Del.*" She dropped the necklaces she was detangling and pressed a hand to her heart. "You scared the bajeezus out of me."

I smacked the pamphlet down on the counter. "I watched *Charmed* like it was my job. I thought I could summon a demon and get this whole town sucked into the ocean. Now, you're telling me the planets brought me back?"

"Okay, this pamphlet"—she paused to yank it out from underneath my sweaty hand with a little grunt—"is not a substitute for professional medical advice."

I ignored the barb and continued my rant. "I'm not supposed to

want to be here. I'm not supposed to *see* myself here. I'm not supposed to forgive my dad, and I am not supposed to fall in love with
Eddie, but *fuck my life*—"

"Wait." She cut me off with a shake of her hand. "Eddie?"

"Yeah." I froze. "Eddie."

"Eddie who?"

I narrowed my eyes at her. "What?"

"What's his last name?" she demanded. *Weirdo.*

"Rodriguez."

"Oh, he's . . ." Meghan blinked hard a few times, like the physical act might dislodge whatever words were trapped behind her
teeth. "H-he's my ex-husband."

My heart dropped into my stomach. "Holy shit," I whispered.

Of course. Humiliation exploded like a pink-red mushroom cloud
over my face. *Of course she was.* Evergreen's population was ten
thousand, on a good day. Narrow that down to anyone under the
age of sixty-five and you were left with, what? Five people?

Meghan dropped her face into her hands and let out a strangled
laugh. "Welp, it all makes sense now." She slammed an open palm
down onto the countertop. I jumped at the quick, rattling *whap.*
"You're the reason he cleaned his dang car."

"I thought he cleaned his car for you—o-or Val."

"Oh, no way," she huffed, fiddling with a stack of papers by the
register then the clasp on her bracelet. Neither one of us knew what
to do with our hands. "No, his car was always a mess."

"I-I'm sorry . . ." I squared my shoulders. "I should go. This
was so wrong of me."

"No. Don't. Hold on." She let out a whine of frustration, rolling
her head on her shoulders. "I *really* like you. Eddie and I . . . He's
not my person, and I wasn't his. I can't take that out on you."

"Seriously, let me get out of your way. You've already helped me *way* too much," I said.

"Stop." Then, she pointed at a chair I'd always assumed was purely decorative—large, velveteen, trimmed with gold paint. "Sit."

I sat.

Through her bronzed glow, Meghan was bright pink. "You're in love with Eddie."

"To be fair," I started quietly, "I've pretty much been in love with him, off and on, since I was fourteen."

"Really?"

I nodded. "We were friends, and we were assholes to each other. It was too much for us, I think. It was hard for us to ever be honest with each other. We both had complicated childhoods."

Her eyes softened. *Recognition*. "He told me."

"He's grown a lot. I'm sorry if it wasn't like that—"

She cut me off with a hard shake of her head. "Don't apologize. He's a good person; I just never felt like . . . like I was his number one. His band, his sisters, his nephews, the bar—they came first. He was still figuring things out, maybe. Then, I got pregnant." Meghan let out a self-conscious laugh, tucking her hair behind a very red ear. "I would joke that if I wanted to spend time with him, I should transform into a condemned building."

"That's a good joke," I noted quietly.

"Thanks." She followed this with a dry laugh. "It was never gonna happen. I just started to resent him—how fast we moved; how little he understood me; how different we were. I wanted to be enough for him." She paused, rolling her eyes around the room. Time had done nothing to stop the sting, I noticed, as tears gathered in her eyes. Quiet hung over us. "Learning that I was enough even if I wasn't enough for him—that was my returning," she added eventually, when she knew her voice wouldn't warble.

"Meghan, I am so sorry . . ." My heart hiccupped in my chest. I wasn't sure if I should reach for her hand or walk directly into the ocean.

"I told you not to apologize." She flipped her left hand around, her pear-shaped diamond ring catching the sunlight. "I've moved on. I don't want to scare you off."

"But what if I risk everything and I'm not enough, either? I don't want to have to start over again. I'm finally . . ."

Meghan smiled a soft, knowing smile. "You finally have something you don't want to lose."

Her words knocked into me, hitting me square in the chest with the force of a shoulder. I grasped at the center of my chest, waiting for a physical ache. *I finally have something I don't want to lose.*

"Look, I can't tell you what to do and, believe me, I never want Eddie to know I even thought about giving you advice but . . ." She sighed. "If he's slowed down and found a way to be still with you? That's special."

I nodded, dropping my eyes to my silly green Crocs. "You can hit me if you want. Like, with your car or whatever."

"*God*, Del." She laughed honestly, from her gut, slumping forward. "No, he's all yours. Have fun with the sisters." Then, she stood and opened a jewelry box next to the cash register, riffling through some scraps of paper and change before pulling out a photo, folded twice over and punctured with thumbtack holes. "I could never bring myself to throw out a picture of my baby, so I hid it." She beckoned me over with a hand, unfolded the photo and slid it over to me. "Take it."

The photo had been folded and refolded enough times to scar

the paper, but I would have been able to recognize his face from a thousand miles away. Eddie, my Eddie. The slope of his nose, the way his lips pulled, his eyelashes, his long fingers and square knuckles. There he was, blown out by the flash, Valerie in his arms, only a few days old.

33

Back of Dad's Truck

The Saturday before I was set to leave for Vancouver, Roger and I packed up the back of his truck and drove out to the dog beach. He agreed it was perfect—for fishing.

He sniffed the air in wistful wonderment. "Sweet water," he announced. "Great for porgies."

He showed me how to line my pole and we stood in the tide, lines cast. Fishing was the perfect bonding activity for an estranged father and daughter—we were together, but there was zero expectation for conversation.

When the sun was blazingly high, we headed back to shore and sat in the back of his truck eating sandwiches.

"I heard you're dating a boy from Evergreen."

"Jeez Louise." I rolled my eyes. "So much for you and Nan not talking."

He chuckled into his can of Diet Dr Pepper. "She said he's a real nice guy, got a kid." He gave me a knowing look. "Be careful with that. You know how it can go."

"Boy, do I. Who was that awful woman you dated? Barbie Jo?"

"BJ," he grunted. "Unfortunate name. Worse woman."

"I'm kind of scared with him—with this guy. He's a good

person, and I'm . . ." I dropped my eyes to the sandy path. "I guess I'm kind of afraid I'm you. Or maybe I'm BJ."

"*What?*"

I glared at him through my eyebrows. "I'm an unemployed co-median, Dad. My life is a mess, I have no idea what I'm doing and it's never not been that way—"

"Will you just stop now?" Roger cut me off, his voice fierce. "You ain't BJ and you sure as hell aren't your old dirtbag father. And you know what?" He took a sharp breath in. "You ain't your mother, either. She could have been a star. She was funny as hell. She had a voice like an angel. And she didn't do anything about it." He shook his head. "We made a lot of mistakes, Delfina, but ain't a single one of them inside the stuff that makes up *you*."

"Mom was funny?" I asked.

He reached over to rest a heavy hand on my shoulder. "The funniest."

I gave his hand a pat before slinking gently away from his touch. "So, next week's my big gig."

"Wrote it down on my calendar," he noted. "In ink. It's the same day as our biweekly fish up by the lighthouse. I was gonna invite you, but then I saw my reminder."

"In ink," I noted fondly. "Well, my new set is a little different— the jokes are a bit more personal. I even wrote some songs."

"Oh yeah?" He took a slow sip of Dr Pepper, green-eyed gaze set on me.

I nodded, unlocking my phone and scrolling through my audio files until I found the folder named BRWAVE_SET_ PRACTICE. "You got me thinking—about Mom and her voice and how you taught me guitar. We were never really family, but if we had been . . . I guess music would have been our thing." I cleared my throat. "Anyway, I wrote some songs about you, and before I play them for the world, I figured I owed it to you to let you hear them first."

Roger pressed his lips together into a taut frown. "Okay, then. Hit me."

I kept my eyes on his, almost daring him to tell me *no*. "Okay, this first one is called 'Shitty Dad Memories.'"

Roger let out a guffaw, head falling forward between his shoulders, like he was a balloon and I'd pricked him with a pin. "Good *Lord*. Alright, alright." Laughter shook through his shoulders, his neck turning as red as a rare steak. "Let's have it, then."

I hit play.

It's noon and he's still sleeping
    on the sofa in Dickies and a flannel
The TV's turned to a channel I fucking hate
Oh, weekends with my dad are super great
Can't find the remote no, can't find the remote
Guess I'll watch—what is this, Celebrity Poker:
    Ephebophile Edition*?*
Whoa, oh, anyway
Keep your words of wisdom, your jokes, and your self-esteem
We've got cold pizza and his new girlfriend Darlene,
    the bike he never bought me and our invisible trip to the lake
A handful of pictures and the rest we forgot to take
He's kind of a douche but you know what they say
They say, that douchebag is your dad
Biologically!
Time is precious when your little girl grows
No more daddy's princess, gonna have to let her go
Well, maybe it's true but that ain't never been us
We're two hard-hearted losers—one of us a boozer

Oh, we'll take sitting in silence over sharing a moment
If all we got are these memories then I guess me and my dad
All we got are these
Shitty memories

I had planned to ask Roger, unofficially, for his approval. But by the time the track ended, I didn't need to. He would have been laughing too hard to respond anyway.

34

En route to JFK Airport

We drove to the airport mostly in silence, my fingers intertwined with Eddie's, resting on the gearshift. Every few miles he'd flit his eyes away from the turnpike traffic and ask, "Nervous?"

As dawn broke, we crossed the Verrazzano-Narrows Bridge, a yawn of orange overtaking the hazy indigo sky.

"Sunrise," I said. "It happens so early."

Eddie cracked a half-hearted smile. "Way before eight."

He was doing his best to act completely fine, and if I hadn't so deeply internalized the minutiae of his body language—memorized every flicker and flit in his brow—maybe I would have believed him. Maybe then I could act fine, too.

We stopped in Bensonhurst to get breakfast sandwiches, which we ate from their humid wrappers as the city blinked awake.

"You're gonna do amazing," Eddie said, eyes fixed on the passing traffic. "This is it, Del. This is your moment. Everything has been leading up to this."

I gnawed my lip until I could taste blood. *This is it.*

The moment I'd prayed for, worked for, trained for. Written, bombed, and workshopped for. I had moved through life the last ten years leaving behind a trail of jokes and punchlines that didn't work, didn't fit, didn't *feel like me;* my trail of bread crumbs through the forest, and if you followed them back far enough, you would end up in Evergreen, on the beach.

There was no way to unknot the way Eddie had become tangled in my life. Every bit of what I wrote in Evergreen held a piece of Eddie.

"Do you believe in soulmates?" he asked me, sleepy gaze still fixed on the road, snapping me out of my thoughts.

I washed down a bite of sandwich with a mouthful of bitter coffee. "I'm not sure. Why?"

"I don't know." He shrugged, his hand finding my thigh. He gave me a firm squeeze. "Seems like the type of thing you and I should believe in."

I dropped a finger to his hand, tracing the peaks and valleys of his knuckles. "Have you ever heard of Saturn's return?"

He shook his head.

"It's this idea that in your late twenties you come home to yourself—your real self," I explained. "That all the dreams and lives you were chasing, that you thought were exactly who you were meant to be, stop working and you have to sit with yourself and figure it all out. And it's inevitable. If you don't stop, the universe will force you. Stop you in your tracks." I lifted my eyes to the street and watched a woman push a cart full of individually bagged apples across a sun-soaked intersection. "I used to think there was only one way for me to live my life."

"What way was that?" he asked.

"Leave Evergreen. Prove to myself that nothing there mattered."

I could feel his eyes on me, tracing down my cheek and neck, until his gaze fell to my hands wrapped around his. He made a small noise in the back of his throat before leaning his entire, broad frame across the console to rest his head heavily on my shoulder, burying his lips into the crook of my neck.

"What's next?" he asked, lips moving like butterfly wings over my neck. I melted into his touch, leaning back against the seat and resting my head against his.

I smiled, even though my chest ached. "I don't know, and I think that's okay. I don't want any promises this time. I don't want . . . to spoil this, you know? I want to remember us like this, how we are right now."

"You're right," he said, linking his fingers with mine and bringing our hands to his chest. "I love you."

35

Vancouver, Canada

Lights up on the Brainwave stage. The moments leading up to this flickered in my mind. Kissing Eddie goodbye. Flowers in my hotel room from Tucker and Cyrus with a note attached that read: *Slay, Bitch.* A call from Nan. Trying to sleep; failing. Sliding on a royal-blue dress.

The lights were bright. Brighter than regular stage lights. I tried to swallow but my throat was too dry.

Panic.

Time went concave. My other senses kicked into overdrive. The air smelled like rubbing alcohol and compact powder. Through the darkness, I could make out a blinking green light that signaled I was on. When the light turned yellow, I had five minutes left. When the light turned red, my time was over. I stepped up to the mic. In my earpiece, a tiny voice:

You're on.

Against my heart, between the material of my dress and my bare skin, was his photo. Pressing into me, steady like a hand on the small of my back.

I forced myself to swallow even if it felt like my throat might rip open.

"Good evening, folks." *Is that my voice?* It echoed over the earpiece and through the room. "You've been hearing a lot of jokes tonight. What if I played you some music?"

They cheered. Loudly. Their energy surged. It rivaled the hammering of my heart. But something inside me flicked on. Stage Del. Fearless Del.

"Great," I said into the mic, confident now. This was the part of my set I hadn't practiced. I'd written it on the airplane in a rush, thinking about Meghan's words.

I'd never been afraid of risk, why start now? I'd managed to stop, for a moment, thinking about everything I had to lose. Suspended ten thousand feet in the air, it was easy to do that.

"I started dating a guy recently and for the first time ever, I fell in love. There's nothing funny about love, you know? It's a pretty humiliating process. Probably why they call it *falling* in love and not *gracefully descending*." Laughter erupted like steam from a pressure valve. The first laugh past us, I could relax into my words.

"See, I had this really concrete idea of who I was and what I deserved. Good things—happy things—didn't happen to me. I was different. I was a fighter, and if I wanted something, it had to come hard with cuts and bruises and regret." I cleared my throat. "But what happens after you get cuts and bruises? It's a stupid question—the metaphor is *so* obvious." A warm, smooth laughter filled the room. I had been playing a short, sweet melody along with my words, willing calm into my heart. "You heal. It's that simple. You get hurt and then you heal. Even if you don't want to, even if you don't think you deserve to."

I paused for a beat.

"Anywho, here's a song about the weirdest thing that's ever happened to me." I adjusted my guitar strap. "It's called 'Oh No! I Think I Love My Dad' and it goes a little something like this."

When I was 13 you forgot my birthday, so you wrapped up an
   old hammer and
The first time I got my period you were so freaked out you
   called a doctor
Not really a real doctor
Just a guy literally named Doctor
And the only time I needed you, you were out on a bender
You left my heart tender, oh but
Lately I've been thinking
That Stevie Nicks said it best
Time really does a number
And you finally got sober
And now I'm slightly panicked because
Uh oh, I'm starting to think that I love my dad
Uh oh, I'm maybe wondering if after all this shit I maybe
Love my shitty dad
When I see you I see my face but older and a man
   and I sort of start to realize
That you fucked up pretty bad
But we can make these next few years
Kind of grand
Because I probably love you, Dad

I sang, and I was free.

AFTER THE show, we all met backstage and drank champagne, and I laughed until my throat hurt. We took a Brainwave Comedy Festival class picture with the professional photographer. Then, we each posed for headshots.

"For trade publications," the production assistant noted as she sprayed my bangs into place. "Smile! Or, don't. Do whatever co-medians do."

"Scowl," the photographer instructed me. "You look *just* like Gene Tierney. And Gene always scowled."

I scowled my heart out.

We were whisked off to an after-party in our hotel lobby, under-neath a twisted Murano glass chandelier, Buddha bar beats thud-ding through our topped off glasses. All around me there were faces I'd only ever seen through screens.

"That song about your dad was so fucking funny," a comedian in a bow tie shouted at me over the music, leaning in so close our glasses almost touched. "How'd you come up with it?"

"Oh, man." I laughed. "It's all true."

"No fucking way," the guy geeked. "Man, you gotta write a pilot. I'm so jealous. If my dad was a piece of shit, I'd be a millionaire."

Indeed. I threw back another glass of champagne.

Conversation partners rotated. I was charming and funny and complimentary in the way I'd trained myself to engage in situa-tions like this: one witty remark followed by one sip. Champagne fizzled on my tongue and in my vision. I wished this bar felt like The Billiards. But the air was too cold, the drinks too weak. The music was too loud, and the bartenders were all wearing matching button-down shirts.

I couldn't keep from trying to steal glimpses at my phone or keep my mind from wandering back to Evergreen. I missed Eddie so much. I missed Nan, I missed Sam and DJ, and after a surpris-ingly strong mint gimlet, I almost missed Roger, too.

Everyone migrated to the dance floor, and I dipped out, slipping off my heels and taking the escalator to my room barefoot, wig-gling my aching feet against the cool metal.

The hallway was silent as I wandered back toward my room. My phone also stayed quiet in my clutch—no word from Eddie or Sam or Nan for hours.

I turned the corner, half expecting in my tipsy state to be greeted by a set of twins in matching blue dresses.

Luckily, no creepy twins.

Just a familiar silhouette.

Taller than I remembered, all shoulders and long limbs, in his navy-blue raincoat. Commanding.

His hair was wet, a nervous hand stroking the curls backward until they sprung back. The slope of his body, folding in on itself as he leaned against my hotel room doorjamb, ankles crossed, was enough to stop me in my tracks. He was talking on the phone in soft, docile tones. Familiar as he'd always been, and yet brand-new every single time.

I guess that's what love feels like.

"Eddie," I called out to him.

All he had to do was turn, a fraction of an inch, at the sound of his name and I took off running full speed at him. He put his phone away and his face broke into a massive, shining grin and he caught me, pulling me against his wet jacket, strong arms around my waist, lifting me against him before we crash-landed into the door, his mouth on mine.

"How did you get here?" I asked through laughter when we finally broke apart.

"Plane," he quipped, lips curling into a small smile before his eyes flickered, every part of us tangled. "After I dropped you off, I felt so awful—I needed to talk to someone. I didn't know who else could help me make sure I didn't screw this up. So, I went to Meghan." He rushed to explain himself, his words tumbling together. "She said she met you a-and she thought you were amazing and radiant, that I should have never let you leave with any doubt about us. She's right. I didn't want to push you to make a decision, but I can't settle for the memory of you, Del."

"Eddie—" I swiped my thumb over his cheekbones, but he cut me off, wrapping his hands around my wrists, begging me with the gesture to listen.

"I know we can make it work," he said, his voice hoarse. "I'll sell the bar and we can move to North Jersey. I'll drive you to New York every weekend if that's what it takes. To every show you're in, every audition. I'll help you sublet a room or pay for hotels. You don't have to pick. I'm here." He dropped his forehead to meet mine, hands wrapped tight around my arms. "I can try to leave Evergreen."

"No, you can't," I said, my voice fierce as I pulled away from him.

"What do you mean? I did—I left. Del, I'm here."

"If you leave . . ." I started slowly. "Who's going to serve me a whiskey-Coke?"

"Wait." His eyebrows snapped together. "What?"

"Who's gonna help me make sure the winter bocci league has funding?"

"Del—" He was trying to ease out of my arms, but I held on tight.

"Who's gonna drive Nan to aquarobics? I barely have a car."

He ceased his wriggling, a sudden slack-jawed joy breaking over his face. "You're kidding me, right?"

"I don't want to go backward, Eddie. I can't do it. I don't want to move back into a shitty apartment in Queens with a shitty commute to a job I hate. If Evergreen gets to move on, why can't I? You were right—this is my new beginning," I pleaded. "I love making things. I love writing jokes and music, and I like it better when I do it with *you*." I leaned up on my tiptoes, sliding my arms up his frame and around his neck. "Let me stay in Evergreen and make a life with you. Please?"

He stared at me for a moment, searching my face for signs of a bluff. "Seriously?"

"Seriously," I breathed. "I can't wait another ten years for you."

Eddie dissolved into my embrace, knees buckling as his arms tightened around my waist, corkscrew curls tickling the side of my face. I shrieked and stumbled backward, bracing myself against the wall with an elbow.

"I promise," he whispered against my neck. "I will love you forever."

Epilogue

THE EVERGREEN DAILY

SUMMER SEASON: Arts & Culture
What's the Deal with The Billiards's New Construction?
Evergreen's Highly Anticipated Live Comedy and Music
Venue Breaks Ground at Historic Local Watering Hole

Evergreen has it all—beach, forest, pizza, and now? Live comedy and music for up to 170 lucky audience members.

After over fifty years of operation, Evergreen's oldest bar, The Billiards, is expanding its back room to include an indoor and outdoor performance space. The bar hopes to welcome acts from across the country by early fall. From up-and-coming indie artists to stand-up comedians en route to Atlantic City, owner Edgardo Rodriguez is saying *yes and* to it all.

"Expanding our space has always been a dream of mine, and now was the right time," Rodriguez, 30, commented.

"Evergreen is a very special place. We want artists to feel welcome here—to live, perform, and play," Delfina Silva-Miller, Rodriguez's business and romantic partner, added. "We want to solidify Evergreen's legacy as a haven for weirdos."

Mayor Johnson's office could not be reached for comment. Disgraced former mayor Jordan Cisco did offer his own opinion, remarking that Silva-Miller's comments were "exaggerated" though ultimately "not wrong, I guess."

"This is just the beginning," Rodriguez noted. "There is still so much more of Evergreen for the world to see."

The Billiards Backroom will open its doors with an unorthodox inaugural event on September 28. The act? Rodriguez and Silva-Miller performing their nuptials, and *everyone* is invited.

Del's Original Songs

Shitty Dad Memories

It's noon and he's still sleeping
*   *on the sofa in Dickies and a flannel*
The TV's turned to a channel I fucking hate
Oh, weekends with my dad are super great
Can't find the remote no, can't find the remote
Guess I'll watch—what is this, Celebrity Poker:
    Ephebophile Edition*?*
Whoa, oh, anyway
Keep your words of wisdom, your jokes, and your self-esteem
We've got cold pizza and his new girlfriend Darlene,
*   *the bike he never bought me and our invisible trip to the lake*
A handful of pictures and the rest we forgot to take
He's kind of a douche but you know what they say
They say, that douchebag is your dad
Biologically!
Time is precious when your little girl grows
No more daddy's princess, gonna have to let her go
Well, maybe it's true but that ain't never been us
We're two hard-hearted losers—one of us a boozer
Oh, we'll take sitting in silence over sharing a moment
If all we got are these memories then I guess me and my dad
All we got are these
Shitty memories

That guy on the news is my dad
That guy who works part-time at Guitar Center?
My dad
Lived out of his trunk for ten months 'cause he broke up with
  Darlene?
Whoo-oh, my dad, dad, dad
We both make music and we're real fuckin' sad
I love making memories with my dad
Even if they're total shit!
Probably traumatic
(Definitely traumatic)
They're all a bunch of shitty dad memories
Boy, they make me smile. They kinda make me smile
They rarely make me smile
Oh, shitty dad memories
Shhhh, he's sleeping off a bender
We'll let him sleep a little longer
Oh, whoa, dad

Oh No! I Think I Love My Dad

When I was 13 you forgot my birthday, so you wrapped up an
  old hammer and
The first time I got my period you were so freaked out you
  called a doctor
Not really a real doctor
Just a guy literally named Doctor
And the only time I needed you, you were out on a bender
You left my heart tender, oh but
Lately I've been thinking

That Stevie Nicks said it best
Time really does a number
And you finally got sober
And now I'm slightly panicked because
Uh oh, I'm starting to think that I love my dad
Uh oh, I'm maybe wondering if after all this shit I maybe
Love my shitty dad
When I see you I see my face but older and a man
      and I sort of start to realize
That you fucked up pretty bad
But we can make these next few years
Kind of grand
Because I probably love you, Dad
Ew! Gross!
I think I love you, Dad
Yuck! Gross!
Oh, whoa
Stevie Nicks said it best in that one song covered by the
      Chicks
I'm feeling kind of bolder and I wonder
when I get older, will I also be a piece of shit?
Never mind, I'm a musical comedian, I know I'm a piece of
      shit
Time really does a number
And you finally got sober
And now I'm slightly panicked because
Uh oh, I'm starting to think that I love you, Dad
Uh oh, I'm maybe wondering if after all this shit I still kind
      of love you, Dad
Gross!

Uh oh, when I see you I see my face but older and a man
And I know, yes, I know
I love my dad
Yuck!

Second Kiss

Summer salt on your lips
When we kiss it's like
French vanilla, cherry bliss
A sunset, disco fever dream
Hot pink, yellow, orange-cream
Ocean sounds trapped in a shell
When only time will tell
Is gonna be real-life thing or just a, just a
Summer fling?
You say my name and it's like a spell
You go first and then I'll tell
You all my secrets
Summer salt on your lips, it's
A sunset hour, disco fever dream
Your mouth on mine and I can hardly breathe
It's summer salt and French vanilla bliss
It's everything and nothing quite like this
It's how you left me standing there
And I'm still wondering
Can we kiss?

Acknowledgments

Behind every author is an army of people basically *Weekend at Bernie's*-ing them over the finish line. I will do my best to adequately express my infinite gratitude to everyone who has gotten me here, but please know— I've failed. Everyone involved is too good for words, too good to be true.

To my agent, Claire Harris, where to start? Thank you for believing in me and my work, not only this manuscript but the one that came before and, hopefully, the ones that come after. While I could quite literally not do this without you, I would never even *want* to.

Thank you to my incredible team at Avon. To my editor, Ariana Sinclair, you have made my wildest dream come true. Thank you for believing in me and in Del hard enough to give us a chance and to continuously, enthusiastically champion us. Thank you to Karen Richardson, Joe Jasko, Alejandra Oliva for your dedication. This book is way better because of you. Thank you to Yeon Kim, Katie Smith, DJ DeSmyter, and Julie Paulaski for bringing this book (and Evergreen!) to life.

Emily, meeting your soulmate in high school is something we would have made fun of in high school. And yet, that was where we met each other. Thank you for telling me about David Sedaris, *RuPaul's Drag Race*, and Upright Citizens Brigade over fifteen years ago. Thank you for being the smartest, wittiest, sharpest writer I have ever met. Thank you for believing in me always and for catapulting me into this world. Thank you for being the Abed to my Troy. Here's to praying that reference ages well.

Andrew, Christine, and Desiree. When people say "the world works in mysterious ways," they are rarely referring to the fact that you might meet three randoms in an improv class and fall in love with their brains. This was the first creative project I worked on in almost a decade without you, and that was really scary. Because any time I've ever written with you, acted with you, or been onstage with you, I've known it was impossible to fail. You've always, always had my back. Thank you, my dearest goddesses.

Dom, I thought about dedicating this book to you, but there was no way to condense my love and gratitude for you and your love into one sentence. You are the reason I am a hopeless romantic. Thank you for making me feel safe enough to come home to my own softness. Theo and I are so very lucky to have you.

To my parents. You have given me so many gifts in this lifetime; you took me around the world, taught me a second language, fed me delicious food, encouraged my various, strange fascinations even when they didn't align with your personal beliefs and/or generally agreed upon ideas of how a little girl should act or be. Mom, thank you for giving me my sense of humor. Dad, thank you for giving me an unwavering commitment to underdogs.

To my earliest readers and cheerleaders: Maggie, Natasha, Miranda, Audrey, El, Lisa, Dervla, and Photine. Your belief in me and this story (as well as others!) carried me through the roughest waters of self-doubt. Thank you for every word of encouragement and every piece of feedback that guided Del and Eddie into a better, truer version of themselves. And to all the other hellions who have been in my pocket through every step of this process, thank you. I love you. Special thanks to Lex Croucher for accidentally starting a cult. Frankly, slay.

Hannah, my oldest friend, I'm so glad the universe brought us together. We've grown from girls to women to gremlins. I can't wait to see what we do next. Thank you for believing in me.

Annie, my bestie. So many pieces of you and your story are tucked into the pages of this book. You always said I had first dibs on your memoir. How was this for a dry run?

Matt DeCaro, thank you for letting me use your incredible, perfect lyrics. The first time I heard you perform "Hot One Weird One" I was on submission with Del's story and it felt like a sign that might be *the one*. I immediately began dreaming of asking you to use your lyrics as an epigraph.

Finally, to the weird girls (gender neutral), the funny side characters, the sassy best friends. When I began daydreaming about Del, there was a very specific trope I wanted to subvert. It's the prototypical rom-com scene: the beautiful, thin protagonist picks up the phone to call her best friend who is supposed to read as less beautiful, less thin, just less. We are in the middle of crisis, and our protagonist needs advice, humor, reassurance, and Best Friend always delivers.

"Go for it, girl!"

"Follow your dreams!"

"You're YOU!"

They hang up. We never see Best Friend again. Protagonist gets her man.

But what happens to the best friend after she hangs up? What are *her* hopes? What are *her* fears? How does *she* feel about the fact that her friends only call her when they need something? That was where Del's story began.

Obviously, it grew. But it started there, with us. With you.

You were neither cheer captain nor on the bleachers—you were doing a weird voice and getting detention. You were watching

Strangers with Candy, researching animal husbandry, collecting cool rocks. You were begging God, every night, for an opportunity to wear fake teeth. You drank too much. You ate too much. You had a weird haircut.

You were perfectly you.

I'm so happy we found each other, here.

Thank you.

About the Author

BETTY CORRELLO is a writer, comedian, and proud Philadelphian. Despite her hardened exterior, she is biologically 95 percent marshmallow. Her greatest passion is writing stories where opposites attract, but love is chosen. When she's not writing, she can be found fretting about niche historical events most have forgotten—or petting her very tiny dog. *Summertime Punchline* is her first novel.